# Too Damn Nice

Kathryn Freeman

*Where heroes are like chocolate – irresistible!*

Published 2018 by Choc Lit Limited
Penrose House, Crawley Drive, Camberley, Surrey GU15 2AB, UK
www.choc-lit.com

A CIP catalogue record for this book is available
from the British Library

ISBN 978-1-78189-421-7

MIX
Paper from
responsible sources
FSC® C018072

Printed and bound by Clays Ltd

*To my amazing mum. She doesn't just read all my books –*
*she persuades everyone she knows to read them, too.*

# Acknowledgements

Behind every book is an army of people who don't get their name on the cover, but without whom the book wouldn't exist. Following is my army.

A huge thank you to my editor. If you'd read the book before she waved her magic wand, you would understand how much I value her insight.

Speaking of reading the book before it is edited, another huge thank you to the Choc Lit Tasting Panel, who supported *Too Damn Nice* for publication and to those who passed it at the Panel stage: Olivia F, Alexa H, Linda S, Lisa B, Purabi, Catherine L, Janice B, Melanie A and Betty.

Speaking of support, a massive thank you to the amazing book bloggers. Their enthusiasm for reading and their kind support of writers is humbling. Thank you for taking the time to help this author.

Speaking of help, a big thank you to those authors, both in Choc Lit and outside, who've been so kind to me, providing advice, help and most important of all, encouragement.

Speaking of encouragement, heartfelt thanks to family and friends for continuing to ask about my next book. Yes, there will be one ☺

Speaking of books, a massive thanks to my publisher, Choc Lit, for believing in this book, and in me. I might have written the words, but they provided the gorgeous packaging, and made it available for others to read.

And speaking of reading, the biggest thank you of all goes to you. Thank you so much for reading *Too Damn Nice*. I hope you enjoy Nick and Lizzie's story.

# Prologue

It was her eighteenth birthday and Lizzie had just signed with an illustrious modelling agency. Really, did life get any better than that? Following a gleeful pirouette she peered curiously at her reflection in the mirror. Silky blonde hair framing an oval face and a small straight nose. Definite plus points. She was also tall, a modelling prerequisite, and slender, another given. But then there was the pointy chin, the cheekbones that were too sharp and the blue eyes that were far too large for her face. Not beautiful then. If she was generous, she might say her looks were striking. She certainly wasn't most people's idea of a model, but then Lizzie had never cared much for what most people thought. If she had, she'd have let the taunts of the boys at school, *Here comes Daddy Long Legs*, crush her ambition a long time ago. Instead she'd laughed in their faces and continued to send her portfolio of photographs off to modelling agents. One day, she'd told herself, what her school friends thought of as ungainly and odd, a modelling agency would see as eye-catching and unusual.

And they had. Here she was, two years on, signed with a modelling giant because of those very same quirky features. Now, as far as Lizzie was concerned, anything was possible. And she was going to try her hand at it all.

With a final grin to the image in the mirror, she slipped on her favourite silver sandals. She'd practised walking in high heels since the age of five, so the journey down the stairs and into the garden in these five-inch sweeties was a doddle. She pushed open the back door and stared in delight at the large marquee in the garden, decorated with twinkling fairy lights and silver balloons, erected in her honour. Tonight was her night. Two celebrations in one. The first, reaching the landmark age of eighteen, her friends all knew about. The second, being signed by the modelling agency, was a secret to all but her family.

'Hey, come and dance with us, Lizzie.'

Her eyes followed the direction of the voice, resting on a group of giggling girls shimmying on the dance floor. Her best friends. Lizzie waved and went to join them.


Nick hovered in the corner of the marquee, watching the girls on the dance floor. Or make that girl, because there was only one who caught his eye. Lizzie. She had done so ever since she'd hurtled into the world eighteen years ago. He knew her by virtue of her brother, Robert. Being best friends with Robert had meant spending a huge chunk of his childhood hanging round the Donavue family home. In the early days, Lizzie had been in the background: the cute baby he and Robert had laughed over as inquisitive five-year-olds; the long-limbed girl with pigtails and big blue eyes. But then she'd grown up. For the life of him he couldn't work out how it had happened, but while he'd been working and touring round Europe with Robert in his gap year, she'd turned from gawky to pretty. Then, during his visits home from university, she'd gone from being his friend's kid sister to the girl he most wanted to kiss. At sixteen she'd been too young for him to act on his feelings so he'd kept quiet, finished university, sowed some wild oats and unknowingly broken a few hearts. As he watched her on the dance floor, he was forced to acknowledge his own heart had been captured years ago.

Now he was back, settled in a job, living in his own place.

Now, surely, it was time to do something about his feelings for her.

Yes, she was eighteen to his twenty-three, but this was Lizzie he was talking about. A girl far older than her years.

Tonight, he was going to ask her out. He was happy to

take things slow – the last few years had given him a lot of practice at slow – but he needed her to know his feelings went beyond those of an honorary big brother. Quite *how* he was going to do that was another matter. If he didn't know her so well, if she'd simply been a girl who'd caught his eye tonight, he'd know the moves. Oh he wasn't smooth – if only – but he'd acquired a fair bit of experience with the opposite sex. Enough to know how to buy a girl a drink. And, if he liked her, how to move onto stage two. He'd taken a few knock backs over the years, but other than a bruise to his ego, it hadn't really mattered.

With Lizzie, it mattered, and not just because he loved her. Her friendship was as important to him as Robert's, and tonight he could seriously screw up both. He had no clue what Robert would think of him fancying his sister. And he had no clue how Lizzie felt, either. She liked him, sure. But liked was a long way from how he wanted her to think about him.

Nick took a final swig of beer, straightened his back, and walked purposefully towards her. He was willing to risk Robert's wrath if it got him Lizzie.

She was dancing with her friends, lost in the music, totally unaware of his approach. He watched, mesmerised, as her tall, sinuous body twirled to the beat. God she was gorgeous. The most stunning creature he'd ever seen, or was ever likely to see. And it wasn't only he who saw it. Scanning the room he noticed other men watching her, young and old alike. She stood out from the crowd. She was unique.

'Nick, there you are,' she said with a smile, holding out her hand to drag him onto the dance floor. 'I wondered where you'd got to.'

He allowed himself to be pulled towards her. Hell, he was so besotted he'd follow her wherever she led him. Off a hundred foot high cliff? No problem. Across an alligator infested river? Bring it on. Even onto a blasted dance floor. Never his forte. Getting his body to dance to a rhythm was well nigh impossible. Call it his reserve, or shyness, or maybe his total lack of musical ability. Whatever it was, next to her he looked stiff and awkward.

'I was trying to avoid dancing,' he replied, shouting to be heard above the sound of the music. 'But it seems if I want to talk to you, I have to dance.'

She laughed, the soft, rich sound rippling through him. 'We can talk anytime. Today I turn eighteen and I want to dance all night.'

He nodded back, though his heart sank in his chest. If she planned on fixing herself to the dance floor all evening, how on earth was he going to get her to himself?

The music moved on to the next track and still they danced, Nick doing a kind of shuffle to the beat while Lizzie whirled around him, her movements graceful and fluid. She danced in the same manner she did most things in life, vivaciously, possessing the confidence of someone twice her age. In contrast he danced awkwardly. He could manage a formal fox trot – set steps that could be learnt – but the loose-limbed gyrating of disco was beyond him. Aware of this he hung back, desperately hoping the music would turn slower. He'd have no problem holding Lizzie in his arms and gliding slowly around the dance floor. No problem at all.

His hopes were dashed as the next high tempo song blasted through the speakers. 'I want to talk to you,' he shouted across at her.

She smiled over at him, her blue eyes glittering and he felt his heart flip in his chest. 'Go ahead, I'm all ears.'

He shook his head. 'No, later. Somewhere quieter.' Declaring his love for her in the middle of a crowded dance floor wasn't what he had in mind. It had an advantage – it would be pretty easy for her to pretend not to hear him. Save them both the embarrassment of her turning him down. But shouting out his intimate feelings on a noisy dance floor wasn't his style. No, he'd take the hit in private, thank you. That's if she ever got off the ruddy dance floor.

The song ended and the music stopped altogether. With a surge of anticipation Nick reached for her hand and gave her a light tug. When she didn't move, he stared at her, puzzled. Then he followed her eyes, catching sight of her father striding towards them, his handsome face beaming. As Nick looked on, the older man whispered something in Lizzie's ear. She grinned in reply, nodding enthusiastically. With a wink at Nick, she let go of his hand and linked arms with her father. Together they walked towards the disc jockey and his microphone.

'Friends,' her father began. 'As you know, we're here today to celebrate my darling Lizzie's eighteenth birthday.' He looked over at Lizzie with the adoration only a doting father can bestow on his most precious daughter. 'What you don't know is we also have something else to celebrate. This afternoon Lizzie received a call from a modelling agency in New York. They want to sign her up.' There was an awed hush as the crowd took in his words. 'Yes, that's right. My daughter is about to go and live her dream. New York here she comes!'

Nick stood, dazed, as Lizzie was besieged by cheering friends, all clamouring to congratulate her. He felt as if he'd been hit in the solar plexus by something large and solid. New bloody York? Could she go much further away? Numbly he watched as she revelled in the attention. He wanted to be happy for her. He really did. But the only feeling he could summon was anguish. There was absolutely no point in spilling out his feelings to her now. Not when she was off to start a shiny new life in America.

He'd lost her before he'd even had the chance to let her know how he felt. Later he'd tell himself it was for the best. That actually the announcement had saved him from almost certain humiliation, because he doubted she saw him as anything other than a friend.

But right now he felt as if life had turned around and spat in his face.

Lizzie couldn't have been happier. She'd had to pinch herself several times tonight to make sure it wasn't all one incredible dream. Going off to New York to model? Wasn't that just a foolish fantasy? How could it actually be happening to *her*? Of course being signed by a major New York agency didn't automatically mean she'd make it. She had years of hard graft ahead of her. An endless succession of go sees, hoping for the elusive contract, the chance to burst out of the pack of unknowns. That great big dollop of luck all top models needed. So no, it wasn't going to be all fun and excitement. There would also be disappointment. And loneliness.

She was going to have to say goodbye to everyone here tonight. To her parents, her brother. To Nick. At the thought of the last name, her heart skipped a beat. Could she really leave him behind, without ever finding out what they would have been like together? God, she'd had a crush on Nick for ... well, forever. While her teenage friends had been idolising pop stars, she'd gone to bed dreaming of Nick Templeton, with his tall, lanky frame, floppy dark hair and steel-rimmed glasses that framed soulful brown eyes. Then he'd disappeared. First had been the year away with Robert, then university. She'd only been thirteen when he'd left, yet she'd believed her life was over. Certainly it had been so much duller without him. As she'd grown older, modelling had become a new outlet for her dreams, but it hadn't stopped her heart lifting each time Nick came home from university to visit her brother.

She watched him now, talking to Robert. At first glance Nick wasn't an obvious choice for a girl's first teenage crush. He didn't have the dashing good looks and easy charisma that caused her friends to fawn over her brother. Neither was Nick gregarious and fun loving. He was far more of an enigma. With Robert, what you saw was what you got. With Nick,

6

every time she looked, she saw a little more. And each bit she saw was even better than the last. He stood taller than Robert and broader, but leaner. The glasses he wore gave him an air of intelligence that wasn't superficial. His first at Cambridge was proof of that. He was the quiet one. Reserved, often serious, but with a dry sense of humour that stopped him from being dull.

Above all, Nick was a strong, stabilising presence. She loved that about him, just as she loved the way his warm brown eyes had watched her tonight. As if she was the only person in the room. Was it possible Nick was finally starting to see her as a woman? God, she hoped so, but if she didn't do something about it now, tonight, she'd be on her way to New York without ever knowing.

Taking a deep breath she walked over to the two men, putting an arm around them both. 'Two of my favourite people.'

Robert tugged at her hair. 'My baby sister, the glamorous model.' He shook his head. 'It doesn't seem possible.'

'Well start to believe it big brother.' She gave him a playful dig in the ribs, making him grunt. 'I won't be around to tease for much longer.' She turned to Nick. 'You wanted to talk? Is now a good time?'

For a brief moment his expression froze, as if in shock. Then he vehemently shook his head. 'It doesn't matter,' he replied hastily, averting his eyes to scan the crowd. They rested on the bar. 'I'm going to grab a drink.' Leaning forward, he planted a kiss on her cheek. 'Congratulations, Lizzie. I pity the New York modelling scene.' He gave her a slightly wonky smile. 'They don't know what's about to hit them.'

Confused, Lizzie watched as Nick was swallowed up by the crowd. 'Was it something I said? Why is he shooting off so quickly?'

Robert narrowed his eyes and regarded his sister. 'If you don't know now, Lizzie, I don't think you ever will.'

'What do you mean? Don't talk in riddles; you know how I hate that.'

Robert simply grinned. 'And you know telling me you hate me doing something is only going to make me do it more.' He grabbed her arm and pulled her onto the dance floor. 'Come on, baby sister. I've always wanted to dance with a model. It's every man's fantasy. I can't wait to be introduced to all your new model friends.'

She danced with her brother, staying on when others joined them. Only when her feet throbbed and her throat felt sandpaper dry did she finally give in and head towards the bar. That was where she found Nick, drinking beer and looking far too glum for a night like tonight. She walked purposefully towards him. Now was her chance. If what she'd read in his eyes earlier was real, and not just wishful thinking on her part, what she had in mind would put a smile on his face.

'What are you doing all alone at the bar?' she asked, draping what she hoped would look like a casual arm around his shoulders. He felt different now. His shoulders were broader and his body stronger than the last time she'd seen him. Every inch a man's body. No doubt with a man's passions. A man's desires. Nerves fluttered in her stomach. Next to him, she still felt very much a girl. Which was exactly why she needed to be strong, she berated herself. A girl would chicken out now. A woman would go after what she wanted.

'I'm drinking.'

It took her a moment to realise he'd finally answered her question. 'And why is drinking making you sad?'

He looked surprised. 'I'm not sad. Just taking some time out.'

She ordered a glass of champagne, wondering how many she'd already had. But, hey, if she couldn't get drunk on her eigthteenth birthday, when could she? Besides, if ever there was a time when Dutch courage was needed, this was it. Her own courage was slipping away by the minute. Taking a deep gulp, she moved in closer to Nick. 'Well, I've got a proposition that might put a smile on your face.'

His deep brown eyes looked wary. 'Oh?'

Smiling she leaned over and whispered into his ear. 'I want you to help me lose my virginity.'

A broad grin was what she'd been hoping for. A slight smile would have done. Even a confused look wouldn't have been a total disaster. Nick did none of these things. Slowly he put down his glass and turned to her, his eyes flat, his expression shuttered. 'You've got to be joking.'

Too late to back down, she had to brave it out. 'I'm deadly serious.'

'Jesus, Lizzie.' He shook his head, looking down at his empty glass. 'Your first time should be with someone special to you. Someone you love.'

'You are special to me.' Couldn't he see that was why she was asking him? Mortified at the way this was panning out, Lizzie wanted to up sticks and run. She hadn't reckoned on having to persuade him. Blithely she'd assumed he'd want this, too.

He sighed and something flickered in his eyes. An emotion she couldn't put her finger on. 'Am I special, Lizzie?' he asked quietly. 'Special in the way a man is to a woman. Not a brother is to a sister.'

She wanted the ground to swallow her up. He was making her feel like a silly girl who didn't understand about sex. Why couldn't he treat her like a woman? Her cheeks stinging with shame, she retaliated as she always did when cornered. She went on the attack. 'I'm going to lose my virginity with somebody before I go to the States. If you're not interested, I'll find someone who is.'

It was as if she'd struck him. He flinched and his face drained of colour.

'Don't be ridiculous,' he replied coldly. 'I gave you credit for being more mature than this.'

9

Ouch, his words hit home, adding to her misery.

'Sex isn't something you have to cross off a list in order to make you a woman.' His eyes narrowed as they bored into hers. 'I know what all this is about. You're worried you won't be able to act sexy to the camera when you've not actually had sex. That's it, isn't it?'

Maybe there was a grain of truth in his words – but there was also so much more to her invitation than that. She *did* want her first time to be with someone special. Him. Yet how could she let him see her feelings now? He'd not just turned her down, he'd as good as laughed in her face.

'So what if it is? Lots of people have sex together for far worse reasons than that.'

Nick hoped to God Lizzie couldn't see through the cold mask he was wearing and into the emotional pit lying beneath it. She was offering herself to him on a plate, and yet here he was, turning her down. And none too gently, at that. But damn it, this wasn't how he'd imagined it happening during those restless nights when he tossed and turned, dreaming of her. If she'd told him she loved him. Wanted him, fancied him, liked him even, as a man, not a friend. That was all he needed. Heaven knew, his body was only too game. But this wasn't anything to do with him. He was just a handy male she happened to trust.

'Thank you for thinking of me,' he ground out, 'but I'm going to decline the invitation to take part in your experiment. You'll have to find someone else. I'm sure you won't be short of offers.'

Stiffly he stood up from the bar stool and walked away. Out of the marquee, out of the party, and into the night. He'd begun the evening planning to tempt Lizzie into a date. Maybe even a kiss. Hopefully, the start of a relationship. Though he hadn't wanted to scare her off, in his mind he'd even pictured marriage and children one day. He was ending the evening walking into the night alone, having just turned down her offer to help rid her of her virginity. As if it was a hurdle to be overcome, not a prize worth savouring, keeping until she could give it to the right man. And God knows, he clearly wasn't the right man. Not in her eyes. She had her heart set on bigger adventures than him.

With a sigh he pulled out his phone, punching in the number of the local taxi firm. He'd had enough of mooning over Lizzie Donavue. She was off to America to start a new life. It was about time he sorted out his own.

As he climbed into the arriving taxi, he was unaware of a willowy blonde figure watching from the house, tears running down her face. Sod Nick Templeton. She didn't want to lose her virginity to a man who didn't want her, anyway. She was off to New York, to the career she'd always dreamed of. She didn't need Nick any more. She didn't need anyone.

*Two Years Ago*

It hadn't stopped raining all day. Perhaps it was fitting. A grim day to match the grim scene in front of them. Not one, but two coffins being slowly lowered into the ground. A simple wreath of white lilies on each. Nick reached out to put an arm round Lizzie's shoulders, desperate to offer whatever solace he could. She flinched from his touch, just as she had when he'd flown out to New York straight after the accident. His heart tore at her rejection, but he pushed away the pain and continued to hold her, needing to offer the comfort as much as he knew she needed to feel it.

He glanced sideways at her face, wondering how she was still functioning. He knew what it was like to lose parents; his own had died during his first school summer holiday. When he and his sister had gone to bed they'd had parents. When they'd woken up, they were orphans, thanks to a faulty gas fire in the master bedroom. It had left him devastated, and he'd been too young to really understand the consequences.

At twenty-four, Lizzie knew exactly what the two oak coffins meant.

Once the brief graveside ceremony was over, the mourners began to move away. Lizzie stayed, head bowed, not bothering to wipe the tears that streamed down her face. Gently he tugged at her arm.

'Time to go.'

Vehemently she shook her head. 'No. I'm not leaving them.'

His heart crumpled. 'You have to, Lizzie. People are going on to the house. They'll expect you there.'

'I don't care.' She glared up at him. 'How can you expect me to leave them? They shouldn't be there, not in that horrid cold grave.' Her sobs grew louder.

He fumbled in his pocket for another tissue, but they'd all gone. 'Look, I understand how you feel—'

She rounded on him before he had a chance to finish. 'No you don't. You can't possibly know how I feel right now.'

'I understand how it feels to see a parent buried,' he reminded her quietly. And damn it, he'd loved her parents, too. Not like she had, sure, but he felt their loss.

'And were your parents coming to see you when they died?' she railed at him. 'And was your sister in the car, as my brother was? No. So don't tell me you know how I feel.'

Briefly he closed his eyes, the pain etched on her face too much for him. Robert had been in the same car as his parents that fateful night, all of them travelling from John F Kennedy airport to visit Lizzie. Her brother, his best friend, had been the only one to survive the crash – if you could call what he was doing surviving. It was early days, but the doctors weren't hopeful of Robert ever being able to lead a normal life again. After seeing him in the hospital last week, wired up

12

to machines and looking totally lifeless, Nick didn't think a miracle was likely.

'Okay,' he conceded, fighting back his own tears. 'I don't know how you feel, but I do know standing here isn't the answer. You need to say goodbye to your parents and come back to the house. Talk to the people who've come a long way to mourn with you.'

He started to pull at her arm, to guide her to the car, but she yanked it away. 'Leave me alone. I don't want you telling me what to do, Nick Templeton. I'll go when I'm good and ready. You can bugger off.'

He bit back a reply, telling himself her rant at him wasn't personal; he was the handy punchbag. Hell, he was happy to take the beating if it helped her get things off her chest. 'I'll wait by the car.'

Desolately he trudged back to the car, leaving her alone by the graveside: a tall, slender blonde, her shoulders shaking as she cried.

Lizzie couldn't think, couldn't function. Her mind was numb. Surely she was acting a role. That of the distraught daughter, the anguished sister. There was no way her parents could be dead. No way her brother could be in a coma, unlikely to ever come out.

But it had to be true, because today she'd watched as two coffins carrying her parents had been lowered into a hole and covered with soil. Relatives she barely knew had trailed through her childhood home, smiling awkwardly and drinking lots of tea. When the last of them had left, she'd scuttled upstairs to her room, looking for the peace and calm she usually found there. After an hour of lying on her old wooden bed, staring emptily out of the window, she still couldn't find it. The house was eerily quiet, as if it, too, was in mourning.

A light tap on the door broke the silence. 'Are you okay in there?'

Nick. Since she'd left to go to America she'd rarely seen him, and certainly not without the buffer of her brother or parents. Her anger at his rejection had cooled over the years, but the brush off still stung and the memory of it hung like an unwanted weight between them. A tension that, so far, time hadn't been able to shift. Yet in those bleak moments straight after the accident when the kind policeman had asked if there was anyone they could call to stay with her, Nick's had been the first, the only name her dazed mind had thought of. Later, waking from a sedative induced sleep, she'd been horrified and called him, interrupting his halting words of sympathy. 'Thank you but I'm fine,' she'd told him. 'There's no need to drag yourself across the Atlantic.'

He'd exhaled a long, deep sigh. 'You're not fine. And I'm in a cab, ten minutes away.'

Of course he'd already dropped everything and flown to see her. That was Nick all over. Kind, loyal. A man who put duty and responsibility before anything else. Even it meant having to deal with a grieving woman, one who'd once asked him to take her virginity.

'Lizzie?'

His voice cut through her thoughts and with a sigh she sat up on the bed. 'It's okay, you can come in.'

The door creaked open and his tall frame moved hesitantly into the room. 'You've been up here a long while. I was getting worried.'

'I was just thinking how the house feels too quiet.' She felt a crushing pain in her chest and pressed her hand to it, despite knowing there was nothing that would soothe it. 'Any minute I expect to hear Mum singing, and Dad laughing at her singing. Or Robert dashing in to ask me, for the hundredth time, when I'm going to introduce him to Kate Moss.'

A small, understanding smile flickered across his face. 'I'm more of a Claudia Schiffer man myself.' He nodded to the bed. 'Do you mind?'

The way he perched carefully on the end furthest from her tugged a wry smile from her. 'Finally I get you in my bed.'

Immediately his face flushed scarlet. 'Look, about that—'

'No.' Horrified, she held up her hand. 'Sorry, I shouldn't have brought it up. We're not talking about it. Not now, not ever.' Why the blazes had she mentioned it?

'Well, obviously, I'd rather not talk about that sort of stuff, either, but ...' He sighed. 'I hate the awkwardness between us now.'

'They say a girl never forgets her first love. I guess she finds it hard to forget her first rejection, too.'

His eyes rested, dark and expressive, on hers. 'It was six years ago. And surely, you have to know, turning you down hurt me far more than it hurt you.'

*Then why do it?* But she was far too emotionally unsteady to have that conversation. In fact, she doubted she'd ever be ready for it.

The quiet she'd started to hate descended on them once again. Outside there was a bird twittering on as if all was well with the world. If only it was. A chill shot through her and she began to tremble, her body juddering uncontrollably. 'Would you mind holding me?'

He didn't hesitate. One minute he was sitting at the end of her bed, the next he was beside her and cradling her in his arms. He smelt like Nick: classic, male, outdoors. He felt like Nick: warm, comforting, steady. 'Thank you for being here,' she whispered into his chest.

His arms tightened. 'Where else would I be?'

He didn't understand her gratitude. He couldn't see how, in his quiet way, he'd got her through the last two weeks. Holding hands with her by Robert's bedside. Arranging the transfer of her parents' bodies to England. Helping her arrange the funeral. Others had pitched in, on both sides of the Atlantic, friends and relatives keen to help. Yet throughout it all, Nick had been the one constant. A rock in the storm of her heartbreak and loss. 'Others came and went,' she told him quietly. 'You stayed.'

'I'm waiting for you to kick me out.'

She smiled against his chest, soothed by the steady beat of his heart. 'I thought I already did that earlier.'

'What, telling me to bugger off? It will take a lot more than that to get rid of me.' She felt his lips as they placed a soft kiss on the top of her head. 'A lot more.'

Nick rested his chin on her soft blonde head, holding tightly onto the haunted woman he'd watched like a hawk all day. He desperately wanted to cry, but she didn't need his sadness, too. She needed his strength.

'I've decided, I'm going back to the States tomorrow.'

He loosened his grip so he could look at her. 'So soon? Are you sure?'

Suddenly restless, she shifted away from his arms and jumped to her feet. 'I can't stay here, in this house, any longer.' Her voice sounded thick, as if she was on the verge of further tears. 'I need to get back to my life. Working again will do me good. Give me less time to think.'

'Don't you need time to grieve properly first?' Or was he just thinking of his own selfish needs? It might have taken a tragedy to bring her back into his life, but he wasn't ready to let go just yet.

'You really think it will help me to stay here and do nothing but think about what I've lost?'

'I think it might help if you took time off work, yes. You don't need to stay here, you can stay with me.'

Her eyes widened. Shock? Horror? It certainly wasn't pleasure. 'I need to go home. Robert is there.'

Much as he wanted to, he couldn't argue with that one. 'What will you do about the house?'

She sighed deeply and gazed around her room. When her

eyes rested on his, they were filled with pain. 'Would you take care of it? Sell it for me.'

Still the besotted fool of six years ago, he found himself nodding. Walk across burning coals? Sure. Sell a much-loved family home and all its contents? Yes, ma'am. 'Is there anything in particular you want to keep?'

Her eyes clouded as she fought against further tears. 'I don't need things to remember them by,' she replied brokenly. 'They won't be coming back. I have to accept that and move on. This isn't home any more.'

As pain lanced his heart, Nick realised with a terrifying feeling of finality that this might be it. The last time he'd ever see her. Now her family was no longer around to keep their tenuous friendship intact, were they fated to drift out of touch?

'You'll still come back, though?' His words sounded desperate, but he couldn't stop himself. 'Or am I destined to be only a name you write on a Christmas card once a year?'

She gave him a wan smile, but didn't contradict his statement. And why would she? He was, and always would be, a reminder of her old life. One she clearly wanted to forget. She was now a high earning supermodel, moving in a glamorous world filled with show business stars and celebrities. It wasn't hard to see why she'd want to focus on that instead of the pain and tragedy of her past.

Especially when that reminder came in the form of a dull English accountant who'd once had the stupidity to turn her down.

The following morning he drove a deathly pale Lizzie to the airport, his mind crammed full of all the reasons why he shouldn't be putting her on that plane. He loved her. He wanted to help her. No, he needed to help her. But what she needed was to return to America. To her work and to her life there. She didn't need him.

As they stood in the departure lounge, just outside security,

Nick dropped her small holdall on the floor. 'I guess this is as far as I can go.'

With a glimmer of a smile, she leaned up to kiss his cheek. 'Thank you, Nick, for being there these last two weeks. I couldn't have got through it without you.'

With his heart breaking apart, Nick squeezed her tight. 'I'll always be there for you. Whatever you need, no matter how big or small, call me. Do you understand?'

She nodded and bent to pick up her bag.

Just before she went through the barrier, he called out to her. 'And don't be a stranger, Lizzie.'

She waved and disappeared out of sight.

# Chapter One

Lizzie drew the duvet back over her head in a pitiful attempt to block out the sound of the buzzing intercom. Three days ago she'd turned off her mobile phone and pulled the landline out of its socket. Why the heck hadn't she worked out how to dismantle the intercom? At least it was only the security desk phoning up. Never had she been so grateful to have moved to this eye-wateringly expensive, but highly secure, apartment block. Pulling the duvet tighter round her ears, she waited for the noise to go away.

When at last it was quiet, she hauled herself out of bed. She needed to take another shower. It was fast becoming an obsession. Something even she, in her shock-numbed mind, could see. Despite the number of showers she'd had though, the stench of sex still surrounded her. It filled her nostrils and clung to her mind, stubbornly determined to hang around. A constant reminder of what had happened. What must have happened, even though she couldn't remember any of it. Shivering with disgust, she turned on the spray, putting it up to maximum heat. If it was hot enough, the steam would surely blast the stench away.

The heat washed over her as she rested against the marble tiles of the shower wall. For three days she'd done nothing, yet she felt drained, physically and emotionally. With a passing interest, she watched the rivulets of water splash over the jut of her hip bones. She had to eat something soon. Even by the too thin modelling standards, she was becoming scrawny. But the thought of food turned her stomach. God, would she ever feel normal again?

Drying herself off, she padded back into her bedroom. She'd bought the apartment two years ago, when she'd made the move from the chaos of New York to the craziness of LA.

All part of a determined effort to put the past firmly behind her. It meant not living in the same city where her parents had been killed. Not living in the city where, on every corner, there was a cafe or a shop she'd taken them to. For a short while the excitement of a new city and a new place had helped. Yet it had been a long time since she'd smiled at the plush cream carpet she'd agonised over buying, or grinned at the gigantic sleigh bed that had cost her a small fortune. A long time since any of it had made her happy. And that was before this latest gigantic, sleazy balls-up.

Clothes. She needed to find some clothes and get dressed. How many hours had she spent lying in bed, crying? She couldn't waste any more time like that. She had to pull herself together. To be strong. Heck, two years ago her family had been all but wiped out on a single, tragic day. This wasn't the worst thing that had ever happened to her. If she could cope with burying her parents, if she could cope with seeing her brother lying comatose in a nursing home week, after week, after week, she could cope with this.

With those thoughts in mind, she reached for the jeans she'd thrown carelessly over the extravagant cerise velvet chair. About to pull them on, her eyes settled on the crushed newspaper lying on the floor. The same one she'd read three days ago. With a wail of anguish she lunged for it, tearing it into shreds. Leaving the tattered remains on the floor she yanked on her jeans, pulled on the nearest jumper – a baby blue cashmere she'd spilt tea down the moment she'd opened the damn newspaper – and walked down the hall towards the kitchen.

'Lizzie? Are you in there?'

She froze, the voice achingly familiar. Perhaps she was hallucinating. She hadn't eaten for days. Her mind must be playing tricks on her.

'Lizzie, it's me. If you're in there, open the damn door.' There was a pause, and a further knock. 'Please.'

In a daze, Lizzie walked slowly to the door. Nobody here called her Lizzie. She was Elizabeth Donavue. She hadn't been Lizzie for years. In fact there was only one person who still called her by that name.

'Nick, is that you?' Her voice came out as a strangled whisper.

'Thank God.' She could hear the relief in Nick's voice. 'Come on, Lizzie. I'm the only one here. Open the blasted door.'

With trembling fingers, she fumbled with the locks. Three days ago she'd secured the door with every security device she had. Now it seemed to take an eternity to undo them all. She barely had time to register it really was Nick standing on her doorstep, before she was bundled into his arms and pushed back into her apartment. He kicked the door shut with his foot and then stood back to look at her.

'What the hell is going on?'

She moved her mouth, but no words came. 'I ...' Shaking from head to foot, she walked away from him. Oh God, she was going to cry. Again. It was all she seemed capable of. She'd only taken two steps when a strong arm reached for her waist and dragged her back, turning her round to face him before holding her firmly in his arms.

'Shh, it's okay. Everything is going to be okay. I'm here now.' Gently he held her, smoothing his hand down her back, just as a parent would comfort a small child.

Lizzie was dimly aware of being lifted and carried to the sofa. Nick sat them both down, cradling her against him, murmuring words she couldn't hear. Despite trying not to, she began to blubber like a baby, all over again. The more she clung to the familiar strength of him, the more she was helpless to do anything but let it all come out. In the end, that's what she did, crying until the tears ran dry and her body stopped trembling.

'I've made your shirt wet,' she whispered, pulling away, totally embarrassed at her meltdown.

'Excuse my language, but sod the bloody shirt.' He narrowed his eyes and scrutinised her face. 'Christ, you look terrible. What have they done to you?'

Tears threatened again. God, it didn't take much. Just a note of concern in his voice and she was filling up again. 'Why are you here?' she asked, ignoring his question. Maybe his arrival was just a fortuitous coincidence. Maybe he hadn't seen …

'I read the newspapers, Lizzie. Saw the photographs.' He fixed her with his serious brown eyes. 'Why didn't you answer my calls?'

Shame washed through her. Now she knew exactly why he was here. Not to see her, but because he'd seen the mess she'd got herself into and felt duty bound to come and dig her out of it.

'Lizzie.' He was still looking at her, pinning her with the force of his gaze. 'At the risk of repeating myself, what the fuck is going on?'

She recoiled at his harsh tone. 'You've seen the articles. You know what's going on,' she replied stiffly, edging away from him.

Nick grabbed hold of her hand and pulled her back to his side. 'Not so fast. Not before you tell me exactly what happened to get you into this state.' He held her face firmly between his hands, angling it so she was forced to look into his dark eyes. 'Damn it, I know what I read isn't the truth.'

The certainty of his words, coupled with the sincerity in his eyes, forced a lump into the back of her throat. 'The girl in those pictures is me, Nick,' she told him shakily, moving to snatch a tissue from the box on her glass coffee table. 'I can't deny that.'

'Did they blackmail you? Force you to do it? Were you drugged?'

Oh God. Dear Nick. 'Thank you.' Another sob wrenched from her. Heaven above, was she ever going to stop crying?

'What on earth are you thanking me for?'

22

'For believing in me.' She sniffed and wiped at her eyes. 'The truth is, I don't know exactly what happened. One minute I was having a drink with Charles and his friend. The next Charles was shoving these disgusting pictures at me, threatening to go to the press with them if I didn't give him a hundred grand.'

'Christ.' Abruptly Nick stood and walked towards the open plan kitchen. 'I think you'd better start from the beginning, but before you do, I need a drink.' His eyes wandered clinically up and down her body. 'When was the last time you ate or drank anything?'

She tried to remember, but the days were a blur. 'I don't know,' she admitted, sinking her head into her hands. 'Oh, Nick. It's all such a bloody mess. When I saw the pictures in the paper, I didn't think of the implications. I just thought, *what a bastard*. Then the phones started ringing and the intercom kept buzzing, all with journalists wanting to speak to me, and suddenly I couldn't cope. I didn't know what to do.'

'So you turned your phones off and went into hiding?' He shook his head. 'Maybe I can't blame you, but it would have been a heck of a lot easier on your friends if you'd just screened your calls.' Across the room, he sought out her eyes. 'You had me worried, Lizzie. You should have phoned.'

'I couldn't. I was too ashamed.' She'd reached for the phone a couple of times, but stopped when she'd begun to rehearse what to say. However she'd phrased it, the words had made her sound like a slut. 'And anyway, I didn't want to burden you.'

'Burden me?' he repeated incredulously.

'Yes. I'm not your responsibility.'

'Bloody hell, Lizzie, since when was helping a friend a burden?' Obviously fighting for control he ran a hand through his hair before swearing again, this time more crudely. 'Don't ever do that to me again,' he muttered finally. 'Look, why don't you go and finish getting dressed while I find us something to eat and drink? Then we can start again, from the beginning.'

Lizzie looked down at her stained jumper, conscious it wasn't the only part of her that looked a mess. Her hair was drying in knots because she hadn't bothered to comb it. She knew if she stared in the mirror she'd see a puffy face and bloodshot eyes.

Squaring her shoulders, she stood. The time for wallowing in self-pity was over. She was a model. Her career might be crashing around her ears right now, but that was no reason not to start looking and acting like one again.

As soon as Lizzie left the room, Nick dropped his head into his hands and sucked in a deep breath. He'd imagined all sorts of things since seeing those disgusting pictures in the newspapers. The photographs of Lizzie and two men, having sex in a hotel bedroom. Dear God, he'd even seen the video of it on the internet. Watched how they'd degraded the only woman he'd ever loved. Of course he'd known straight away it wasn't really Lizzie. It might have been her face and her body, but it wasn't her free will. Yet if he knew it, why did nobody else realise it? The way it had been reported had implied she'd been a willing participant. One of the men in the photographs, the one claiming to be her boyfriend, had expressed outrage at his private life being made public. Then gone on to announce they often enjoyed three in the bed sessions. That in fact the Elizabeth Donavue he knew was a raunchy sex kitten, very different to the angelic image she portrayed in the media.

Nick had wanted to wring his bloody neck.

Beneath all the lies though, one thing was true. Lizzie was no longer the young innocent girl he'd fallen in love with. In his heart he'd known that, but knowing and having evidence of it thrust in his face were two different things. Over the years he'd got used to seeing her linked to a string of good-looking men. Most recently to some her mother would have been shocked at. But whatever her dubious choice in members of the opposite sex, he was sure the raunchy image being portrayed in the press was a false one. Lizzie might have grown up, become more sophisticated, but at heart she was still the girl he'd loved for most of his life.

Clenching his jaw, Nick opened the fridge door, horrified by how empty it looked.

He wouldn't rest until whoever was responsible for hurting Lizzie was made to pay.

Lizzie hesitantly brought a forkful of scrambled eggs to her lips.

'Come on, eat up,' Nick encouraged. 'You're nothing but skin and bones under those clothes.'

She gave him a small smile. 'Thanks. Your lavish compliments always did blow my mind.' But she nibbled at the toast, took another mouthful of eggs, and gradually began to find her appetite. Within minutes she'd cleared her plate and washed it down with a large glass of orange juice.

Feeling slightly more human, she sat back on the chair and glanced over at him. Despite the trauma of the last few days, she felt the familiar tug on her heart. Age had only made him better looking. He still wasn't dashingly handsome, not by the standards of the models and TV stars she mixed with, but he was, oh so quietly, extremely attractive. In fact, he was more than that. He was quietly sexy, which was a pretty breathtaking combination. Tall and lean, his thick dark hair was shorter than the last time she'd seen him, highlighting his seriously deep brown eyes. His long thin face still shrieked of intelligence, even without the glasses she was used to seeing him wear. Now she thought about it, this new, glasses free face was altogether more eye-catching than she remembered. His brown eyes larger and more eloquent. So no, he wasn't extravagantly handsome, but she'd take his serious, intelligent good looks over those of the men she'd dated any day.

He looked up and caught her staring. 'What's wrong? Have I got egg on my chin?'

For the first time in days, Lizzie found herself wanting to giggle. Sitting at this table with Nick might be escapism, but for a few short minutes she was going to push all the crap into the background and just enjoy him being here. 'I was trying to work out what had changed about you. Where are the glasses?'

He dropped his gaze back to his plate and started clearing up. 'I decided to give in to vanity and have laser surgery.' He shrugged. 'Mainly I got fed up with losing them down the back of the sofa. I still haven't got used to the fact that I don't need them any more. The first thing I do when I get up in the morning is reach for the blasted things.' Having piled all the plates into the dishwasher, he turned back to her. 'Feeling better?'

She nodded. 'A bit, thank you.'

'Strong enough to tell me what happened?'

Was she? Lizzie took a deep breath and reached for the glass of wine he'd poured. 'Yes,' she said quietly. 'But let's do this somewhere more comfortable.'

Nick followed her back to the sitting room. There she curled up on the end of the sofa while he chose to sit in the armchair. He leant back and made himself at home, throwing one long jean clad leg over the other. 'Why don't you start by telling me who the hell Charles is?'

# Chapter Two

At the sound of Charles's name on Nick's lips, Lizzie shivered. 'Charles is a bastard. I'm ashamed to say, he was also my boyfriend.'

She risked a glance at Nick. His expression was serious, concerned, but there was no judgement. Whatever else had gone on between them, he was still her friend. He was on her side. He nodded for her to continue.

'Charles started off as my personal trainer.'

Nick's lips twitched. 'Very show biz.'

'Yes, I know, but, hey, I'm a model. I'm paid to look good.' She fidgeted with her hands, more embarrassed than she'd thought at discussing her love life with him. And this was only the start of the story. 'I thought Charles was different to the guys I'd been dating. Less shallow. Less inclined to make sure his best side was facing the camera when we went out.'

'It wasn't anything to do with his rippling torso then?'

'Well, that might also have been a factor,' she had to admit. 'But, in all honesty, mostly I liked him because he was attentive and easy to be with. Don't laugh, but he seemed genuine.'

'Yeah, a genuine low life.'

She snorted. 'Yes, well, clearly when it comes to men, my judgement is shot to pieces.'

'You won't get any argument from me over that statement,' he muttered darkly. 'Go on.'

'A few nights ago Charles and I arranged to meet up in the bar of the Beverly Wilshire.' Nick whistled and without thinking, she stuck her tongue out at him. It took her back to her childhood, when life had been simple, uncomplicated by the surge of puberty and emotions other than friendship. 'It's the only place in town, honey,' she drawled. 'Charles and I had a couple of drinks together and he seemed in good form.

27

I remember thinking, this is pleasant. Then another man came up and introduced himself. One of Charles's friends.' The lightness of a few moments ago vanished and sickness and disgust crept back. She'd had sex with that man – someone she'd only just met – and she couldn't remember any of it. 'Sorry, I don't think I can do this.'

Nick unfurled his body from the armchair and walked towards her, arms outstretched, but Lizzie jumped to her feet and moved away. How could she talk about the sordid things she'd obviously done with one man, while being comforted by another? Even more so, when that man was Nick.

A mixture of hurt and frustration flashed across his face as his rejected arms fell uselessly to his side. 'I know this is hard for you, but I need to know what happened,' he told her stiffly as he sat back down in the armchair. 'If I don't, I can't help.' His eyes pleaded with her. 'I want to help.'

She understood, but God, on a scale of 1 to 10 of the most cringe-making things a woman could discuss with the man she had a crush on, this must rate somewhere near 100. Perching on the side of a small table, her legs like blancmange, she cleared her throat and tried again. 'I can't remember the friend's name. Matthew, maybe? All I know is it wasn't long after he joined us that I started to feel funny. Like I was drunk, though I'd only had two glasses of wine. My head felt as if it was spinning off my shoulders so I told Charles and he checked me into a room at the hotel, telling me I needed to lie down.' Her hands were trembling so she clasped them in her lap. 'That's it. The rest is a blank until I woke up in the hotel room the following morning. There was a note on the bedside table from Charles saying he hoped I felt better and that he'd come round later that evening to check up on me.'

'You don't remember *anything* of what happened during the night? No flashbacks, no blurred images?'

'No. When I woke I was naked and I knew I must have had sex. The smell ...' She shut her eyes, still smelling it now. 'I remember wondering what sort of man Charles was that he'd made love to a woman so clearly out of it.' Her voice grew smaller and smaller. 'I didn't have to wait long to find out. He came round that evening and handed me an envelope full of photographs.' Finally she raised her eyes to Nick. 'You said you'd seen them?'

He nodded. 'And before you ask, yes the video clips as well.'

Swallowing hard, Lizzie blinked. There were thousands, maybe millions of people watching her have sex at this very moment. With not one, but two men. And Nick had seen it, too – Nick, who hadn't even found sex with her appealing enough when she'd been a virgin. Right now he must be thinking she was only one step up from a whore.

'Charles threatened to take the pictures to the press if I didn't pay up.' She rushed the words now, desperate to get to the end of the sordid tale. 'I could have found the money, but I remember thinking *bugger him*. He'd already degraded me. He wasn't going to make money out of me, too. I had no thought for the consequences. I just didn't want to let him win.'

'So you didn't pay up and Mr Genuine followed through with his threat.'

She flinched. 'I didn't need the reminder of how gullible I was.'

He leaned forward and ran a hand across his face, instantly contrite. 'No, you didn't. Sorry.'

'I wasn't aware of what he'd done until I read the newspaper the next morning.' For the rest of her life she'd remember the horror and disgust, the disbelief when she'd turned to that page. 'The phones started ringing then and they just wouldn't stop.' Shaking away the memory, she remembered what had puzzled her earlier. 'How did you get past the security downstairs? I explicitly told them not to let anybody upstairs without buzzing me first.'

'The guard did buzz up, but you didn't answer. I told him I was your lawyer, and that if he didn't let me up, I'd have him done for kidnapping.' His mouth curved at the memory. 'It was the best I could come up with at the time.'

'Are the press still out there?'

'Oh yes, in force.' He gave her a direct look. 'I don't think I realised quite how famous you are.'

'After this fiasco I'll be a damned sight more so, and for all the wrong reasons.' Tears threatened again. Angrily she rubbed them away. 'God, what a mess.'

'Lizzie, have you contacted the police?'

Vigorously she shook her head. 'No. What good would it do? I haven't got any evidence to prove I didn't wilfully go to bed with the pair of them. Charles was my boyfriend, for heaven's sake. I can hardly cry rape. Not when the pictures show how much I'm apparently enjoying myself.'

'You were drugged,' Nick stated quietly.

'Yes, I think I was. Either that or I'd had a lot more to drink than I thought.' She let out a frustrated sigh. 'I've got no proof of that, though. It's been too long after the event. There won't be anything in my bloodstream any more.'

Nick had done his best to sit quietly while Lizzie had been speaking. She would never know what it had cost him to remain outwardly calm, while inside he'd swung between wanting to shake her and wanting to find Charles and shove a fist into his smirking face. Then haul him up by his fancy lapels and punch him again. Why had she lowered herself so much to go out with that snake in the first place? Didn't she realise how special she was? Far too special to be sleeping with a glorified bodybuilder.

He tried to rein in his anger, but some of it seeped out as he spoke. 'Why didn't you go to the police straight away? As soon as the bastard turned up with pictures?'

She recoiled sharply. 'Oh sure, that was my first reaction. Charles, thanks so much for showing me those photos. Do you mind if I call the police while you wait here? Oh and do help yourself to a drink.' She let out a humourless laugh. 'I wasn't thinking, damn it. I was too stunned, too shocked. And, oh God ...' Tears once again flowed freely down her cheeks. 'I was ashamed. There were pictures of me naked, having sex with two men. I couldn't bear the thought of talking to a starchy police officer about it. Heck, to anyone about it. Plus I never for one moment thought Charles would do as he'd threatened.' She grabbed the last tissue from the box. 'I thought I meant something to him. Even when I realised he only wanted me for a meal ticket, I stupidly believed what we'd shared would be enough to stop him from humiliating me. Guess I was wrong.'

Nick's gut twisted as he stared at her puffy blue eyes, the blonde hair that hung limply around her shoulders. It was humiliating to realise he was as much in love with her today as he had been all those years ago, yet in her eyes they were so estranged she hadn't even bothered to call him when all this had kicked off. He'd had to barge over uninvited, uncertain of his reception. He couldn't even haul her into his arms because she was sitting on that blasted table, as far away from him as she could possibly be, her body language screaming *leave me alone*. He was left sitting on the armchair, looking at her helplessly. 'We'll work all this out, Lizzie.'

'I don't see how. I've been such a bloody fool.' Agitated, she pushed off the table and began to pace.

'If you're guilty of anything, it's being too trusting.' He clasped his hands together to stop from reaching out to her. 'What about your contact at the agency? Don't you have a manager or agent or whatever the term is? Someone who can handle the press for you?'

'Yes, yes I do.' She laughed sadly. 'I didn't even think of calling her. Too terrified of her reaction, I guess.'

He scowled at her. 'This isn't your fault.'

'No. Deep down, I know it's more to do with one man's greed than my naivety, but ...' She buried her head in her hands. 'God, I've just signed a contract to be the face of a new perfume. Innocence.' She began to laugh uncontrollably.

Simmering with anger he walked over and grabbed her by the shoulders. 'Get ahold of yourself, Lizzie,' he told her tersely. 'This will all blow over.'

'Easy for you to say. You don't earn a living from your face.'

He'd never hated her job more. 'You're worth more than just your face,' he snapped. 'Even if this ruins your career, so what? There are other things you can do. Jobs that use your brain instead of your looks.'

'Like what, Nick? If you can think of another job for a woman like me, with no qualifications and no experience other than smiling in front of a camera, that can earn me what I'm earning now, don't keep it to yourself. Spit it out.'

Great. Now he'd managed to make her angry. Still, better angry than feeling sorry for herself. He rubbed at his eyes. Crikey, he was tired. The time difference was finally catching up with him. 'Okay, I'm sorry. It won't come to that, anyway. For the time being you need to talk to your agent and get her to issue a statement that puts your side of things. We also need to talk to the police.' He saw her look of horror, but didn't back down. 'Charles drugged you, raped you, then tried to blackmail you. Yes, the police need to know.'

'I don't want them involved.'

Her shoulders set in a stubborn line but he ignored them. 'Tough. We're calling them. And then I'm taking you back to England for a while.'

At that casually dropped bombshell, she gasped. 'Oh, you are, are you? Who on earth suddenly made you my keeper?'

'I'm not your keeper, but I am going to take care of you.'

'Thanks, but I can take care of myself.'

He thought about retorting that on current evidence she wasn't doing a great job of it, but held his tongue. She was no longer the young girl he'd dreamt of protecting. She was a grown woman, capable of making her own choices. Still, she needed to face the truth. 'You're a mess,' he told her bluntly. 'You're not sleeping or eating properly, which means you're also not thinking clearly. I'm taking you back to give you time to recover, both mentally and physically. The press won't know you're there. It will give you some breathing space.'

'And if I don't want to go?' The stubborn glint that he knew of old was back in her eyes.

'I can't force you. It's your decision.' Then he fixed her with a glare of his own. 'But make sure whatever you decide, you do it for the right reason and not because you don't like being told what to do by me.'

Lizzie took a long, hard look at Nick's strong profile. When she'd been young, she'd had him wrapped round her little finger. As soon as she'd grown up, that had stopped. Evident the moment she'd asked him to make love to her and he hadn't. Now he was glaring at her, daring her not to do as he'd said. 'I want to tell you to butt out,' she admitted, surprised by the tremor in her voice. 'I know I've made a spectacular mess of things right now, but up to this point I've done pretty well, actually. I've made it to the top of my profession in one of the toughest cities in the world. Without your or anyone else's help.'

'I know that. You're strong and determined. Always have been. But admitting you need help doesn't make you less capable. It simply makes you sensible.'

She acknowledged his comment with a small smile. 'Low blow.'

'I can fight dirty if the outcome is important to me.'

Beneath her chest, her heart fluttered a little. The thought of leaning on someone else for a while, especially if that someone was Nick, was making her feel almost giddy with relief. 'Okay, I'll come back with you, but because I want to, not because you're telling me to.'

'Good.' His dark brown eyes warmed with amusement, as if he knew exactly how much it had cost her to say that. 'First things first though. Call the agency.'

'They're going to kill me,' she muttered as she plugged the phone back in. 'My career has been built on a squeaky clean, ice maiden, butter wouldn't melt in my mouth image. It doesn't exactly fit with lurid newspaper photographs showing me engaged in three in the bed sexual romps. I'll probably never work again.'

'Bollocks,' Nick cut in tersely. 'You will. Charles isn't going to win this one. If the police don't have enough evidence to lock him away, we'll attack from another direction. By the time we've finished with him, it will be Charles that nobody will want to work with again, not you.'

As she dialled the agency number, Lizzie wondered if she'd ever seen Nick this angry. He was the calm, mild-mannered one. As a child she'd soon learnt not to bother winding him up; he never rose to the bait. Robert, on the other hand, she'd been able to wind up like a top, getting him to flare into anger at the slightest provocation. What she wouldn't give to have her brother do that again. 'I don't expect you to help me with this, Nick,' she asserted, waiting for the agency to pick up. 'I've got money. I'll find an attorney to handle it.' The last thing she needed was to be indebted to him even further.

'I know you've got money,' he replied tightly. 'But I've got connections. I know a good lawyer, or attorney as you Yanks call them, and he happens to be based in LA. If anyone can get you justice, Dan Rutherford can.'

Just then the receptionist answered. Figuring now was the time to put her effort into saving her career, rather than arguing with Nick, she turned away and asked to speak to Maria. Agent and friend. At least she had been before this mess had hit the headlines.

# Chapter Three

Several hours later Lizzie's external face was back in the right sort of direction. Maria, bless her, had been amazingly supportive. Between her and the PR agency they used, plus a few corrections from her newly-acquired attorney, courtesy of Nick, they drafted out a statement saying simply that Lizzie was horrified by the leaked photographs and had no recollection of what had happened that night. The matter was now in the hands of her attorney and she would not be making any further comment except through him.

Now was the tougher part – talking to the police. Bad enough recounting the sordid details to Nick. At least he'd been a sympathetic ear. The hard-faced cop was something else. Maybe she was being paranoid, but the officer seemed to be going through the motions. Oh, he made a show of taking down her story, and asking lots of questions, but she sensed he was doing it only because it was expected of him. Not a flicker of sympathy crossed his stony face, not a hint that he believed what she was saying.

'Somewhere at the newspaper office there will be an envelope with Charles's fingerprints on it,' Nick insisted. 'Or at least CCTV evidence of him leaving the package there. That'll help prove he wasn't an innocent bystander in all this. And what about the other guy? Maybe he'll talk. Or the staff at the bar? They had to have noticed Lizzie going from having two drinks, to suddenly falling off her chair, paralytic.'

'We'll follow up every lead,' the officer reassured him wearily. 'But you have to understand all this happened several days ago. Any evidence there might have been is likely to have been lost by now, and eyewitnesses are unlikely to remember a lady appearing drunk in the bar. It's hardly an unusual occurrence.'

Lizzie's hackles rose, but Nick's clearly rose faster. 'Are you taking this seriously?' he asked coldly. 'If not, you damn well should be. We're not talking about a petty dispute between lovers, here. This lady has been raped and blackmailed. She needs to trust you'll do everything in your power to make sure the man who did this is punished.'

It was odd, hearing herself being referred to in the third person. Odder still to have someone fighting on her behalf.

Ruffled by the accusation, the previously laid back officer glowered at Nick. 'I'm well aware of what you say has happened, Mr Templeton. But you and your friend need to understand you've done yourselves no favours by waiting until now to report it. We'll do what we can. I can't say more than that.'

While Nick showed him out, Lizzie sank wearily onto the sofa, glad to see the back of the man. 'He didn't believe a word I said,' she commented when Nick walked back into the room. 'He thinks I've had a row with my boyfriend over the photographs, and now I'm pissed because he's leaked details of our torrid sex life to the press.'

'It doesn't matter what he thinks,' he replied quietly, coming to sit down next to her. 'We know the truth. And the truth always comes out in the end.'

With that he leant back against the cushion and shut his eyes. For the first time since he'd arrived, Lizzie noticed how tired he looked, a fact emphasised when he rubbed first at his eyes and then at the dark stubble across his chin. He had good hands, she noticed. Strong and capable. She bet they could excite a woman just as well as they could soothe.

Embarrassed at the turn of her thoughts, she glanced quickly back at his face, grateful to find his eyes still closed.

'Nick,' she whispered, causing his eyes to flutter open. 'You're exhausted. It must be the early hours of the morning for you. Have you booked into a hotel, or do you want to crash here?'

Wearily he threaded a hand through his hair. 'I came straight from the airport. My bag is down with security. I'd rather bunk here, if it's all the same to you.'

Taking hold of his hands she pulled him to his feet. 'It's the least I can do. Go fetch your bag. I'll check the spare room has some bedding in it.'

That night she slept better than she had done in days. Odd, because in effect, nothing had changed. Her life was still in exactly the same God-awful mess it had been three days ago. The only difference was now someone was sharing the burden with her. It had been a long, long time since anyone had done that.

As she filled the kettle the next morning, her stomach grumbled, reminding her she was hungry. Another giant step forward. She rummaged in the kitchen, but all she could come up with were tea bags and stale bread. A pretty damning insight into how well she'd been looking after herself recently.

'You haven't turned into a real American yet then?'

Unused to people in her apartment, she jumped at the sound of the voice. A moment later a sleepy Nick wandered into the kitchen. His hair resembled that of a hedgehog, his face still needed a shave and he wore yesterday's jeans and a wrinkled T-shirt. One he must have slept in. All in all he looked decidedly crumpled – a far cry from his usual classic, tidy appearance. God but he looked sexy though. Sweet vulnerability combined with an edgy maleness. It made her heart sigh.

He nodded over to the teapot she'd just filled.

'Ah, you mean I haven't succumbed to starting the day with a cup of coffee instead of tea.' She grimaced. 'Ugh, no way. In fact when I go on a shoot I drive them mad because I always ask for a cup of English breakfast tea. They roll their eyes and call me a typical English brat, but, hey, you can take the girl out of England, but you can't take England out of the girl.'

'Good to see some things don't change.' In his progress

towards the breakfast bar he paused to study her, his brown eyes skimming over her face. Quietly assessing. 'How did you sleep?'

Though she'd spent most of her life having her looks scrutinised, she squirmed under Nick's careful study. 'Better, thanks.' She turned away before he could find further fault. 'How about you? From what I can see, not for long enough.'

'I'm probably not looking my best,' he acknowledged with a wry smile, scraping a hand over his dark stubble. 'You, on the other hand, look a lot better than you did yesterday.'

Lizzie winced at the memory. 'I needed to.' She poured the tea into two giant mugs and added milk. She didn't have to ask Nick whether he wanted sugar. She'd made him countless cups of tea over the years and his taste had never changed. Strong, white, no sugar. 'Do you still mean it, about me coming back to England with you?'

'Yes. Why, are you having second thoughts?' He accepted the steaming mug and plonked his tall frame on the nearest bar stool.

Lizzie bit her lip. 'No, of course not.' She'd mulled it over again last night, before nodding off to sleep.

'I sense a but.'

'There is no but. I was just thinking how it would probably do me good to get away from this place for a while. I've not been back to England for years. Not since the funeral.' She flinched at the word. Saying it out loud made it real. There were times she liked to live in a fantasy world. One in which her parents were still at home and she could fly back and see them when there was a pause in her manic schedule. A world with no grief … and no guilt. It worked, until she reached for the phone to call them and realised they weren't there.

'Have you ever really given yourself time to grieve, Lizzie?'

Avoiding his eyes, she turned her attention to the toaster and began to fill it with the stale bread. 'Truthfully? No. I threw myself into every venture offered so I *didn't* have time to think. Because thinking is too damn heartbreaking.' The need to cry clogged her throat as she busied herself with finding some butter. Suddenly all she wanted to do was get away from this stifling apartment. Away from California where she was being hounded by every journalist with a pulse.

It was time to go home.

Prising Lizzie out of her apartment and onto a plane had been easier than Nick had anticipated. Of course they'd had to use a bit of creativity to get her out of the building without the press getting wind of it. Nick had walked out of the front with their bags and picked up the hire car. Wearing a dark wig and disguised as one of the cleaners, Lizzie had sneaked out of the rear exit where he'd been waiting. Only Maria, her agent, knew she was leaving the country.

'Nick, before we go to the airport there's somewhere I need to visit. Just quickly.'

He glanced over. Wearing large sunglasses and a black baseball hat, she looked stunning but solemn. 'Robert?'

She nodded. 'I know it's stupid, that he can't understand, but I always like to tell him when I'm going away.'

'It's not stupid,' he replied softly, indicating to pull off at the next junction. A manoeuvre that caught her totally by surprise.

'How did you know to turn off here?'

'I've been there before.'

'You have?'

'Why are you so surprised? He was my brother, too. At least in spirit.'

'Yes I know, but ...' She shook her head and stared out of the window.

'I've only been to see him twice. Both times I called you first. Both times you weren't there.'

'I've done a lot of travelling in the last two years.' He watched as she played with her bottom lip. 'If I'd had some warning, I would have changed my schedule.'

39

Nick shifted his eyes back to the road. She was right. Only phoning her the day before he was due to fly out hadn't displayed a great deal of effort on his part. The truth was, he'd been torn. Half of him desperate to spend time with her. Half of him desperate not to go down that route again. So in the end he'd fudged the issue and called at the last minute, appeasing his conscience, ensuring minimal damage to his heart.

When they entered Robert's room, Nick was shocked to see his friend looking thinner, more gaunt than he had eight months ago. The staff were meticulous in keeping his hair trimmed, his face shaven, but they couldn't do anything about his still, lifeless appearance.

Nick stood behind Lizzie as she sat by her brother's side and held his hand, calmly talking to him as if he were really listening to her. He didn't know how she did it. As quickly as he entered the room, he always wanted to leave. The sight of his dashing, larger than life friend reduced to such a hollow shell was too painful to watch for long.

She was quiet on the way to the airport and he left her to her thoughts. What could he say? It cut him up to see Robert like that, but he'd only been his friend. To Lizzie, Robert was the only family she had left.

They managed the whole trauma of airport check in and departure without Lizzie being spotted. Now settled in first class, she'd kept her wig on and was, outwardly at least, captivated by the inflight magazine. She looked beautiful – even with the wig, the exhausted pale face – but so fragile. Nick had to fight the urge to snake his arm around her and snuggle up. Sadly the last thing she needed at the moment was another man coming on to her. What she desperately *did* seem to need was a good friend.

'Are you sure there's nobody else you want to tell you're leaving LA?'

Slowly she eased back on her seat. 'Is that your roundabout way of asking me if I've got any real friends?'

'Yes.'

A wry smile twitched at her mouth. 'I've got lots of friends, thank you, but none I feel the need to contact right now.'

It struck Nick that who she thought of as friends, he called acquaintances. If they'd been real friends, why hadn't she phoned them at the first sign of trouble? And if they weren't close enough to lean on, why the hell hadn't she phoned him? His conscience pricked. He hadn't exactly overwhelmed her with calls himself.

'I'm sorry I haven't been in touch as often as I should have over the last two years.' He gave her hand a quick, awkward squeeze.

She slipped the magazine into the seat pocket, and his hand fell clumsily onto the armrest. 'You've been busy. I've been busy. Life often gets in the way. You phoned me on my birthday and at Christmas. That meant a lot.'

His efforts sounded pathetic, even to his own ears. If he was honest, his attempts at keeping in touch had stopped after he'd glimpsed Lizzie on American TV during a visit to Robert. She'd been hanging on the arm of a famous actor and in a flash all the hard work he'd put into trying to forget her had decimated into a million tiny, jealousy-filled pieces. He'd wanted to dive into the TV set and knock the man's straight white teeth down his neck. To his shame he'd dashed off home and not contacted her since.

'I'm going to get some sleep.' Lizzie called for the flight attendant to turn her seat into a bed and was soon snuggled down, her head tucked under the duvet.

Wearily Nick rubbed his eyes with the heel of his hands. Even dog-tired as he was, he knew he wouldn't be able to sleep. It was a combination of the noise of the engines and the absurd notion they were suspended in a silver tube, thousands of miles up in the sky. He reclined his chair back a little and accepted the drink offered by the stewardess. Sipping at his whiskey, he gazed at Lizzie's sleeping form, unable to shrug off the feeling that he'd let her down. It shouldn't have mattered that visiting her would have hurt his already damaged heart. Lizzie bloody well deserved to have someone in her life looking out for her, checking everything really was going as well as it appeared on the surface. Instead he'd taken things at face value and stayed away, licking his wounds, trying to move on.

With a start he remembered Sally. Colleague, friend and occasional sleeping partner when it suited them both. He should warn her he had a friend staying with him for a while. The last thing he needed was Sally turning up at the barn and Lizzie opening the door to her. The thought of the pair of them meeting sent an unpleasant shudder through him. Lizzie and him weren't together, neither were Sally and him a real item. Still, he wasn't sure he wanted the woman he loved but wasn't sleeping with to meet the woman he was sleeping with but didn't love.

He must have dozed off, because the next thing he knew they were announcing the approach for landing. Gently he gave his companion a shake. 'Time to wake up, sleepyhead.'

She groaned and pulled herself up, peeling off the eye mask, blinking her large blue eyes. It was so odd to see her with curly dark brown hair. It kind of suited her. Then again, so would a pink, frizzy wig.

'Are we landing already?'

He grinned. 'If you call *already* ten hours later, then yes, we are landing already.'

'Wow, I must have slept the whole way.' She pulled off the blanket and immediately the cabin crew glided over to sort out her seat.

'Some company you are,' he told her when they'd finished. 'Remind me not to sit next to you on a plane again.' He inspected her face. 'You needed it though. In a couple of days you might look half decent.'

She gave him a quick dig in the ribs before shifting to look out of the window. 'London. I never thought I'd miss it. But here I am, looking at the grey sky and the brown Thames weaving through the city like a fat worm, and thinking it's the most beautiful sight in the world.'

'I can think of more beautiful sights,' Nick replied quietly, his eyes on her profile. 'But I agree, London's one heck of a city. I hadn't planned on us staying in it though.'

She snapped her head round. 'Oh? Where are you planning on taking me then? Do I get a say?'

'Yes, of course you get a say,' he answered hastily. 'We can stay in London if you like. I've a two bed flat in the City, which I use during the week because it's handy for work. Alternatively, we can drive a couple of hours west and stay in the barn.' He smiled at her raised eyebrows. 'Converted barn. It's even got running water. There's more room there and I thought fresh air and countryside might be a better place to wind down.'

Lizzie studied him for a few seconds. 'I didn't know you had a place in the country.'

'I don't know how many places you have,' he countered, trying not to feel too defensive.

'Three.' Pride filled her eyes. 'And I don't care if that sounds boastful. I paid for them all with my own earnings. There's the place in LA, a house in the Nappa valley and a lodge in the mountains for when I go skiing.'

'Obviously,' he said dryly, pushing aside the stab of guilt as he remembered something he hadn't told her. There was time enough for that later. 'I can't compete with that, though you can keep your ski lodge. I wouldn't get on a pair of skis even if you paid me. The London flat is actually my parents' old place. The barn is all my own. Sheep on the hills, no other house in sight, a walk through the field to the pub—'

'Okay, okay,' she interrupted, laughing softly. 'It bugs me to say it, but you're right. The barn sounds lovely.'

'Let's hope you're still thinking that when you've stepped in your third cow pat.'

They shared a smile, just before the wheels touched down.

# Chapter Four

As Nick drove through the country lanes, Lizzie felt the tug on her heart. The villages they drove through looked very familiar.

'We're not far from where we used to live, are we?'

He shook his head, though his eyes remained fixed on the road. 'The barn is about half an hour from your parents' old place.'

The ache in her chest, the one that never really disappeared, just quietened when her mind was busy, started to gnaw at her. It felt wrong to be driving to another home. To know that even if they were heading to her old home, her mum and dad wouldn't be there.

Another family would.

Suddenly a warm hand found hers, clasping it tightly with his strong fingers. She glanced up and Nick gave her a quick, understanding smile, his eyes full of sympathy. *I know*, he told her silently. *I'm here for you*.

Emotion shot into the back of her throat and she took a deep, steadying breath. For the first time in years she realised she didn't have to cover up what she was thinking. Pretend everything was okay. Not with Nick.

That thought alone was enough to steady her.

Ten minutes later, Nick turned the four-wheel drive down a dirt track. Ahead of them was a stunning glass-fronted barn conversion, nestled between the rolling hills. As a place to hide away from everything, and everyone, it was damned near perfect.

'Wow, is this really it?'

He nodded.

'But it's gorgeous.' She was already itching to jump out of the car and take a look inside. 'You let me rabbit on about the places I've bought, all the while knowing you were taking me to this.'

Nick gave her a sideways glance. 'Property isn't too expensive out here. It's not a big deal. Not compared to what you have.'

Was there a trace of bitterness in his voice? She studied him as he manoeuvred the car round the potholes. No, it wasn't that. He'd never coveted what others had. Yet there was something. Resignation? Anger? Sadness? 'Don't put yourself down. You're a partner in a thriving accountancy practice. It's what you always wanted to do. I can't imagine you'd be jealous of my career.'

'Jealous? No. It's just you live in a world a million miles away from mine.' The wistful tone to his voice had her scrutinising his face, but he quickly masked whatever he was feeling with a quick smile. 'Anyway, there's no way I'd want to earn a living by taking my clothes off and pouting at the camera.' She delivered a smart thump to his arm. 'Ouch.'

'It's the least you deserve,' she told him, opening the car door. 'I'll refrain from delivering the riposte you warrant, which goes something along the lines of *who on earth would pay you to do that anyway*, because I'll be relying on your generous nature for a while.' Jumping down from the car she took in a lungful of fresh air. 'Wow, you can't beat the smell of the English outdoors. A combination of grass and sheep poo. So, are you going to show me round this country pad of yours, or do I have to nosey by myself?'

Nick fetched her case out of the boot, commenting, 'Mulberry, I see,' and went to open the front door. 'Nosey all you like. I'm going to check what there is to eat.'

Lizzie needed no further encouragement and dashed towards the barn like a greyhound after a hare. It was definitely different from the sleek modern places that littered LA. The door opened into a small hallway, but her eyes skipped over the flagstone floor, the local paintings that lined the wall, drawn instead to the room at the end. Her mouth gaped as she walked into the main living area. Weathered oak beams dominated the vaulted ceiling, and huge windows looked out onto the garden and across to the neighbouring fields, flooding the interior with light. To one end was an inglenook fireplace, complete with wood-burning stove and lined with row upon row of neatly stacked logs. The sight made her smile. It was so Nick: prepared for a blizzard, even in spring.

To the side of the living room, where Nick was opening various cupboards, was the kitchen. All granite and gleaming stainless steel, with windows overlooking the hills.

Comfortable yet tasteful was how she'd describe it, which wasn't a huge surprise. Just as Nick himself was good-looking, yet understated, traditional but not dull, so was his barn.

'Am I allowed upstairs?' she called out.

'As it's where you'll be sleeping,' his voice floated back to her, his head now inside the fridge. 'It's probably a good idea.'

Eagerly she climbed the sturdy oak stairs to the first floor where she found two bedrooms, both with en suite bathrooms. It wasn't hard to guess Nick's bedroom. The biggest, dominated by a giant wooden bed, the navy duvet stretched neatly across it without a single wrinkle to be seen. Feeling slightly sneaky she opened the wardrobe door. Jumpers and T-shirts were meticulously folded on the shelves, ironed shirts and several smart jackets hanging from the rail.

Smiling again to herself she took a peek at his en suite – and her heart stuttered at the Clinique bottles on the shelf by the window. The second toothbrush in the holder. So he did have a woman in his life. Not one who stayed here often enough to leave her clothes in the wardrobe, but a regular enough visitor to leave a second set of toiletries in his bathroom.

*You can't have seriously expected him to live like a monk*, she told herself crossly. She certainly hadn't.

The sharp reminder of why she was here brought a sting to her eyes. No, she wasn't going to cry. She'd done enough of that.

Closing the door to the en suite she walked briskly past the second bedroom, which she guessed would be hers so would check out later, and onto the last room. A study; clearly where Nick worked when he was away from the office.

She broke into a grin on discovering the framed rugby shirt on the wall and the antique leather ball in an oak display cabinet. He'd loved all sport, but rugby had been his passion. Robert's too. Many an hour she'd spent on a field in the pouring rain, watching the pair of them being tackled into the mud. A wave of nostalgia swept through her. Happy, happy times.

Fighting back the emotion she took several deep, steadying breaths and started to walk back down the stairs. The sight of Nick bending down to light the stove made her hesitate. Suddenly she was struck by how intimate this was. She was going to be sharing his home. Just the two of them. Yes, he was someone she'd known all her life, a man she had once looked on as a brother. But that had been a long time ago. He wasn't her brother, and the feelings he stirred in her were far from those of a sibling. There was still this incredible pull whenever she looked at him. Something time, and a string of supposedly gorgeous hot dates, hadn't managed to dim.

As if aware of her presence, he turned round and smiled. That was also something that hadn't changed. It still licked at her heart, turning his otherwise slightly serious face into one that was dimpled and boyish. It made her want to smile back and as she did, some of her unease disappeared.

'Got your bearings?'

'I think so.' She shuffled herself down on the large scuffed leather sofa. 'So, how long have you had this place?'

Nick turned to poke at the fire, more in a bid to steady himself than to encourage the flames. Lizzie was here, in his home. It was a dream come true.

*But think why she's here, you dimwit.* Not because she'd suddenly realised she loved him. Not even close.

He forced his attention back to her questions. 'I bought it a few years ago. I was fed up with living in London all the time. Great during the week, but at weekends I couldn't turn off. I'd find myself popping back to the office for some reason or other. Before I knew it, Monday had come round and all I'd done was work.' Satisfied with the fire, he stood and rested his arm against the mantelpiece. 'Now I try to come here every Friday. If I have to work, I can, but mostly I try to relax.'

'And what do you do here, with your precious time off? It seems it could get pretty lonely.' She didn't quite look him in the eye. 'Of course that assumes you don't have any regular company?'

He huffed out a breath. 'You're not usually so subtle. Ask the question you want to ask.'

This time her eyes looked straight into his. 'Do you have a girlfriend?'

And now she'd asked, he wasn't sure he wanted to answer. 'I have a female friend who visits occasionally,' he said carefully.

'A friend with benefits?'

He winced. 'And now I'm wishing you'd stuck to the subtle approach. Sally is a fellow partner at the accountancy practice. We enjoy each other's company,' he added lamely, hoping it didn't sound as shallow as it sometimes felt. He did like seeing Sally, even outside the bedroom. It's just she would never be It for him.

And that was the fault of the woman staring at him now, he thought with a rush of anger. If only she wasn't so damn beautiful. So strong and funny and refreshingly direct.

If only he wasn't still so hopelessly in love with her.

With a quick, jerky movement he went to sit on the opposite sofa. Ignoring the unasked questions in her eyes, he made a play of stretching his legs out on the Union Jack footstool. 'Anyway, I quite like my own company, as it happens. If I get lonely, I go to the local pub. There's always somebody there ready to chew my ear off about all these city boys who come and buy up properties in the country.' In a desperate display of nonchalance, he put his hands behind him and cupped the back of his head. 'What about you, Miss Los Angeles? What do you do to relax?'

As if she was mirroring him, Lizzie stretched out on the sofa. 'I go to the cinema, run along the beach, have a drink with my friends, party.'

'That's what you call relaxing? Don't you ever stop and do nothing?'

Lizzie laughed. 'No way. Life's too short for standing around. I'm too scared I might miss out on something.'

'That's one of the many differences between us,' he mused, wondering if she was already thinking what he was about to say. 'You're extrovert and party loving. Me? I'm a quiet night in front of the television type of guy.' Abruptly he got to his feet. 'Do you want a drink? Anything to eat?'

His swift change of subject earned him a questioning look, but thankfully she didn't follow it up. 'You don't have to wait on me, Nick. If I'm staying here, I have to do my share of the chores. And since you cooked for me yesterday, it's only fair that I give it a go today.'

He snorted. 'I cooked scrambled egg on toast. I don't think that counts.'

'It does in my book. Do you have any requests, or shall I see what I can come up with, bearing in mind my limited repertoire?'

'Why don't we work something out together?' He started to walk into the kitchen, turning his head to check she was following. 'If you watch and learn from the master, you might even get to expand that repertoire.'

'You, the master?' This time she was the one who snorted, though it was more a delicate noise than he'd managed. 'Since when did cooking become one of your areas of expertise?'

'Since I had to fend for myself and became bored of takeaways.' It had surprised him how much he'd started to enjoy it though, his stint in the kitchen turning from a chore into a world of discovery. It was one of the things he looked forward to about hooking up with Sally: cooking for someone other than himself for a change.

And now, for a week, maybe even two, he would have Lizzie to cook for.

The thought brought a rush of pleasure. He wasn't going to think of the hole she'd leave in his life when she left. He was going to enjoy the time he had with her.

In the end Lizzie watched as he prepared his signature dish, prawn linguine, courtesy of a well-stocked freezer. Drawing up two stools, they ate in the kitchen at the granite-topped island.

'I can't remember the last time I had a home cooked meal,' she said, in between mouthfuls. Not small ones, either, he noticed with satisfaction.

'Seriously? I wouldn't have thought models were great fans of takeaways.'

She gave him a slightly embarrassed shrug. 'We're not. I eat out a lot.'

He gave himself a mental slap round the head. Of course that was the other option to cooking or takeaways. 'And this confession from the woman who was going to cook for me. Are you ready to concede my mastery in the kitchen then?'

She gave him a thoughtful study. 'I am prepared to admit you make a fantastic prawn linguine.'

'And the scrambled eggs?'

'Okay, you're a master of linguine and scrambled eggs. But for all I know, that could be all you live off.'

Nick considered her. 'That sounds like a cunning move to get me back in the kitchen again, just to prove you wrong.'

Her lips twitched, telling him she knew exactly what she was doing. 'Well, you do seem happy cooking. I'd hate to take that pleasure away from you.'

Shaking his head, Nick started to clear away the plates. 'You always were an expert manipulator, even as a child. You had your whole family wrapped around your little finger.'

At the mention of her family, Lizzie's smile faltered. He watched as sadness filled her eyes and cursed himself for mentioning them. It was something they needed to talk about, as was the situation with Charles and the photographs, but he'd promised himself he wouldn't raise either subject just yet. He wanted her to take time to simply relax and start to feel at home.

He scratched around in his mind for the right words to say but came up with nothing, so instead he went with instinct. 'Come here.'

He held out his arms and, to his intense relief, she stood and moved unhesitatingly into them. 'I miss them so much,' she mumbled against his shirt.

'I know. So do I.' He lifted her head so she was forced to look at him. 'I think it would help us both if we talked about them. Not now,' he added hastily as she stared at him in horror, 'not when we're tired and jet-lagged, but maybe over the next few days.'

'Okay.' She studied him, her expression pensive. 'I forgot you loved them, too.'

'They were like parents to me, and Robert is the brother I never had. Yes, I loved them, too.' Her face was pale, her eyes heavy. 'Come on, you look done in. Why don't we call it a night?'

Nick carried her case up the stairs and placed it in the spare bedroom. 'I think there should be everything you need in here,' he told her, poking his head into the cupboards to check there were spare blankets and towels. 'Will you be okay?'

Lizzie sat tiredly down on the bed, glancing round at the room. Suddenly she burst into tears.

'Hey.' Alarmed, Nick crouched down in front of her. 'I didn't think the room was that bad. I even had my sister advising me on colours.'

She rolled tear-filled eyes at him. 'It's perfect.'

'Then why the tears?' God it hurt to see her so miserable. 'We'll sort it all out. You don't need to worry.'

'I know.' She fished a tissue from her pocket and dabbed her eyes. 'It sounds daft but I wasn't actually thinking about all that crap. It just struck me how much better everything seems now, here, than it did when I woke up on my own yesterday.'

'If you'd phoned me earlier you wouldn't have had to go through any of it alone.'

'You're right, I should have buried my pride and done exactly that.' She laughed softly. 'Then again, you came anyway, even without the call.' Gently she kissed his cheek. 'You're a special man, Nick Templeton.'

Nick swallowed back the lump in his throat. Special was good. If only he could be happy with that. If only he didn't crave more. Giving her a last reassuring squeeze, he pushed himself to his feet. 'Goodnight.'

He shut the door gently behind him. The next few days, maybe weeks if he was lucky, were going to be bittersweet. Somehow during that time he was going to have to work out a way to be happy with special.

# Chapter Five

When she woke the next morning, Lizzie's first thought was that she was at home. Not the apartment in LA, but the home she'd once shared with her family. It was the sound of the sheep that tricked her. She'd grown up in the country, accustomed to waking to the bleating of lambs and the chatter of birds. The regret, when she realised she wasn't waking up there, indeed that she'd never wake there ever again, was sharp and painful.

Needing the distraction she quickly drew back the blue and white check curtains. Okay, she wasn't at home, but this wasn't a bad place to wake up. There was a similar sense of peace to home. In fact the longer she stared at the tranquil country view, the more she could kid herself the shambles going on in LA was just a bad dream. And Lizzie was pretty good at kidding herself. If she was capable of pretending her family were still with her, then she could have a bloody good go at putting all that chaos to the back of her mind. At least for a while.

Shrugging on her robe she walked onto the landing, wondering if Nick was awake yet. As she tiptoed past his study, she heard him talking to someone on the phone. The door was ajar so she carefully pushed it open. He was sitting behind his desk, his back to her, but turned and smiled when the creak of the door gave her away. Quickly she backed out, shutting the door after her.

*How stupid*, she berated herself as she walked down the stairs. Worse, *how selfish*. Wallowing in her own self-pity, thinking only of what she wanted, what she needed, she'd conveniently forgotten Nick had a job to do. One that probably didn't fit too easily with having to drop everything, jump on his white charger and dash across the Atlantic to rescue her, then babysit her.

Sighing deeply, she filled the kettle. It was, what, Thursday? Well, she'd stay till Sunday. That would give her long enough to get her head screwed back on, whilst not causing Nick too much further disruption. On Monday he could go back to his office, and she … the kettle wobbled in her hand. Cold dread, the type that had clung to her in LA, curled its way into the pit of her stomach. She would go back to hell. But hopefully, by then, she'd be feeling strong enough to face it.

'You look very pensive,' Nick remarked as he joined her in the kitchen. 'Did you sleep okay?'

She glanced over. He had the look of a man who'd been up for a while – clean-shaven and dressed in jeans and a crisply ironed sky-blue shirt. He seemed to fill the kitchen, looking taller and broader than she'd remembered. And smelling gorgeous. It drifted up her nostrils: a hint of ocean, a sniff of fresh air, a waft of something sexy. *The question, Lizzie. Answer his flipping question.* 'Err, yes thanks, I slept like a log.' She indicated to the kettle. 'Do you want a cup?'

'Sure.' He sat on the stool and waited while she poured the water out into the mugs, frowning when he saw her hands weren't quite steady. 'Don't tell me you've been thinking about Charles and those flaming pictures again?'

Carefully taking the tea bags out of the mugs, and adding the milk, Lizzie pushed one over to him. She had been, yes, until he'd come into the room. Perhaps she was better off thinking of Charles.

'Coming here is great, Nick. Exactly what I needed, but I've got to go back and face it all some time.' She took a sip of tea. It was hot enough to almost scald her lips. Just how she liked it. 'So I was thinking, I'll go home Sunday. If that's okay with you, of course. Me staying here until then.'

Slowly Nick put down his mug and stared at her. 'That's really what you want to do?'

His eyes drilled into hers and she almost told him the truth. *No, of course it isn't.* But she'd been selfish and needy before and it had cost her parents their lives and Robert any sense of normality. Abruptly she spun away. 'Do you want some toast?' She began to forage in the bread bin.

'Lizzie, forget the flaming toast for a moment. I want to know what your plans are. I had thought, well, I'd hoped ...' He let out a deep sigh. 'Heck, I intended for you to stay a lot longer than that.'

'Really?' She nearly squeaked with joy.

'Of course, really,' he replied quietly. 'I don't want you going back until we've sorted out this mess. Hell, I won't let you. If I need to, I'll lock you in your bloody room. The speculation won't stop until we've proved what Charles did, Lizzie. You can't go back to living like you were when I found you.'

Tears threatened again, tears she didn't want him to see because she'd drowned him enough already. 'But you have a life,' she told him haltingly. 'I can't expect you to suddenly stop everything to help me out. I know you think you have a duty to look after me. Some sort of promise to Robert.'

'Rubbish.'

His vehemence rocked her back on her heels. 'Well, I didn't mean to upset you. I just wanted to let you know I really appreciate everything you've done for me already and—'

'Lizzie, will you shut up for one blasted moment and give me a chance to speak?' His voice was still raised, the words enunciated slowly and clearly. Perhaps he wasn't angry, but exasperated.

She shut up.

'Firstly, yes, I do have a life, but there's no reason I can't continue it with you here. On the days I need to go into London, you can choose to come with me, or stay at the barn. It's up to you.' Though he was back to calm and controlled, an edge of steel ran through his words. 'Secondly, how on earth can you think I'm only helping out of duty? I'm doing this because I care for you, Lizzie. I care and I want to help. Okay?'

Oh boy, the tears were falling fast and hard and the

tightness in her throat was making speech almost impossible. 'Okay,' she whispered, wiping her cheeks. 'I guess if you put it like that.'

He stretched out his hand to squeeze hers. 'Of course I also need to consider that if your parents are watching over us, they'd have my guts for garters if I didn't look out for you.'

'If they are watching, they're already livid with me for getting into this flipping mess in the first place,' she said with a sniff. 'God, I seem to have this habit of blubbering all the time.'

He smiled. 'Better to let the emotions out than keep them bottled up.' Looking up at the clock, he shifted off the stool. 'Right, I've got to make a few more calls and then I figured we could go for a walk. I know a pub that does a great lunch.'

'Sounds good.' She put a hand on his arm to stop him dashing away. 'But please, Nick, if I start to get in the way ...'

He flashed a grin at her. The one that made her knees buckle. 'Don't worry. I'll let you know.'

The walk to the pub was over the hills, and Nick strode off at his usual brisk pace. It was one heck of a day for it. The sun was shining high in the sky and the spring weather warm enough to allow them the luxury of being unburdened by coats. Lambs bleated on either side as they rambled steadily through the fields. It always made him smile when he looked at them, their cheeky faces watching intently as they monitored the humans going by. Turning to ask whether she knew when a lamb became a sheep, he was surprised to find his companion – blonde hair once again covered by a dark wig, glasses shading her eyes – was several yards behind him.

'Nick Templeton, for pity's sake, will you slow down,' Lizzie shouted at him, then cursed as she lost her footing down a rabbit hole.

Grinning, he waited for her to catch up, noting she finally had some colour in her cheeks. Combined with the wig and the oversized sunglasses, she looked like a glamorous film star; a present day Audrey Hepburn. She'd lost none of her unique sparkle, that was for sure. In fact it seemed she was growing even more stunning with age. What was she now? Five years less than him ... that would make her twenty-six. Yes, she was now a truly beautiful woman. *And way out of your reach*.

'If I'd realised we were going on a yomp, I'd have worn my combats,' she complained as she drew alongside him. 'You might have the long legs of a six foot man, but I don't.'

'Six foot three,' he countered. 'And yours look pretty long from where I'm standing. But that's irrelevant. I do believe you're unfit, Ms Donavue.'

'Unfit my arse,' she replied crossly, her breath coming out in fast pants. 'When I was with Charles ...' She bit her lip and looked down at her mud-covered boots.

'Oh yes, the personal trainer.'

'Exactly.' Shrugging, she lifted her eyes back up to his. 'I should have realised then, when he was practically dragging me round the park, that he'd turn out to be a bastard. I called him one often enough, once my lungs had recovered.'

'He can't have been much of a personal trainer if a short walk over a few hills has you panting.' And yes, that was meant to be a dig at Charles, not her, but her cool tone told him his aim was off.

'I'm a bit weak from not eating over the last few days, that's all. I could do with walking a little slower.' Dutifully he fell in beside her. 'Are you still as obsessed with exercise as ever?'

'If you mean do I continue to believe in the benefits of exercise, then, yes, I guess I do,' he clutched gratefully at the change of subject.

She smiled then, just a glimmer, but at least it had stopped her thinking about Charles. 'And do you still take part in those ridiculous marathons?'

'Hang on a minute, since when did it become ridiculous to challenge your body?' She tipped up her glasses and the twinkle he saw in her eye told him she was playing with him. 'I've not done as many recently,' he admitted reluctantly. 'When you get to my advanced age, the recovery takes a lot longer.'

'You poor old thing.' As she used to when they were growing up, she threaded her arm through his. 'I admire you for taking part, though. I find it hard enough dragging myself out of bed for a three mile run, never mind the thought of doing that eight times over.'

'I haven't got any other reason to stay in bed.' His eyes rested on her, staying there just a little too long. With an effort he dragged them away. What the hell was he doing, drooling over her like that? She'd run a mile if she guessed how he really felt. Probably even run twenty-six of the ruddy things.

'Not even for Sally?'

Guilt rushed through him as he realised he'd been thinking of Lizzie in his bed, and not the woman he was, albeit only loosely, sleeping with. 'I told you, Sally and I aren't ... we're not ...' he trailed off, annoyed with himself. His relationship with Sally wasn't something he should be ashamed of. So what if it was just about sex and convenience? It wasn't as if he was leading her on. Sally felt exactly the same way. 'We're not serious,' he settled with. 'And anyway, never mind my love life, what on earth were you doing dating a slimeball like Charles?'

Lizzie's expression told him she didn't want to discuss her love life, either. 'He was a mistake.'

'There seem to have been quite a few of them.'

She glanced at him sharply. 'I'm not good at reading men.'

'Hey, I wasn't judging,' he told her hastily, kicking himself for his bluntness. 'It's just I've noticed a certain, shall we say, type.'

'You've been checking up on me, have you?'

Busted. He tried a casual shrug. 'I'd prefer to call it taking an interest. Your dates seem to have become meaner and tougher looking each time.'

Her expression tightened. 'So, I like a bad boy. It's not unusual, you know.'

Wham. It felt like being punched in the gut. Her words couldn't have been clearer. *I don't fancy you.* Nick knew he could put on black leathers and shove a stud through his nose but he'd still look like the blasted boy next door.

'Sorry.' He let out a long, slow breath. 'I didn't mean to pry or to criticise.'

They walked on, but now the atmosphere between them was charged and Lizzie looked as tense as she had in LA. *Change the bloody subject.*

'The pub's not far. In fact, if you look over to your left, you'll see the roof peeping out from between the hills.' He slid a sideways glance at her. 'Hopefully after you've eaten you'll be sufficiently revived to keep up on the way back.'

'Funny man.' With a toss of her head she marched out ahead of him. Distracted by the sight of her trim behind, Nick stepped straight into a mound of sheep dung.

# Chapter Six

Barring their altercation on the way to the pub – and how upsetting had that been, hearing Nick talk about this Sally woman. The one he appeared to be seeing for a quick shag when he felt in the mood, and then in the next breath criticising her own choice of companion. Apart from that though, it had been a good day. In fact Lizzie wondered if it might even go down in her diary as one of the best she'd had in recent memory. What it had lacked in sparkle and glitz, had been amply made up with fresh air, laughter and blessed peace. Back at the barn now, and having eaten Nick's excellent steak and chips, washed down with half a bottle of very nice Merlot, she lay on the sofa, pleasantly exhausted. Nick had disappeared off to his study a while ago and she was summoning up the energy to climb the stairs to bed. It made her laugh to see it was only ten o'clock. In LA the evening would only just be getting started. Here, in the English countryside, all she was fit for was curling up and going to sleep.

Reluctantly she tore her body from the too comfortable sofa and climbed up the stairs. Nick's deep voice echoed from his study as he talked to someone on the phone. She came to an abrupt halt when she realised he was talking about her.

'Dan, I don't have to remind you how much we need to sort this out, for Lizzie's sake. Are you really going to tell me you haven't found anything on this guy?'

Her hackles rose. Why hadn't Nick told her he was going to be discussing her situation with his attorney friend tonight? Not only that, why hadn't he let her join in? Angrily she pushed open the door. Nick acknowledged her with a frown before turning his attention back to the person on the phone.

'Sorry, mate, I know you're trying your best. I'll mull it over again this end and call you back later.' With a hiss of frustration he ended the call and turned to face her. 'Dan's been following up on some leads, but it doesn't look as if any have been successful so far.'

'And when, exactly, were you going to tell me about this?' Her voice sounded horribly shrill, but she was cross.

'I'm not sure, *exactly*, but some time tomorrow morning.'

'Don't you think you should have consulted me before discussing my private life with one of your friends?'

'Hey, that's not fair.' He leapt to his feet and moved to touch her shoulder but she shrugged off his hand. 'That's not how it was,' he replied stiffly. 'You agreed to let Dan be your attorney. All I'm trying to do is help. Can't you see that?'

'Yes, I can. What I can't understand is why you think you can do this without talking to me. It's my mess, my life.'

He sighed deeply and turned to look out of the window, leaving her with a view of the rigid set of his shoulders. 'Today you looked happy. The torment had disappeared from your eyes. I didn't want to bring it back again so soon.'

Oh God, what could she say to that? The sincerity of his quietly spoken words knocked the anger from her. But it didn't mean he was right.

'Nick.'

He glanced back over his shoulder, his dark eyes watchful.

'I understand you were trying to protect me, and I thank you for it. But I'm no longer a little girl who needs you to look after her. I'm a grown woman. I don't need wrapping in cotton wool and cosseting.'

'Message understood.' Slowly he moved to sit back at his desk. 'I guess it was naive of me to think you might need rescuing. You've always been strong, not to mention fiercely independent.' Once seated, he smiled, though his eyes were … sad? That was it. Why on earth was he sad? 'I promise not to exclude you from now on.'

The last thing she wanted to do was upset him, but he looked so drained, defeated almost, she knew she had. Maybe one day she'd understand what was going on in that super brain of his, but clearly it wasn't going to be today. 'I didn't mean to sound so mean. You know how grateful I am for everything you're doing.'

Nick tried to smile at her, but his face was so tight he couldn't manage it, so instead he turned his attention to his computer. Gratitude. That was all she was ever going to feel towards him, and it was about time he got the bloody message. He'd been trying to come to her rescue like a flaming superhero – erase the bad man, win the girl. He should have known better. All Lizzie needed was a friend to advise her. Not Superman to take over. He had to stop morphing into this moping, lovesick fool every time he saw her. It was really starting to piss him off – God knows what it was doing to her.

'Why don't you go to bed, Lizzie,' he replied finally, aware she was still hovering. 'I promise I'll run through everything with you tomorrow morning.'

She gave him a curt nod and left the room. To give her space – give them both space – he took a few minutes to go through his emails. Just as he was gearing up to go to bed, his mobile rang. He looked at the caller ID and sighed.

Then sucked in a breath and shoved a smile on his face. 'Sally.'

'Well, hello stranger. You're answering your phone so you can't have totally disappeared off the planet.'

This time his smile was more genuine. 'Yes, sorry. Something came up.' He cringed at his awful phrasing.

'Something?'

And yes, he deserved that question. Time he had the conversation with her he should have done the moment he'd brought Lizzie here. 'A friend of mine is in trouble. She's staying with me at the barn for a while until we can sort it out.'

'She?'

Damn, why was he feeling so guilty? 'Yes. She.'

There was a brief pause before Sally replied. 'I'm sorry to

hear that.' Another pause. 'Is this friend the same one you once mentioned to me? The one who headed off to the States and broke your heart?'

He'd spilled his feelings to Sally one drunken evening, not long after Lizzie had returned home following the funeral. What had started out as a quick drink after work had ended with them both having too much to drink, and going back to his flat. Sally had listened, made sympathetic noises, then told him she'd just had her own heart broken by a guy who'd cheated on her. Drowning in their shared misery, they'd gone on to have sloppy, drunken, consolation sex. After that it had become an unspoken agreement that when one of them needed cheering up, or someone to share something with, they'd hook up. 'Yes,' he admitted. 'It's the same friend.'

'Ah. Is she okay?'

Nick had never told Sally exactly who his 'friend' was, and he certainly wasn't going to start now. 'She will be,' he said firmly.

There was another silence and Nick guessed Sally was put out that he was being so tight-lipped, but even if he hadn't wanted to protect Lizzie's privacy, he still wouldn't have wanted to talk to his sometime lover about the woman he loved.

'So, I guess me popping over this weekend is a bad idea then?'

Nick shut his eyes, leaning back on his chair. 'It would be better if you didn't come over, yes.' Christ, this was awkward. He felt like he was cheating on her, and in effect he was, even if just with his mind. It didn't matter that Sally knew the score. She was a great woman. She deserved more than being someone's occasional shag. 'Look, Sally—'

'It's fine,' she interrupted. 'Whatever spiel you were going to give me about this not being fair on me, you can forget it. I went into this with my eyes wide open. I hope you manage to help your friend. I'll still be here when she goes back to the States.'

'That's not right.' He let out a long, deep sigh. 'You deserve more than this.'

'I think you've forgotten what I said at the beginning. I'm not after any more than this. I'll see you in the office?'

'Yes. I'll be in next week.'

When he put down the phone he felt sadder than he had in a long, long while. What was wrong with him that he was pining after a woman who didn't want him, not like that, when he should be out there looking for someone who did? And why, instead of doing that, was he making do with some half-baked relationship where they were both using each other, rather than supporting each other, protecting each other? Loving each other?

Lizzie wished she hadn't listened to all that. Wished instead she'd walked away as soon as she'd heard Nick talking on the phone again. She'd only come back to his office to apologise again for being such a bitch to him.

She turned to move, and the damn floorboard creaked.

'Lizzie?'

Forcing a smile on her face, she opened the door. 'Sorry. I just came back to apologise again, and then I heard you on the phone, so ...' *I listened in, like a nosy cow, and now wished I hadn't.* 'I didn't want to intrude.' She twisted her hands, feeling stupid. Not only was she putting on him in terms of his hospitality, his work, now she was getting in the way of his love life. 'Look, I can go away for the weekend. Give you and Sally some privacy.'

He exhaled harshly, shoving a hand through his hair. 'I don't know how much you overheard, but I have no interest in seeing Sally while you're here.' His dark eyes rested on hers. 'You are far more important to me.'

Inside her chest her heart stuttered, then did a long, slow flip. Funny how none of the men she'd ever slept with had told her that. Determined not to think about how important she would remain when she went back home, and he picked up his affair again, Lizzie went up to him and kissed his cheek. 'Thank you.'

# Chapter Seven

When Lizzie walked down to the kitchen the next morning, Nick was nowhere to be seen. She knew he wasn't in bed, because he'd left the door to his room wide open. The king-sized bed was rumpled but empty and there had been no sound of a shower. For the briefest of moments she wondered if he'd decided to drive into the office to avoid talking to her about his late night chat with Dan, but when she looked out of the window his car was still on the drive. It was then she noticed the lone runner, making his way across the fields towards the barn. Even from a distance, she could tell it was him. A tall, rangy figure dressed in T-shirt and shorts. The sight made her smile. He'd never been one for all the gear, something that had always amused her and Robert. Here was a man who did so much exercise he needed the lycra leggings and climate control vests, yet he was happier wearing tatty T-shirts and shorts, leaving the latest athletic fashions to the fair weather joggers.

She opened the door for him and he stood on the step, panting slightly. About the same way she panted when she walked up the stairs. 'Morning.'

He eyed up her dressing gown clad figure. 'Morning, sleepyhead. When are you going to get up early enough to come and join me?'

Her eyes strayed to his legs. Used to seeing male legs smothered with fake tan and waxed hairless, Nick's were a novelty. Pale and covered in a fine layer of dark hair, they were muscular and most definitely male. 'It all depends on how far, and how fast, you're planning on going.' Reluctantly she shifted her gaze back to his face.

'Worried it won't be fast enough or far enough?'

'Of course.' Both of them knew she was lying.

'Well, come out with me tomorrow and I'll try and keep

up with you.' He bent down to yank off his trainers. When he stood back up, his expression was serious. 'I'll grab a quick shower and we can talk over breakfast.'

As she watched his retreating back, the tension returned to her stomach once more. Perhaps he'd been right to keep this stuff to himself. At least he'd given her yesterday.

By the time Nick came back down, freshly showered and changed into black jeans and a black T-shirt, Lizzie had managed to scramble together a pot of tea and several rounds of toast.

'Does the dark attire have any bearing on what you're about to say?' she remarked as she poured out the tea.

He glanced down at his clothes. 'I can assure you I have enough trouble finding tops that match bottoms, without having to factor in matching them to my mood.' Sliding effortlessly onto a stool, he reached for a mug. 'You're getting good at breakfast, Lizzie. Maybe soon you'll be proficient enough to move onto lunch.'

She sat down opposite him and glared. 'Ha ha. If you want me to continue to make breakfast, I suggest you rapidly change the conversation. We can start with what on earth you and Dan were talking about last night?'

'Fair enough.' He took a huge mouthful of toast and Lizzie was forced to wait while he chewed then swallowed. 'I told you when we were in Los Angeles that we'd clear your name. Before we start, I need you to understand that no matter what it takes, that is what we're going to do.'

She opened her mouth to speak, then shut it again when she saw the fierce determination flaring in his eyes. Somewhere in her chest, her heart lifted and lodged itself near her windpipe.

'Okay,' he continued, stretching his hands out in front of him, as if he was getting down to business. 'Here is where we're at. Your attorney, Daniel Rutherford, otherwise known as Dan the Man—'

She nearly choked on her toast. 'Seriously?'

'Seriously. The guy's a legend. Anyway, he's been working on a few angles he'd hoped would provide the police with sufficient evidence to nail Charles, aka, the bastard.' Nick's face turned sombre. 'Disappointment number one, it appears nobody at the bar remembers you acting oddly or appearing drugged. The guy on the reception desk remembers you, Charles and another guy coming to get a key for the hotel room, but only because he recognised your face. He said you seemed perfectly happy and he had no reason to think there was anything unusual going on.'

The toast she was chewing started to taste like cardboard. How could she not remember willingly going to that hotel room? Willingly having sex with two men? Not just willingly but, according to the pictures, *happily*.

'Hey, are you all right?'

Nick reached across the breakfast bar and held her hand. Clearing her throat she brought her mind back to the here and now. 'Yes, sorry. For a moment I started to think back.'

He swore and clutched her hand tighter. 'That's exactly why I didn't want to discuss this with you yesterday, or last night. I wanted you to have time to be you again. Without all this crap getting in the way.'

'I know, but I can't continue to put my head in the sand. It's my life we're talking about. The real one, not the fantasy one I'm living here.'

Point taken. Sadly Nick let go of her hand. For the first time he acknowledged his desire not to mention this yesterday hadn't been entirely selfless. He, too, hated the reminder of her life in LA. Of what that git had done to her. He wished instead of talking about this, he could sweep her into his arms and take her to bed. Make both of them forget everything. But that was *his* fantasy, and the likelihood of it happening was about the same as him winning the London marathon. On one leg. Dressed as a flamingo.

'Okay. Where was I?' He took a swig of his tea and tried to collect his thoughts. 'Dan managed to acquire the original photographs from the newspaper group and gave them to the police for fingerprinting. Disappointment number two, it seems there were so many prints on them there was no hope of getting a match with anyone.' The hand that had been holding her mug jerked and Nick kicked himself. 'Sorry, that was pretty tactless.'

She gave him a wan smile. 'Don't worry. It's not like it's only the newspaper staff who've seen the photos, is it? They've been in all the papers, splashed all over the internet. Probably somebody, somewhere, is eating fish and chips off them. I hope it doesn't spoil their appetite.'

At that, Nick had to chuckle. 'It won't put any men off their appetite, trust me. Far from it.'

Her cheeks instantly turned red. 'I don't want to think of hoards of men lusting over pictures like that. It's different when I'm modelling. Then I'm acting the part of the model, Elizabeth Donavue. And wearing clothes, damn it.' She jumped to her feet and began to load the dishwasher, clattering the plates into each other.

Shit. 'I'm sorry,' he muttered inadequately. 'When they dished out sensitivity, I must have been at the back of the queue.'

'No. I probably just got a double dose. I need to develop a thicker skin.' She slammed the dishwasher door shut. 'So, where do we go from here?'

He tried not to wince, telling himself the machine was probably still under warranty. 'Where did you get Charles's name from? Was he recommended? I mean as a personal trainer,' he added hastily, tugging a reluctant smile from her.

'He's been on the scene for the last few years. Loads of actresses use him and some of the models I work with, so, yes, he was recommended. What are you thinking?'

'It seems odd to me that this man, who has presumably

been working with other women at least as wealthy as you, suddenly decided to target you for money. What if you weren't the first woman he'd blackmailed? What if he'd already played the same trick on some of the others, but they paid up, rather than risk the exposure?'

Lizzie, who'd moved to taking out her anger on the work surface, stopped scrubbing at it for long enough to glance at him. 'It's a thought,' she replied slowly, 'but wouldn't they have warned me off?'

Nick shrugged. 'Maybe that was all part of the deal. They paid up, kept quiet and recommended him to other clients. He promised to keep the sordid photographs out of the papers.'

'It seems like a stretch. Then again, in LA a lot of things seem too incredible to be real. What's the plan? Ask Dan to interview every woman who's used Charles?'

'Why not? If you can list the names of those you know had him as a personal trainer, Dan can start from there.' Unable to resist, he reached over to frame her lovely face with his hands. 'Help him nail the creep, Lizzie.'

Her big eyes widened as they stared into his and his heart seemed to stall. What was going on behind those huge blue windows of hers? Was she, too, thinking how wonderful it felt to have this connection? To feel skin on skin for a few precious moments? Or did she want him to get his big hulking hands off her delicate face?

The ring tone from his phone crashed into the moment and with a sigh he delved into his pocket to answer it. 'Templeton.' Mouthing *write that list* at Lizzie, he walked slowly back to his study.

He worked there for the rest of the morning, wandering down once to fetch a drink, only to find Lizzie gazing out of the window, seemingly lost in thought. Did she see the daffodils bobbing in the breeze, or was she seeing those blasted photographs? He wished to God he knew.

Finally it was lunchtime and he headed straight for

the kitchen, reaching gratefully for the sandwiches she'd pulled together, and even more gratefully for the large mug of caffeine-filled coffee sitting next to them. Following the awkwardness of his conversations last night – first Dan, then Lizzie overhearing him with Dan, rounding it all off with Sally, and Lizzie overhearing *that* – he hadn't had much sleep. Lizzie sat down quietly opposite him.

'How's the list going?'

'I've left it on the coffee table.'

She looked so down. Vulnerable, too, though he knew she wasn't nearly as fragile as she appeared. His conscience pricked, reminding him there was something they hadn't spoken about since the funeral. A rather large something that weighed heavily on his mind. Now was as good a time as any to stop cosseting her, as she would put it, and face up to it.

'Lizzie, there's something I want to show you this afternoon.'

She stopped chewing and quirked an eyebrow. 'Really? That sounds exciting.'

He pushed his empty plate to the side. 'I'm not sure exciting is the right word for it. In fact, I'm pretty certain it isn't. It's going to involve a car journey.'

'Do I get to know where to, or is that all part of the mystery?'

As her eyes danced, clearly amused, Nick wanted to put his head in his hands and howl. Why had he set it up this way? Like some blasted adventure, when he knew damn well as soon as she realised where they were going, it was going to cut her in two. Then again, if he told her, she'd never get in the car. 'You'll find out where we're headed soon enough.'

Lizzie sat beside him in the car, still wearing the air of a schoolgirl going on an outing. Nick gritted his teeth and concentrated on driving the route he knew off by heart. It was another beautiful day, hardly a cloud in the sky, but for once the sun failed to lift his spirits. The further he drove, the more he doubted the advisability of what he was doing, and the heavier the feeling of dread in his stomach. He should have waited longer. She was still a long way from recovering from a traumatic episode in her life. It was hardly the time to remind her of another, even more horrific one.

'Oh my God. You're taking me home, aren't you?' Lizzie's voice trembled as her eyes caught sight of the signpost to the village she'd grown up in.

'It's about time, Lizzie.' And it was, but his stomach clenched as he realised it was highly likely she was going to hate him for what he'd done. At the very least, she'd never trust him again.

# Chapter Eight

Fear ripped through her. It was ridiculous to be afraid of looking at the house she'd grown up in, but Lizzie didn't want to see it and know her parents weren't there. She especially didn't want to see another family living in it. 'I don't want to do this,' she told him harshly.

He must have heard the terror beneath her anger because he took one hand off the steering wheel and reached for hers, clasping it tight. 'I know,' he replied quietly, 'but I think it's time you did. There's also something I need to tell you.'

'Oh God, what?' Her mind flashed through all the possibilities. The house had changed beyond all recognition. It had been turned into a restaurant. It had been bulldozed and a block of flats put in its place. 'The new owners haven't painted it pink, have they?'

He shook his head but didn't smile. Giving her hand a final squeeze he placed his back on the steering wheel. 'No, nothing like that.'

'What then?'

They were nearly there. Lizzie knew it was just round the next corner. With her heart beating wildly in her chest, she briefly considered wrenching the steering wheel from Nick so he would be forced to turn round. How dare he spring this on her? Why hadn't he asked her first, let her build up to it, rather than forcing the issue? She opened her mouth to scream at him, but the words died on her lips. There it was, right in front of her. Her childhood home.

Oh God, it looked so pretty. The pink roses her mother loved so much were budding round the door. The front lawn was neatly trimmed, the paintwork shone. Whoever had bought it clearly loved it. She took some solace in that.

Nick surprised her by pulling up into the driveway. 'What are you doing?' He wasn't going to force her inside, was he? That was too much. She couldn't bear to see how things had changed.

'That something I need to tell you is … err, you see …' He broke off with a hiss of frustration, his whole body vibrating with tension, his eyes not holding hers. 'I bought the house.'

She gaped at him. 'You … what?' Surely she hadn't heard him right. 'You sold the house. That's what you told me. I received the money into my bank account. It helped me set Robert up in his nursing home.'

He darted the briefest of glances in her direction. 'Technically, that is what happened. What I didn't tell you was I sold the house to me.'

Dumbfounded she continued to stare at him. 'What on earth for?'

'I know you asked me to sell everything, but …' Finally his eyes met hers. Brown pools that welled with sadness. 'God, Lizzie, I just couldn't. I'm sorry.'

Her mind hurtled back to the day of the funeral; the last time she'd stayed in the house. She could vividly remember wandering through it, knowing her mother would never again cook in that kitchen. Her father would never get round to fixing the squeaking door to the living room. Robert would never again sleep in his old bedroom. 'You lied to me, Nick,' she choked out. 'I asked you to sell this house, but you didn't.' Acutely aware of the greatness of the loss she'd tried to put behind her, she buried her head in her hands.

His arm circled round her, but she slapped it away. 'Don't you dare touch me,' she screamed. 'How can you pretend to be my friend, when you've sliced me in two?' Nick jerked back, clearly stung by her words, but Lizzie didn't care. She was hurting, and he was the cause. 'What did you think you were going to achieve by this, Nick? Are you enjoying watching me fall apart?'

'Of course I'm not,' he shot back, then swallowed hard and sucked in a deep breath. 'I thought it might do you good to come back here. To allow yourself to grieve.'

'You stupid man,' she spat back. 'Don't you think I've done enough grieving? Do you honestly think I went back to the States and just got on with my life without a second's thought for them?'

'No, I don't.' His voice was heavy with misery. Slowly he reached into his pocket for the keys. 'Clearly I've cocked up here, big time, and for that I'm truly sorry. But while you're here, do you want to go in and take a look?'

At the sight of the familiar keys dangling from his fingers, she froze. Part of her wanted to get behind the wheel, turn the car around and drive away as quickly as she could. That was after shoving Nick out and leaving him stranded on the damn driveway. But the house, despite her initial dread, looked lovely. And she'd always been one to face her fears, not run from them. 'What have you done with the contents?'

'I took the clothes to the charity shop, but after that ...' He sighed. 'I didn't know what to keep, and what to get rid of. So I guess I took the easy option and just kept it all. I thought you should be the one who decided what to keep and what to throw. I always knew one day you'd come back.'

'I've only come back because you've given me no alternative,' she replied coldly. 'I told you at the time I didn't need their things to remind me of them. I have enough memories in my head to last me a lifetime.' Memories and great bucketloads of guilt. How many times did she close her eyes only to find that conversation with them running through her head? The one where she pleaded with them to come over as soon as they could because she was lonely. And how many times did she recall the knock on the door, the grim looking police officer informing her of a car accident? Three members of her family as good as wiped out. All because of her.

'I've got the message. You're not happy with what I've done.' Pointedly he waved the keys in front of her nose. 'But are you going in, or not?'

In that moment, she hated him. He was forcing her to

74

remember things she'd rather bury, but she didn't really have a damn choice. Cursing under her breath, she snatched the keys from his hand and climbed out of the car.

Nick opened his door and waited for her to come round the bonnet of the car. 'Do you want me to wait out here?'

'Yes. If you value your head, and don't want it chewed off, I'd keep away from me for a while.' With her heart thumping and her legs trembling, she walked up to the front door. Once there she took a deep breath, slid the key into the familiar lock, turned three times, a quirk that had driven them all mad, and stepped inside.

Her first thought was how bright and cheery it looked, totally at odds with what she'd expected. She'd been imagining their beautiful furniture covered with dust sheets, so it was a pleasant surprise to find the house as well maintained on the inside as it was on the outside. There were no dust sheets and, incredibly, no dust. In fact, everything was very much as it would have been had her family been alive. Only tidier. Hesitantly she wandered through the rooms, almost smiling at how shiny everything looked. Her mother would have been delighted. When she caught sight of the big old chair her father used to sit in she faltered, tears welling in her eyes. God, he'd loved that scruffy chair. If anybody else dared to sit on it, they were treated to a steely glare and quickly scuttled off. Despite the tears though, her lips curved at the memory. In reality, Dad had been a big softie. Putty in his daughter's hands, so her mother liked to tell her.

Slowly she climbed the old mahogany staircase, memories crowding through her. Her and Robert zipping down on metal tea trays. The day they'd brought their parents breakfast in bed for the first time. Chasing the puppy up the stairs after it had scampered off in disgrace, having peed on the living room carpet.

On reaching the landing, she took another deep breath and braced herself for the bedrooms.

First was Robert's room. Her heart pounded as she slowly opened the door. It was exactly as she'd remembered it. Unusually tidy, because he hadn't slept in it properly since going off to university. Despite later buying a house of his own, many of his much-loved possessions had remained in this room. The model aircraft on the shelves, the signed football, the framed pictures of Formula One race cars. Oh God, there in the middle of the bed was his battered old bear. Her eyes welled again as she reached across for it, fingering the worn ears. Robert was five years older than her but he'd always tried to act even older. Except when it came to that shabby bear.

Clasping it to her, she entered her parents' bedroom. The big wrought iron bed still had their duvet on it. The one with pink rose petals her mother had loved and her father had put up with. Some of her mother's necklaces were carefully displayed on a jewellery stand. Her father's old trilby hung jauntily on the end of the bedstead.

The rush of tears came upon her so abruptly she had no chance to stop them. As the twin bonds of grief and guilt wrapped themselves tightly round her, slowly suffocating her, she threw herself onto the carefully made bed and wept her heart out.

Nick looked at his watch for the umpteenth time. She'd been in there for twenty minutes now. Should he go and check on her? Okay, she'd made it excruciatingly clear she didn't want him in there with her, but surely by now she'd had enough time alone? He remembered the coldness of her voice, the hard expression on her face when he'd told her what he'd done. If there had been a decent sized rock, he'd have crawled under it. So, no, it was probably best he stayed out of the way.

He glanced again at his watch. Twenty-four minutes had passed. Approximately. His fingers drummed impatiently on the dashboard.

Twenty-five minutes. It was no good. He couldn't wait out here any longer.

Clambering out of the car, he walked briskly up to the house and pushed open the door. His heart nosedived at the sound of crying. No, not crying. Heart-wrenching wails of anguish. He didn't stop to think about whether she'd want him intruding on her grief – his mind was powerless to prevent him following the clamour of his heart. Bounding up the stairs he thrust open the door to the master bedroom.

He found her curled in the foetal position in the centre of the bed, hugging a scruffy teddy bear, her whole body shuddering. She looked so alone, so utterly lost, his heart shattered. Uncaring of how she'd react, he moved onto the bed and dragged her into his arms. She stiffened but didn't resist. Moments later she was clinging to him, crying even harder.

*Well done, Nicholas.* What a way to treat the woman you love. Literally bring her to her knees. He tried to soothe, rocking and running his hands over her hair, all the while feeling like the meanest bastard that ever lived.

'I'm so sorry,' he murmured, lying down on the bed and bringing her against him. 'So very sorry. I shouldn't have brought you here without warning. It was too much.' When at last he felt her tears begin to lessen, he kissed the top of her head. 'You've got full permission to hit me wherever you think will cause most pain.'

'I don't have a desire to hit you,' she sniffed, fumbling around to try and find a tissue. He handed her the wedge he'd put in his pocket before leaving the car. 'At least not at the moment.'

'Well, you should. As if you haven't been through enough recently, I decide to take you back here. Christ, I should be up for moron of the year.'

'Moron is a bit harsh.' Her face was blotchy, her eyes filled with pain, but her lips wobbled in a half-smile. 'Twit, maybe.'

Hell, he'd take twit any day. 'I let you down, and I'm sorry. I don't regret not selling the house,' he qualified quickly. 'At the time you were too raw with grief to know what you really wanted. But I do regret not telling you. At first I didn't want to upset you by talking about it. Then, well, our conversations on the phone were so brief.'

'I was always hurrying you up, wasn't I?'

'You did seem to be very busy. I tried to tell myself it wasn't that you didn't want to talk to me. Maybe I always phoned at the wrong time.'

Lizzie shuffled so she was sitting up on the bed. 'Now it's my turn to apologise. It wasn't that I didn't want to talk to you, it was just …' Her breath caught. 'Oh, Nick, whenever I spoke to you, it reminded me of Robert. I deliberately brushed you off because it was too painful. Then, after I'd put the phone down, I was so angry with myself. You were kind to phone me, and I was rude.'

He sat up, moving so they faced each other. 'Hey, don't worry. It wasn't the first time in my life a woman had given me the brush off.' She gave him a tremulous smile and for a moment his heart lightened. Maybe, just maybe, they would get through this with their friendship still intact. 'Come on. If I remember correctly, there's a great little pub around the corner. Let's go and have a drink.'

# Chapter Nine

They found a quiet corner of the village pub, far enough away from the other drinkers that Lizzie, after hastily donning the dark wig she permanently kept in her handbag now, wouldn't be noticed. Checking nobody was watching, she removed her sunglasses and waited while Nick fetched the drinks. A small beer for himself and a large glass of wine for her. She figured she deserved it. Shrugging off her jacket, she glanced around, the familiar surroundings sending prickles down her spine. She might have gone off to America almost as soon as she'd been old enough to drink in here, but still there were plenty of good times to remember. Nick's sombre-looking face, on returning with the drinks, told her he was thinking the same.

'Did you used to come in here a lot?' she asked, taking a big gulp of wine.

He nodded, his eyes taking in the unchanged deep red walls and dark wood beams. 'I think it's fair to say Robert and I have drunk many a pint in here. Your father, too. We used to get together during the breaks from university. Robert and I would arrange to meet here, and your dad would sneak in later, telling us he was supposed to be walking the dog.'

Lizzie was amazed to find herself laughing. 'Well, that explains why the poor thing grew so fat.'

For once Nick didn't laugh with her. Instead he fiddled with one of the beer mats. 'About the house. I know you wanted me to sell it, and at first I did try. But once I'd cleared out all the obvious stuff I knew you wouldn't want, like the clothes, well ... I couldn't work out what to keep and what to discard. You'd said you didn't want anything but ...' He sighed. 'To be honest, I couldn't bear to throw it away. I kept going back and each visit was slightly less painful. I started to think, what if she wants to buy a house in England one day? Surely she'd want something from her old home? Perhaps a mirror, or a table, her father's chair.'

Lizzie placed a hand over his arm. 'I was wrong,' she told him softly. 'It was unfair of me to ask you to do what I did. How could you possibly decide what I needed?' She shook her head. 'And you were right. At the time I was too numb with shock and grief to make any sort of rational decision. I couldn't bear the thought of seeing any of their things ever again. I just wanted it gone so I could try and look forward, not back.'

He sipped at his beer. 'I do think it was important for you to come back here, Lizzie. Granted I should have warned you first—'

'But then I might not have come,' she added, cutting him off.

'I would have made you, eventually.'

'Oh, yes?'

He laughed. 'I'm meaner now. Not the same pushover I used to be.'

'I didn't mean it like that. You were never a pushover.'

'I was where you were concerned.' For several heart thumping moments he held her gaze and her heart began to dance. Wasn't there more to his words, to his look, than those of a brother?

But then he stared back down at his beer and she knew she was reading too much into his simple statement. If he'd seen her as anything other than Robert's kid sister, he'd have taken her up on her offer all those years ago. Maybe if she hadn't gone to America, things would have been different, but she couldn't dwell on that. During the last two years she'd spent too long running *what if* scenarios through her head. *What if* she hadn't asked her parents to come and see her? *What if* she hadn't sent them that limo but they'd got into a taxi instead?

All it did was magnify the pain and intensify the loss.

'Who looks after the house?' she asked after a while, speaking into the now awkward silence.

Nick finally raised his eyes from his glass. 'I found a local couple happy to go over every week and check up on it. The husband sorts out the garden and the wife cleans inside and tends to the flowers.' He shrugged awkwardly. 'I didn't want it slowly falling into disrepair. I always had in mind that at some point you'd come and see it, and then decide what you wanted to do with it.'

'But how could you afford all this?'

His expression tightened. 'I had the compensation money from my parents' accident.'

She vaguely remembered being told they'd died from a faulty heater. 'Didn't you have it earmarked for anything else?'

'For a long while I didn't want to touch it. Profiting from their death ...' He grimaced. '... it seemed wrong.'

'But it wasn't like that. The money was to try and make up for their death.' Even as she said the words, she realised she knew where he was coming from. No money could ever come close to helping.

'I didn't need it. I already had their London place, and my salary can easily cover the mortgage on the barn.'

'What about your sister? Isn't the London home half hers, too?'

'We did a deal. Charlotte had our aunt and uncle's place when they died, and I kept our parents' home.' He raised his eyes to hers. 'She was too young to remember them but I wanted to keep something of theirs to keep my memories alive.'

Finally she became aware of what an incredible thing he'd done for her. It wasn't what she'd asked, but he'd anticipated that what she'd asked of him, and what she'd needed, were two different things. Money, as he'd demonstrated, wasn't important. Memories were.

'Nick, I said some harsh things earlier, things I regret. What you've done, buying the house, looking after it ... I ... oh heck, I'm going to cry again.' She wiped at the tears hovering on her lashes. 'I should have thanked you, not yelled at you.'

Surprise flashed across his face. 'Are you telling me I really did do the right thing, after all? Because I can tell you, I've gone to hell and back in my own mind, wondering if I wasn't making a colossal mistake. Especially when I saw you crying your heart out on the bed.'

'Well, the way you communicated the whole thing to me was a bit of a dog's breakfast.'

'Accepted.'

'But, yes, on the whole, though it kills me to admit it, you definitely did the right thing.'

A broad smile spread across his face, lighting up his chocolate-brown eyes, slashing a groove down his cheeks. 'Well, hell, who'd have thought it?' Still shaking his head in bemusement, he raised his glass. 'Let's drink to that.'

Hand on her glass, she hesitated. 'You will sell it back to me?'

He touched his glass with hers. 'Of course. For the right price.'

For the briefest of moments she froze, staring at his deadpan face. But then the laughter shone in his eyes and she relaxed. 'I bet I can make you an offer you can't refuse.'

His eyes held hers, though some of the laughter faded. 'I bet you can.'

The rest of the day was much less traumatic. They revisited the house, together this time, and Lizzie's heart actually lightened as they talked through shared memories. Though the band of guilt remained firmly in place – something she would always have to live with – it felt as though the constraints of grief had loosened, freeing her slightly. With Nick's help, the horror and blame were pushed into the background for a while and she was able to remember happier times. Sitting in her father's chair, tears falling freely down her face, felt strangely comforting. Looking through old photograph albums was poignant, yet fun. For the first time since the accident she spent time appreciating what she'd had, rather than focussing on what had been taken away.

'You know maybe sometime we'll have a day together when I don't burst into tears at some point,' she remarked as they ate pizza that evening. Takeaway, her treat. That weight she'd lost was definitely coming back. Soon she'd have to get on those flipping scales.

Nick scooped up another slice, ignoring the cheese running down his chin. It made her smile. He was so grounded. Unconcerned with the trivial things that so many of her male friends obsessed about. Designer labels, how his hair was styled, whether his face looked tired/sallow/more wrinkled than yesterday.

'I'm not unused to women crying on me,' he said, bringing her back to their conversation. 'In fact, it's the tearful ones who seem to hunt me out.'

'Maybe your broad shoulders make us feel you can carry our burdens.'

It was the tiniest of compliments, but she was interested to see a slight flush appear on his cheeks.

'Or maybe I just have sucker scrawled across my forehead.'

Her attention snared, she snuggled back on the sofa. 'Come on then, how many women have cried on you, before me?'

His eyebrows nearly scooted off his forehead. 'You can't be serious. I'm sure we can find something more interesting to talk about.'

'Oh no, don't disappoint me now. You know how we women love a good sob story.'

He winced. 'Bad joke. Really bad. Anyway, if we have to discuss tears, how about other men you've cried on?'

Lizzie waved her slice of pizza at him. 'No way are you turning the tables on me. I asked first.'

He let out a resigned sigh. 'Okay, let me see. At university there was a girl called Anne. She was definite fruitcake material. Her parents were splitting up while we were together. Trust me, there wasn't anything I didn't know about that divorce.'

Putting her empty plate down on the coffee table, Lizzie smiled at him. 'That's part of your trouble. You're too good at listening. Not many men do.'

'Maybe I've not got anything interesting to say.'

'Ah, poor Cinderella, Nick, eh?'

He flinched. 'Thanks.'

'Hey, come on, I was kidding.' He didn't really think he was boring, did he? 'I love to hear you talk. If I've got a complaint, it's that you don't do it enough. Which is why I'm determined to squeeze information out of you while I've got you on a roll. So, other women who've cried on you.'

Nick cast his eyes over the remaining slice of pizza, but his stomach didn't fancy it any more. Lizzie was right – he didn't like talking about himself. Compared to a lot of people he led a pretty dull life. But compared to Lizzie? He was, as she'd so eloquently put it, like flaming Cinderella. As for this topic – *women who'd cried on him?* – he bet she didn't discuss this type of crap with any of her showbiz men. 'Well, I guess we'd have to include your mother,' he told her, taking peevish pleasure from her shock. Well, she had asked.

'My *mother*?'

Of course now he wished he'd kept his gobby mouth shut. 'It was soon after you'd left to go to New York. She'd just had a letter from you when I came to visit. I guess I was handy.'

'Wow. That must have been a moment for you.'

'Actually, it was one of the only times I've been *pleased* to have a woman cry over me. She wasn't really upset, just missing you. The fact that she felt comfortable enough to let me hug her, well, it made me feel like I was really part of the family.' Now he sounded pathetic, yet when he dared to glance at Lizzie, her eyes were full of understanding.

'You never really talked about your other life when we were kids. You know, the one you spent in your real home with your aunt and uncle. I always got the impression from Mum that you didn't get on with them much. Was that right?'

How the blazes had he got onto this subject? 'They preferred my sister, if that's what you mean.' Only eighteen months old when their parents had died, Charlotte had been the apple of their aunt and uncle's eye. Nick, a rapidly growing boy, old enough to remember his real parents, had been a complication his guardians hadn't bothered to try and understand.

'Mum always looked upon you as her second son, Nick,' she told him softly. 'I know she did.'

He felt his eyes prick and bit the inside of his cheek. He was not going to make a fool of himself in front of her. 'I miss them more than I thought I would,' he finally confessed. 'To lose one set of parents is bad luck. To lose two.' Shit, he was choking up. Swiftly he rose to his feet and legged it into the kitchen. There he grabbed at the tea towel, wiped his eyes and took a quick slug of water.

When he returned she eyed him watchfully but thankfully didn't comment on what she could read in his face. 'Do you remember much of your real parents?' she asked instead.

Wearily he collapsed back onto the sofa. He wanted to tell her he'd had enough of this conversation, but he'd probed into her private life enough over the last few days. He couldn't object now the tables were turned. 'Not as much as I'd like. Dad was a giant of a man, but soft-hearted. I don't remember him ever raising his voice to me. Mum was a typical mum, I guess. She liked to cook, maybe that's where I get it from, and hugged a lot.' He gave her a wry smile. 'I missed that, more than anything. Aunt Sarah didn't hug me once. I think she thought I was too big for that sort of thing.'

Before he knew it, Lizzie had climbed off the armchair and was sitting next to him, wrapping him in her slender arms. 'That's to help make up for what you missed out on,' she told him, squeezing him firmly. 'Perhaps that's why you're such a great hugger. You know how much it really means. So, any more women who've cried on you?'

Nick had stopped listening. His mind was back in that cold, sparsely furnished house he'd lived in with his aunt and uncle. Childless themselves, they were older than his parents had been, and set in their ways. Clearly having a pair of kids dumped on them had meant a lot of adjustments. He guessed he should be grateful they'd taken to Charlotte, at least. Still, the lack of love, support, even affection, had made life pretty bleak. Even worse had been the snide remarks, the continuous undermining of anything he'd ever achieved. If he'd come second, why wasn't he first? If he was first, why had he dropped those three marks? He wasn't trying hard enough. God, it was no wonder at times he was an insecure screw up. And then, to top it all, when his uncle had become aware of his obsession with Lizzie, there had been the incredulous laughter. *What are you thinking, boy? You've got no hope there. Just look at yourself.* Nothing his uncle had ever said had hurt more than that. Probably because, even then, he'd been aware of the truth in the words.

Amazingly though, that very same girl, now a stunning young woman, was at this moment holding onto him as if she'd never let him go. She smelt so wonderful, like blossom in the spring, and she felt even better. Nestled against him, soft and warm, she felt so bloody fantastic he'd happily freeze the moment and stay like this forever. But he couldn't, and any minute now his body was going to betray the far from brotherly feelings he was experiencing.

On the pretext of clearing up the pizza boxes, he reluctantly eased her away. 'I think it's your turn,' he countered when he'd deposited them by the front door and filled up both their wine glasses. 'Men you've cried on, or men who've cried on you. Take your pick.'

Lizzie curled her feet up under her and stared at the rim of the wine glass. 'I've not had any men cry on me, not unless you count Tommy Potter in the second year of primary school.'

'What did you do to him? Break his heart because you wouldn't kiss him?'

'Nope. I accidentally broke his Action Man. He wouldn't stop blubbering and I felt so guilty I tried to console him. It was like hugging a toad.'

Nick laughed. 'Okay, how about men you've cried on?'

'My dad, countless times. Robert, when Dad wasn't around.' She gave him a small smile. 'Sorry, but the only other man I've cried on has been you.'

'You must be really happy then, living the American dream,' he replied quietly.

'I didn't say there hadn't been tears. Just that I hadn't cried on anyone else.' Before he had a chance to wonder why not, she was talking again. 'But to answer your question, yes, I am happy. At least I was. I enjoy my work. I know it sounds shallow to someone like you, but I get a buzz from being in front of a camera. One I couldn't possibly begin to explain.'

'What do you mean, someone like me?'

She rolled her eyes at him. 'Wow, you're really going to make me say this? I mean someone intelligent.'

'A degree doesn't make me more intelligent than you, Lizzie. It just means I went on to study, while you went out to work.'

'If you can call what I do work, eh?' He opened his mouth to protest, but she cut him off. 'It's okay, it doesn't feel like work to me, either, which is what I love about it. I get paid silly sums of money to travel the world, meet amazing people from all walks of life and work with hugely talented designers, making their creations come alive for them. It's an incredible feeling. I'm also starting to toy with acting.' She glanced at her watch. 'But you don't want to start me on that subject, not at this time of night. If it's all right with you, I'm going to hit the sack. I'm shattered.'

Nick watched her go upstairs but stayed where he was, gazing broodingly into the flames that flickered through the window of the stove. When she'd spoken of her modelling, her eyes had lit up for the first time since she'd been here. A stark reminder that as soon as her name was cleared, she'd be off. Back to where she belonged in the glitz and glamour of LA.

Lurching to his feet, he went to take his disappointment and frustration out on the fire.

# Chapter Ten

Lizzie woke reasonably early the next morning – a Saturday, though the days were beginning to blur. Apparently it wasn't early enough to catch Nick though. When she padded into the kitchen she found a note in his bold, stylish handwriting, telling her he'd had to go out – he'd promised the neighbouring pub owner he'd go through his accounts – but would see her after lunch. Without him, the barn seemed eerily quiet. Odd, because when he was working in his study, she couldn't hear him anyway. She'd probably heard dormice noisier than he was. She smiled, thinking how totally different he was to her. He liked the peace and quiet to study and think. When she had paperwork to do she had the radio on, full blast. In her world silence wasn't golden, it was boring.

She missed him. It was hard for someone as independent as her to admit that, but she did. He was so solid, so together. Amazing, considering his childhood. When he'd admitted how much he'd missed being hugged, her heart had nearly split in two. In her teenage eyes he'd always been special. Now she was just starting to realise quite how special.

After downing a quick breakfast she acknowledged she wasn't going to be able to stay at the barn all day. Not knowing Nick wasn't there. Within an hour she'd taken delivery of a hire car and was driving back over to her parents' house.

She wobbled slightly going up to the front door, but was soon immersed in going through their belongings, picking through what she wanted to keep. She shed tears, but there was no repeat of the wracking sobs of yesterday. Altogether she felt calmer and more at peace.

When she finally set off back to the barn it was later than she'd intended, but she was quietly pleased with what she'd achieved. In the boot was a suitcase filled with memorabilia to take back to America. And in her heart, along with the inevitable pain, were now some good memories. She'd never be able to forgive herself for her part in their deaths, but her grief no longer felt quite so raw.

Finally the little rental car bounced down the long lane towards the barn. Grinning ruefully at her driving incompetence – was there a single pothole she hadn't hit? – she swung the car round the corner and experienced a quick spike of pleasure at the sight of Nick's car on the drive.

Nick opened the front door. 'Where the hell have you been?'

The suitcase she'd been in the process of dragging out of the boot clattered back down. 'What's wrong?'

He stood with hands on hips, an almost palpable anger emanating from his rigid frame. 'I'll tell you what's wrong,' he thundered, striding over to snatch the case from her hands. 'I came back to an empty house, with no note saying where you were. I tried to phone your mobile, but it was turned off. Damn it, Lizzie, I was worried.'

'I ... well ... I'm sorry,' she mumbled, stunned by his reaction. 'I suppose I didn't think you'd be concerned.'

'Didn't think I'd be concerned?' he repeated incredulously. 'The last I knew, you didn't have a car. I figured you must have gone out for a walk and got lost. Or fallen down a ditch and broken your leg, or worse.' He dropped the case to the floor, biting off any further doom filled scenarios. 'I was seconds away from calling the police when I heard the car coming down the lane.'

Now he'd started to calm a little, Lizzie dared to look at him. He did, indeed, look like a man who'd had an anxious moment or two. His hair was ruffled, as if he'd been constantly thrusting his hands through it. Traces of worry lingered in his eyes. She felt terrible, though a selfish part of her was warmed by his concern.

Reaching up, she planted a kiss on his cheek. 'I'm really

sorry, Nick,' she whispered. 'I didn't think. It's been a long time since anyone has cared where I was.'

Nick's heart had undergone a thorough workout during the last hour. It had lifted when he'd entered the barn, looking forward to seeing her, only to be squashed when he'd found no trace of her. Then it had started to thump noisily as he'd scoured the place, desperate to find a note or any sign of where she had gone. Now, as she kissed his cheek, it went into free fall. For a moment he closed his eyes and imagined that the kiss was the start of something more. Then reality crashed down on him. She was offering an apology, pure and simple.

'Yes, well, next time leave me a note,' he replied rather too harshly.

Lizzie nodded once before walking stiffly ahead of him into the house.

Exhaling in frustration, he bent to lift up the case. She'd looked so pleased with herself when she'd first climbed out of the car. Almost happy. Before he'd gone and torn her off a strip. 'So where have you been all day?' he asked her rigid back. 'And what on earth is in this case? It weighs a tonne.'

She spun to face him. 'Open it and see.'

He laid the case on the coffee table and fumbled with the old lock. When it opened, his mouth gaped in astonishment. 'You went back to the house, I take it.'

'It would seem so. I thought I'd take some things back to America. Memories for me, mainly, but I've got a few of Robert's things for him, like his bear and his model plane.' She shifted her slim shoulders, clearly trying to keep herself together. 'I know it's stupid after all this time, but maybe it could spark off a memory. At least bring him some comfort.'

Her sad eyes tugged at his heart, though not half as much as the thought of her going back home. 'That's a great idea, and I'm glad you felt able to go back.' Shutting the case, he stood. Her face was inches away from his, those soft lips so inviting. Reluctantly he kissed the top of her head instead. 'You look like you need cheering up. Why don't I take you out for dinner?'

Lizzie hesitated. 'It's Saturday night, restaurants are likely to be busy. Isn't there a chance I'll get recognised?'

'Nobody looked at you when we had lunch in the pub. Put your wig on and you should be fine.' He brushed a hand over her satin smooth cheek. 'Come on, what do you say? My shout.'

Finally he glimpsed her smile. 'Well, I guess it beats either of us having to cook. I'll go and magic myself into a brunette once more.'

Lizzie tried not to look too conspicuous as they sat down at a table near the back of the restaurant.

'It's okay, nobody's noticed you,' Nick whispered as he drew in his chair.

'Am I that obvious? I was trying to act casual.'

'You are. Now relax and have a glass of wine. I need to update you on where we are with project Charles.' He put up his hand before she had the chance to come back at him. 'Before you say anything, Dan phoned me just after I'd got back. I had planned on us both catching up with him this evening, but it didn't happen that way.'

He looked so pained, she had to smile. The tongue-lashing she'd given him had obviously struck home. 'You're forgiven.'

'The bad news is the police don't have any evidence to convict Charles, so I'm afraid they've rubbed their hands of the case.'

She hadn't really thought they would be able to do anything, but her heart still sank at the confirmation. 'Is there any good news?'

He smiled and her heart did a slow flip. Honest, sincere, impossibly cute, though he'd hate to be told that, his was a smile totally without guile. And though his teeth weren't quite straight, and weren't quite brilliant white, it had the ability to make her heart yearn for more. More smiles, more closeness. More of everything.

A waiter hovered and they quickly gave him their orders. 'So,' Nick continued when they were on their own again, 'Dan says he can't get Charles through the criminal courts, but he can go through the civil courts instead. There the standards of proof aren't as high. They usually use the preponderance of evidence standard.'

Lizzie looked at him blankly. 'Err, the per— What? Stick to straight English, please.'

'Sorry,' he acknowledged the slip with a wry grin. 'If you hang around with lawyers long enough, some of their language starts to stick. In a criminal case, it has to be proven beyond all reasonable doubt that the defendant is guilty. In a civil case, usually it only has to be established that, on the balance of probabilities, the defendant is guilty.'

'I see, I think. But how does that help me? He won't get convicted, will he, even if we can prove that, in all probability, he did it?'

Nick's face turned grim. 'It's true there isn't enough evidence to convict him, but if Dan can prove Charles was guilty in a civil case, he can at least clear your name. You'll also have the satisfaction of making him a social pariah, ensuring he never works in Los Angeles again.'

Umm. She must be a hard bitch because she was really warming to that idea. 'Does Dan honestly think there's a chance?' She was almost too frightened to hope.

Nick reached across to clasp her hand, his grip warm and reassuringly strong. 'Yes, he does. Apparently Charles has form. It seems you aren't the first person he's tried to blackmail. Thanks to your list, Dan was able to track down an actress who finally admitted Charles had tried the same trick on her. It didn't hit the press because she paid him off. Dan said she took a bit of convincing, but having seen what Charles has done to you, and knowing he's probably got another victim already in his sights, she's agreed to testify. Dan's certain there'll be others.'

Nick paused as they were served their food.

'I thought models ate carrots,' he whispered when the waiter had walked away, nodding over at her rather huge portion of lasagne.

'We do. But right now I'm not modelling and I'm making the most of it.'

He chuckled. 'Well, hell, eat away. You could do with putting on a few more pounds.'

She knew he meant the words kindly, but they still stung. It was a fact that dress designers loved thin girls, but men preferred curves. 'So, you were saying. Charles has done this before?'

'Yes, and there's more. A background check on him revealed he's got a record for having drugged a previous girlfriend, back in his home town of Denver.'

Funny how that knowledge didn't surprise her. 'Well, at least I wasn't the only dumb blonde taken in by him.'

'You may be blonde, but never dumb,' he told her quietly. 'None of this was your fault.'

'Thank you. Though I can't help thinking I should be more careful with my choice in men.'

Something flared in his eyes. 'I agree.' He looked like he wanted to say more, but instead he took a sip of wine and moved the conversation back to his discussion with Dan. 'Anyway, Dan says he has enough to build a case. If he can also add some witness statements from your previous boyfriends, confirming three in the bed sessions are totally out of character for you, we could be home and dry.'

It was good news, but her desire to eat had vanished. It would mean more dissection of her sex life, even though this time those doing it would be on her side.

'It will all be over soon.'

She looked up to see his gentle brown eyes gazing back at

her. 'I know.' With a small sigh she pushed her plate away. She'd had enough, in every sense.

Suddenly the hairs on the nape of her neck stood to attention as, from behind Nick's shoulders, she spotted two men approaching their table. They were grinning in the cocky manner of men who thought they were funnier, cleverer and better looking than everyone else. 'You look just like that blonde model,' the taller, heavy set one announced. 'What's 'er name?' He turned to his friend. 'Elizabeth someone or other.'

'Yeah, the one who likes to have pictures taken of her while she's having sex,' the other one replied loudly.

Opposite her, Nick stiffened. He made to stand up but she placed a hand on his arm, stopping him with a look. 'I'm flattered you think I look like a model,' she told them both with a sweet smile. 'But I'm just an ordinary girl out on a date with my boyfriend. So if you don't mind leaving us alone?'

They gawked at each other and Lizzie was half afraid they'd simply grab her wig and pull it off to prove they were right. Thankfully they thought better of it and stalked away.

'That was close,' Nick muttered when they were out of earshot. 'You're good. Maybe you should pursue that actress idea, after all.'

She tried to smile, but the encounter had left her more than a little uneasy. 'Can we go back now, please?'

Within minutes he'd settled the bill and they were walking outside.

'It is you, isn't it?'

Her heart plummeted as the two men, who'd been smoking outside, approached them once more.

The shorter one leered at her. 'How do you fancy a little session with me and my mate? I hear you're into threesomes.'

Before Lizzie had a chance to speak, Nick grabbed him by the neck and shoved him, hard, against the wall. 'Say one more word and I'll wring your scrawny little neck.'

The heavier man went to pull Nick off, but Nick twirled round fast, catching him unawares. He delivered a single, hard punch to his generous stomach, leaving him doubled over in agony.

That was it. She'd had enough. 'Stop it, Nick,' she screamed, pulling him off before he could do any further damage. 'These two delusional men can think what they like. Please, take me home.'

Wordlessly Nick took hold of her hand and helped her into his car, anger still simmering in his dark eyes.

The journey back to the barn was quiet, both lost in their thoughts. Lizzie was emotionally wrung out. Everything she thought she'd escaped from was now staring right back at her again.

Nick cursed himself all the way home. What had given him the bright idea to think he could take Lizzie to a busy restaurant and she wouldn't be recognised? He shuddered at the thought of the potential repercussions of his stupidity. Sure the men had sloped off quietly now, but they didn't look the type to keep an encounter like that to themselves. Certainly not if they could make money from it by blabbing to the press.

He pulled into the drive, killed the engine and turned to face a very withdrawn Lizzie. Nearly back to the girl he'd seen at her apartment a few days ago. 'I'm sorry.' He seemed to be saying that a lot these days.

She shook her head. 'It's not your fault.'

'I don't see how you work that one out. I was the one who insisted everything would be okay, that you wouldn't get recognised. I was stupid.'

'Not half as stupid as me, getting myself into this mess in the first place.' She put a hand on his arm to stop him saying anything more. 'I just want to go to bed.'

Silently they climbed out of the car and walked into the barn. What had started as a way of cheering her up had badly backfired. He could only hope this was the lowest point. It would all start to get better from now on.

# Chapter Eleven

The next morning Lizzie threw open the curtains as she always did. This time the beauty of the morning countryside was marred by a sight that sent shivers down her spine. Frantically she tugged the curtains shut again, blocking out the sight of dozens of reporters and cameramen camped outside on the drive. *Shit*. If only getting rid of them was as easy as shutting the curtains. She slumped back on the bed, eyes tightly closed. This was her reality. Not the relaxed walks with Nick, or the cozy evenings spent in front of his fire. No, that was just a pleasant diversion. Reality was a boyfriend who'd sickeningly betrayed her, a reputation that was in tatters, and a career that was rapidly heading down the plughole.

All of which she probably deserved. Why had she suddenly started to believe she was entitled to something good happening for a change? God, she'd even begun to believe in Nick's story, that everything would be okay. *Lizzie, come back with me to my lovely barn and wait there while I wave my magic wand and make all the bad stuff disappear.* Next she'd start believing in Father Christmas and the flipping Tooth Fairy.

For a while she buried her head in the pillow, trying to block out what was waiting for her downstairs. If lying down and feeling sorry for herself was the answer to her problems, she'd have cracked this days ago. But it wasn't. So she forced herself out of bed and into the shower. Then, in a well-established routine, she styled her hair, put on her make-up and prepared to face the press. Today she would adopt another role in front of the cameras. That of the top model whose career was ruined by a sordid affair with a low-life scumbag. Viciously she slammed the palm of her hand against the bedroom door. Yes, that was better. Anger beat wallowing in pity, any day. Even if her hand was smarting a bit.

With her anger still simmering Lizzie walked down the stairs, ready to face the music. That was when she saw Nick, sitting on the sofa, scribbling away on a sheet of paper.

'I see we have company,' she remarked.

He looked up with a start. From the look of him, he hadn't had much sleep. His eyes were slightly bloodshot and strangely flat. 'It seems our friends from last night weren't content to keep the knowledge of Elizabeth Donavue's appearance to themselves.'

'Maybe I should have stayed in Los Angeles after all.'

His jaw tightened. 'I'm sorry you feel that way. I realise I was wrong to insist we went out last night, but I'm damned if I'm going to apologise for taking you away from the media circus that was LA.'

'Except now I'm facing the same circus here. So what's the difference?'

'I'm here with you.'

The words were so softly spoken it took a moment for them to register. 'Well, that's just great. Now I can cock up your life as well as my own. Brilliant. Bloody fantastic.'

He came to stand in front of her, his eyes searching hers. 'Who said anything about either of our lives being cocked up?'

Unable to bear his kindness, she moved away. 'You can seriously stand there and pretend to me that everything is going to work out? Charles is still out there spouting his lies. Photographs of me in compromising positions continue to be splashed across the papers. Now I'm in danger of being hounded in two countries, not one. *And* you've been dragged into it, too. That's real progress. Remind me to listen to you more often.'

Nick stepped back from her metaphorical slap round the face. 'Well, I'm just about to put an end to at least one of your problems,' he muttered darkly.

It was then that his eyes seemed to notice her. Since arriving at the barn she'd settled on her preferred style – ponytail, jeans and a jumper. Now she was in model mode. She'd lightly curled her hair so it flowed loosely down her back and she'd put on a silk blouse and soft cream trousers that flared from her hips, making her legs look longer than they were.

'Wow, you look stunning.'

'I figured if I'm going to talk to the press, I'm going to do it as Elizabeth Donavue, not Lizzie.'

'Oh no you're not.' He moved towards the door, blocking her path. 'You're staying right here. I'm the one going outside to talk to these morons.'

'I hate to disappoint you, Nick, but they aren't going to be interested in what you have to say.'

'Interested no, but they'll damn well take notice. That's if they want to avoid a lawsuit for trespassing and harassment.' With that he yanked open the door and slammed it behind him.

She stared at the closed door for a moment, then sighed. The man had no idea how hard it was to get rid of the press. Still, he was obviously determined to act as her personal protector, so she'd give him a chance to do it his way. And having him take control, watch out for her, try and guard her from harm, was a pretty incredible feeling. It would be even more incredible if he was doing it for reasons other than duty and honour. He cared about her, yes, but did he feel any more for her than that? Because her feelings for him were becoming gradually more complex. What had started out as a simple crush was fast developing into something more scary. When he looked at her now, he didn't just melt her insides, he melted her heart.

As if she needed the addition of that confusion to her already chaotic life.

In a bid to distract herself, she started to make a cup of tea. God, she really was so very English still.

'They're going,' Nick announced as he stormed back in. 'I don't think we'll see them again.'

'What, that easily?'

'Yes,' he replied somewhat tersely. 'This is my private property, both the driveway and the land surrounding it. They can't hang around here without my permission.'

Lizzie felt very contrite. She'd overreacted again. Big time. That was her all over. A real drama queen. Using Nick as a punchbag when she should be venting her anger at the man who'd caused it. 'Thank you,' she said inadequately.

'You're welcome. There aren't many things I've got right recently. At least this was one of them. For now at least.' There was no accompanying wry smile. Just a tight, almost grim expression.

'You've got a lot of things right,' she argued hotly. 'I've not always been gracious enough to recognise them.'

'No. Until Charles is found guilty, I haven't done a damn thing.' He thrust a hand into his jeans pocket. 'I'll be in the study if you need me.'

Lizzie watched him stride away with an ache in her heart. She was falling in love with a man who must see her as nothing but trouble. It was time she kept away from him for a while and gave him a break from her overly cruel tongue.

They kept to their separate ways for the rest of the morning. Nick waited until he'd heard Lizzie make her lunch and return to her room before going down to make his. It was the first time they'd spent the day together, yet not shared a meal. He knew she was still angry with him. Why else would she not offer to feed him? With a sigh he went to forage in the fridge.

The knock on the front door took him by surprise. He rarely had visitors here. He'd deliberately kept quiet about the place, wanting to keep it as a private bolt-hole. In fact apart from Lizzie, only three people knew he had it; the lady who looked after it for him, Sally and his sister. Please God let it be one of them and not more sodding journalists.

Though if He was listening, perhaps he could see to it that it

99

wasn't Sally? He really didn't need that potential drama right now.

'Charlotte.' Relief flooded through him as he opened the door. 'What on earth brings you here?'

'Is that any way to greet your sister? Especially as she's driven over an hour to get here.' The pretty, smiling woman on the doorstep wagged her finger at him. 'A big hug and the offer of a drink would be more appropriate, don't you think?'

Laughing, he reached out and gave her the hug she'd demanded. Then he thought of Lizzie, who no longer had a sibling to wrap her arms around, and tightened his hold. As children they hadn't been that close. Mainly because his aunt and uncle had demanded all Charlotte's attention, leaving him the odd one out. There had been many times, in those early days, when he'd felt like he'd lost his sister, along with his parents. It was one of the reasons he hung around at Robert's house so much. There, between his friend, Lizzie and their parents, he received the attention he missed out on at home. As time had moved on though, and Charlotte had grown older, her appeal to their aunt and uncle had waned. The picky teenager was far less interesting than the pretty toddler. Nick had tried to fill the hole they'd left, giving Charlotte his time, his attention, his love, and their bond had grown. As they'd moved into adulthood it was Charlotte who'd proved better at keeping in touch, at giving him her time. And her love.

'You still haven't told me what you're doing here,' he told her as he put the kettle on.

'Well, there I was, catching up on the celebrity gossip in a terribly indiscrete newspaper, when I read that a certain leggy model, subject of a recent sex scandal, had returned to England and was hiding away somewhere in the country not too far from London.' The mug he'd been holding slipped out of his hand and rolled dangerously close to the edge of the worktop. 'I'm not sure if you know who I mean? Long blonde hair and a stunning smile? Someone you grew up with and had a rather large crush on, if I remember correctly.'

Nick snatched at the mug. 'Thanks, Charlotte. And if you could dial your voice down from embarrassingly loud to a little more discreet, I'd be enormously grateful.'

'Oops, sorry, I forgot your crush was always a secret, though why on earth you never told her, I don't know. You were always so close.'

'I never told her because she went off to effing America to become a bloody model, remember?' he hissed, hoping Lizzie couldn't hear. 'Anyway, you're right,' he continued in a more normal voice. 'Lizzie is staying with me at the moment, until this issue blows over.'

'Poor thing. She must be seesawing between livid and humiliated.'

'Actually, I couldn't have put it better myself.' Lizzie appeared in the doorway, surprising the heck out of both of them.

Nick died a few deaths but she didn't look at him any differently than she did normally, so either she hadn't overheard, please God, or she was going to be one hell of an actress.

Charlotte dashed towards her. 'Lizzie, it's good to see you again.'

There was an awkward moment, when neither seemed to know whether to hug or shake hands. They hadn't seen all that much of each other, really. Nick had usually visited the Donavues alone. But clearly they *felt* they knew each other because when Lizzie reached out her arms to hug Charlotte, she hugged her warmly back. 'It's good to see you too, despite the circumstances.'

Turning to Nick, Charlotte gave him her winning, baby sister smile. 'Be a sweetie and make me a drink. We girls need to catch up.'

It seemed like hours before Nick managed to manoeuvre his

sister towards the front door. 'Thanks for coming round,' he said again, hoping this time she really was going to leave.

'My pleasure. It's not often I get to talk to a famous model.' She lowered her voice. 'I can see why you were so besotted.'

Nick felt the telltale flush creep over his face. Hell, shouldn't he have grown out of this blushing habit by now? He tried to look away, but his sister had razor-sharp eyes.

'Oh God, Nick, you're still besotted, aren't you?'

This time he physically moved away, walking out ahead and into the driveway, not giving her the opportunity to read the depth of his feelings in his eyes. 'Don't be ridiculous. I'm helping out a friend in need, that's all.'

'And putting yourself through all kinds of torture in the process.'

He felt a pair of arms wind their way around his waist, forcing him to stop. How he wanted to deny the truth of her words, but he couldn't. Not now she was standing in front of him, scrutinising his face for every trace of emotion. 'What else am I supposed to do?'

'You could tell her how you feel. You never know, she might feel the same way.'

He raised his eyes skywards. 'We're talking about a world famous supermodel here. Have you taken a good look at your brother recently?'

Charlotte looked him straight in the eye. 'Yes. Have you taken a good look at Lizzie recently? She's no different to the girl you hung around with, you know. Not inside. Why do you assume she's more interested in flashing good looks than brains and personality?'

Amused, he cocked his head to one side. 'I'm not sure whether to be insulted that I haven't got the looks, or flattered that my sister thinks I'm smart and funny.'

Laughing she climbed into her car. 'You've got it all, big brother of mine. Not only that, you're a good man. Good enough for any woman you set your heart on, be it a brain surgeon, a princess or a supermodel.'

With his head feeling several inches wider, he waved Charlotte goodbye. As a gawky adolescent, trying to find his feet as a young man, he'd have given his eye teeth to hear such a compliment. Instead, all he'd ever heard was how he wasn't good enough. He wondered if he'd ever be able to believe the words of his sister, over those of his uncle.

'That was nice of Charlotte to come round.' Lizzie was waiting in the kitchen when he came back into the house.

'She probably just wanted a nosey.'

Lizzie shook her head. 'No, she was looking out for you. She loves you so she wants to take care of you. That's what siblings are for. I used to have that with Robert ...' Her words trailed off, and he ached for her.

'Well, now you've got me,' he replied roughly.

'Even when I yell at you, like I did this morning?'

'Yes, even then.' *You've got me forever*, he wanted to shout, but despite his sister's words, he knew he couldn't. Maybe there would come a time when he'd be able to, but it certainly wasn't now. She needed a friend, not another male complication. So he accepted the warm smile she gave him, and told himself it was enough.

They ate dinner on their laps in the living room, the conversation flowing easily between them once more. Nick was loath to break the harmony, but there was still a matter that needed to be dealt with.

He cleared his throat. 'Lizzie, I need to ask you something. A delicate something.'

'Go ahead,' she replied easily. 'There can't be any more embarrassing conversations left for us to have, surely?'

'Ah.' He rubbed a hand across his chin and prayed the right words would come to him. 'I mentioned yesterday that it would help if Dan could contact your previous, err, boyfriends, to give a character witness. It would be good if we could give him those names this evening, so he can move things along.'

Her fingers tightened on her wineglass. 'Well, lucky me. It looks like I do get a further chance to humiliate myself. You know what, why don't I tell you my favourite sexual positions as well, and be done with it.'

Briefly he shut his eyes and tried for calm. 'I know this is embarrassing. It won't surprise you to know I'm squirming over here, too, and all I'm doing is listening. Would it be easier to tell Dan directly? You know, someone who doesn't know you personally?'

'I'm a public figure, Nick. Telling anyone, whether it's Dan or you, the names of previous boyfriends feels like kissing and telling. It's sordid and cheap.' Bleakly she looked at him. 'Do you need to know everyone?'

Nick wanted the ground to open up and swallow him. He didn't bloody want to know any of them, let alone all of them. And it wasn't just because his toes were curling with embarrassment at it all. He didn't think he could bear to be reminded of all the men who'd touched the body he wanted to touch. Who'd kissed the lips he longed to kiss. 'No.' His vocal chords sounded like they were being pulled out of his throat. 'Only those you think would be happy to testify on your behalf.'

She fixed her eyes on a point over his left shoulder and took a deep breath. 'Okay, in the last few years there was ...'

She proceeded to reel off the names of one baseball player, and three leading actors. All of them A-list stars. All of them with big, flashy appearances and bad boy reputations. He wrote the names down grimly, his pen nearly scorching the paper with the ferocity of his scrawl. At least now he had a real feel for her taste. And it sure as hell wasn't quiet, ordinary looking accountants.

When she'd finished, he scrambled to his feet, desperate to

put some space between them. 'I'll give Dan a call with these names right away and let you know how it progresses.'

'Thanks.' Her eyes refused to look at him. They stared, unseeing, through the large barn windows and into the dark night. She looked so vulnerable, a reed thin figure on his huge, sprawling sofa. He wanted to comfort her, but right now he didn't think he was strong enough. Not with the names of her past lovers burning a trail across his damn notebook.

'Goodnight,' he called out gruffly.

She didn't reply.

# Chapter Twelve

Lizzie woke up drenched in sweat and with a man's arms clasped firmly round her shoulders. She experienced a moment of blinding terror, before she realised whose arms they were.

'It's okay, Lizzie. You're having a bad dream.'

As her eyes fell on Nick's anxious face she quit the struggle she'd been having with the man in her head and lay back weakly against the pillow. 'Sorry,' she whispered when she finally found her voice. 'Did I wake you?'

Nick smoothed back the hair that stuck to her damp forehead. 'Generally speaking I do wake up when I hear a woman scream.'

'Oh God, I wasn't, was I?'

'Well, maybe not so much screaming, more shouting.'

'Crap.' She ran a hand over her face, horrified to find it clammy. 'What did I say?'

'Get your fucking hands off me, you bastard.' He smiled gently down on her. 'I heard that one clearly enough.'

Embarrassed, she shrank further back into the pillow. 'Not very ladylike.'

His smile disappeared. 'I expect, at the time, you weren't being treated like a lady.'

Images from the nightmare flashed through her mind. Her lying prostrate on a bed. Two men on either side of her, fighting her, slapping her round the face. Telling her she was a whore.

'Hey, come back to me.'

'Sorry.' Her voice sounded small and fragile. 'I was just remembering what woke me.'

Nick shifted her along the bed, making room so he could sit down next to her. 'Come here.' Putting an arm around her shoulders, he pulled her towards him. 'You're safe now. Go back to sleep.'

'I'm not sure I can. Every time I close my eyes, the same images keep running through my mind.'

His arms stiffened. 'I take it those images have something to do with those bloody photographs.'

'Yes.'

'Do you think what you saw was a true memory?'

'Definitely not,' she reassured him. 'The scene is from the photographs Charles took, but it's muddled, the faces morphing from ex boyfriends into those of the men who harassed us at the restaurant.'

He eased them both further down the bed so she was lying down next to him, her head resting on his chest. It felt natural. So perfectly right. 'We're going to have to get you thinking about something else then. Something pleasant.' His heart was a steady, comforting beat beneath her ear. 'What do you *want* to picture when you close your eyes? A mountain of chocolate? A flashing row of cameras?'

She managed a weak laugh. 'Nice try, but neither of those is going to help me sleep. The first gives me hunger pangs. The second kick starts the adrenaline.'

'Okay, okay. Let me think. How about a warm, sun-kissed beach? Glistening white sand, clear turquoise water?'

'Any sharks?'

She felt him shake his head. 'You're not playing fair. Come on, close your eyes. Feel the sand beneath your feet, the warmth of the sun on your back.'

Slowly she shut her eyes. 'Umm, now you mention it, that sounds lovely. I've not been on holiday for years.'

'You live by the beach,' he pointed out.

'That's not the same as going on holiday. Nothing to do but read books in the sun and paddle in the sea.'

'Now you're getting there.'

As she listened to him describing her dream holiday, she instinctively snuggled closer. Through his thin cotton T-shirt she noticed how beautifully solid his chest felt. Athletic and muscular. He certainly didn't feel like an accountant, not that she could say she was an expert in that field. The longer Nick's deep, steady voice washed over her and his strong arms transmitted safety and security, the less the nightmare taunted her. Gradually she began to relax.

It was a while before she realised he'd stopped talking, though his hands still stroked her arm. Soothing, calming. She moved, wrapping her arms more tightly around him. Warm and strong, he felt heavenly. Male and spicy, he smelt heavenly, too. Dimly she became aware that his hand had moved from her arm to her back, the strokes still slow and steady.

But now she wasn't feeling sleepy any more. In fact her breasts were starting to tingle, her pulse to flutter. His movements were no longer sending her to sleep. They were turning her on.

Oh God, she wanted this, but she didn't want this. Wanted this because she'd fancied him forever and was now starting to fall in love with him. Plus if anyone could banish her fear of being intimate with another man, Nick could. Didn't want this, because she was rubbish when it came to men and relationships, as her recent track history had proved. Sleeping with him would only poison what they had. She was better suited to men in the limelight. Those who craved the attention she could give them. Who treated her as she deserved to be treated. Men like those on the list she'd given Nick last night.

Automatically she started to shift away, but the motion brought her head up close to his. Her mouth on a level with his mouth. Her lips inches away from his.

The inches disappeared, and Nick kissed her. Gently at first, softly enough that she had time to move away, had she wanted to. Her mind might believe she should, but under the persuasive heat of his lips, her body had other ideas. She was helpless to do anything other than melt. Seductive, arousing, his mouth caressed and teased. He didn't demand, but rather coaxed, enticed. As he increased the pressure her head fell back against the pillow and his body eased across hers. She inhaled sharply at the feel of long, hard, male lines and a hot, heavy arousal against her thigh. But even as his mouth trailed sexy kisses over her face and down her neck, inside a voice niggled. Is this really what they *both* wanted?

'Nick?' Gently she pushed him away.

Dark brown eyes snapped sharply into focus. The flare of passion drained away, replaced with a look of horror. 'Shit.' He leapt from the bed with the speed of a man who'd touched a live wire. 'I'm sorry.' With another oath he yanked open the door. 'I'll leave you in peace.'

Nick stumbled back to his bedroom, disgusted with himself. Had he really thought he'd be able to lie next to her and simply soothe her to sleep? When only a few strips of cotton separated her slender body from his, her soft breasts from his chest? Clearly when it came to Lizzie, all his brain cells disappeared.

With a groan of frustration he lay on his bed, hands over his face, body as stiff as a board. He'd blown it. There was no way he could mistake the puzzled look on her face, the confusion in her eyes when she'd tried to push him off. Hell, he was supposed to have been comforting her, not forcing himself on her. He shuddered at the thought of what he'd done, after all she'd been through. How was he meant to steer their friendship back on an even keel after a move like that?

For several hours he lay awake, staring into space. By the time the soft light of dawn crept between his curtains he knew he couldn't stay in the house any longer. Pulling on his running shorts and a T-shirt, he crept downstairs. Perhaps a long run would help to rid him of some of this terrible ache he had inside. The ache of wanting something he could never have.

Lizzie didn't manage much sleep, either. Hard to, when she knew two doors down the hallway, Nick was in his bedroom. Impossible to, with the memory of his tender kisses still lingering on her lips and her body a mass of sensitised nerve endings, crying out for him to finish what they'd started. But it didn't matter what she wanted. It hadn't eight years ago when she'd first propositioned him, and it didn't now. Nick didn't want her. Oh, his body had been keen enough, but when he'd realised what he was doing, or more precisely who he was doing it with, he'd not been able to get away from her fast enough. Wearily she rubbed at her eyes, wishing she hadn't had a nightmare. Wishing Nick hadn't tried to comfort her. More than anything, wishing he hadn't been horrified at the thought of making love to her.

At the sound of a door closing she peered out of the window, only to see Nick running down the drive. Who was he running away from? Her or himself? With a groan she slumped back onto the bed and willed herself to drift back to sleep.

A few hours later she woke to a grumbling hunger. Unable to ignore it, she grabbed her dressing gown and crept downstairs, feeling stupidly nervous about bumping into Nick. But after peeking into all the rooms, she soon realised he wasn't in. Was he still running? Surely not – she'd last seen him hare off down the drive *two hours* ago.

Just then his exhausted, bedraggled form stumbled through the front door.

Bent over, hands on knees, shirt streaked with sweat and legs caked in mud, he heaved in several, ragged lungfuls of air.

'I was starting to wonder where you'd disappeared to.'

Slowly he stood to his full height. 'I needed to clear my head.' His voice was tight as a drum, body held rigidly taut. He was probably cringing just being in the same room with her.

'How far did you go?'

'Over the hills and back. Nearly twenty miles.'

She baulked. 'Wow, that's harsh medicine. I think I'll clear my head with a cup of coffee, a piece of toast and a sit in the sun.'

He released a tiny glimpse of a smile. 'Enjoy. I'll catch you later.'

Later turned out to be a lot later, because apparently Nick needed to go into the London office today. And though it was Monday and probably to be expected, she couldn't help thinking it had more to do with what had happened last night than his work.

She also couldn't help wondering if Sally would be there. If they'd meet for lunch. If Nick would admit to her that he'd kissed another woman.

And if Sally would forgive him when he reassured her he'd stopped the kiss as soon as he'd realised who he was kissing.

It was after nine when Lizzie finally heard his car scrunching back down the driveway.

'I've made us some chilli,' she announced when he walked through the door. It had been therapy, of sorts. A few precious moments when she hadn't thought of last night and how he'd fled from her.

'Oh, um, thanks.' He rubbed a hand over his weary face. 'I'll take a bowl up to the study. I've got a bit more stuff to finish.'

'You wouldn't be trying to avoid me by any chance, would you?'

Like a child caught in a lie, Nick skirted over her eyes, taking a great interest in the wall above her right shoulder. 'I've just got a lot on, that's all.'

'Fine,' Lizzie replied coolly. God, the man was exasperating when he wanted to be. 'Take your meal to the study. Do your work. Put your head in the sand for a while longer. But after that you need to pull it out and come downstairs. We have to talk.'

He gave her a quick, bleak look before spooning chilli from the steaming pot into a dish and legging it up the stairs, two at a time. Lizzie turned back to the empty kitchen, ladled some chilli into a bowl for herself and sighed. Nick could run from her, but he wasn't going to be able to hide for much longer.

It hurt that he didn't want her like she wanted him, but she wasn't about to lose his friendship over it. Even if it did mean having to pin him down for a very awkward conversation.

Nick, cowardly custard that he was, sat huddled over his computer in his office, no longer pretending to work. He just couldn't face her. Not yet. Not when his mind was still trying to figure out what to say. *Oops, sorry I forgot we were only supposed to be friends.* Yeah, that was real classy. Or how about the truth. *I've been in love with you forever. Every time I see you, I want you more. I would die to make love to you all night long, until you're convinced you'll never want another man.* Like she was going to want to hear that after the shocked way she'd looked at him when she'd pushed him away.

So, instead of going downstairs and talking to her, like a decent, honourable man, here he was, holed up in his study. Afraid to confront the woman he loved. Afraid to face up to what he'd done. Could he be more pathetic? Even he couldn't invent any more work now, and his office smelt of stale chilli from the remnants of the bowl he'd finished over an hour ago. He needed a drink. A bloody large, alcoholic one. With any luck Lizzie had given up waiting for him and gone to bed.

Of course she hadn't. Giving up wasn't part of Lizzie's vocabulary. She was the most determined person he'd ever met. It was what had brought her such world-renowned success. That and her breathtaking beauty. As he walked down the creaking stairs, she turned and looked him straight in the eye. That was another thing about her. She was direct and honest. Almost painfully so. Though he loved and admired that about her, right now he vehemently wished she was cowardly and evasive, like him.

'Nick,' she began as he reached the bottom of the stairs. 'About what happened last night …'

'I said I'm sorry.' He winced at how defensive he sounded. 'What more do you want me to say?'

'There's nothing to be sorry about,' she replied crossly, looking at him with those stunning blue eyes of hers.

'That's not true. I took advantage of you. One minute you were having a nightmare, the next I'm all over you like a rash. That doesn't score any nobility points in my book.' He went to pour himself the drink he needed.

'That's not how I saw it. One minute we were enjoying a kiss, the next you couldn't get away from me fast enough.'

'What?' She'd been *enjoying* it? Or was she just being kind? Letting him down gently?

'Do you really think of me that way, Nick? Or were you imagining I was someone else?'

'Hell, no. I mean, yes.' He exhaled in frustration and moved towards the fireplace, clutching the whiskey as if his life depended on it.

'Which one is it then? Yes or no?'

His head started to pound. 'Both. No, I wasn't imagining you were someone else. Yes, of course I think of you that way.'

Her eyes widened. 'I always thought you saw me as a silly young girl. Your little sister.'

Buying himself time to formulate a reply he went to sit on the sofa, leaning forward so he could rest his hands on his knees. 'It can't have escaped your attention that you stopped being a little girl a long time ago.' Unable to resist, he looked directly into her stunning blue eyes. 'Now you're a beautiful woman.'

To his astonishment, she blushed. 'Thank you.'

He gazed into her eyes, mesmerised. She was so bloody gorgeous he almost couldn't breathe, yet she'd flushed at his compliment? Unbelievable. It was only when she broke the contact, dropping her gaze to her hands, that he realised he'd been staring. No wonder she was embarrassed. 'But you'll always be Robert's sister to me, Lizzie,' he told her gruffly. 'So you don't need to worry. I can appreciate your beauty and still keep my hands off you.' He bloody hoped.

He took a final swig of his drink and stood up. 'Last night was a temporary blip. I won't let it happen again.' His words sounded harsh, as if he was blaming her when the fault was totally his. To soften them, and to reinforce his elder brother status again, he bent down and kissed her lightly on the top of her head. 'Goodnight.'

Lizzie stared at Nick's departing back, totally baffled. How could he tell her she was beautiful and then promise to keep his hands off her? Kiss her like he had last night and then promise not to let it happen again? God, he scrambled her brain so much, she wanted to scream. She was in half a mind to tear up the stairs after him, throw herself onto his bed and show him exactly how she thought of him. And it wasn't as a flipping older brother. But her life was a mess and however she might want him, dragging Nick into that chaos wasn't fair.

So instead of following her heart, she hung around downstairs a while, giving them both some space. Soon she'd be heading back to America. It was going to be hard enough to leave Nick as it was. If they started an affair, she'd never want to return. And she had to go back. For Robert, for her career. Besides, Nick was her one true friend; the only one who knew the real Lizzie. She couldn't afford to risk complicating their relationship with an affair. If she lost him, she'd lose herself.

Her heart tightened and tears filled her eyes but she resolutely brushed them away and padded up the stairs to bed.

# Chapter Thirteen

Nick knew the only way he could stick to his promise to keep his hands off Lizzie was to put some distance between them. A lot of distance. So he submerged himself in his work. It was a long way from how he'd hoped to be spending his remaining days with her, but he had enough stacked up to kid himself he needed to disappear off to London every day, and lock himself up in his study at night. He wasn't hiding from Lizzie, of course. Just working really hard.

When they did occasionally bump into each other, he could almost convince himself things were back to where they had been before *the kiss*. Almost, because the awkwardness was still there. On both sides. It was one thing him knowing he wanted to make love to her. It was quite another *her* knowing that, too. But though she occasionally looked at him as if she was wondering what he was thinking, he ignored the unspoken question and kept all conversation bland and trivial.

On Sunday though, Nick couldn't escape into London. Well, he could, but even he considered that one gutless step too far. Working yesterday had been sad enough. So instead of heading off in his car, he went for a run. Once the physical exercise, combined with the ice cold shower, ensured his hormones were under control, he ambled downstairs. The patio doors had been flung open and he spied Lizzie sitting on a lounger, enjoying the sunshine. Deliberately he went to join her.

'Good morning.' He pulled out a chair and sat down, casting a casual eye over the papers she was reading. It was better for him than looking at her legs, which were stretched out gloriously in front of her. Long, shapely, smooth. He dragged his eyes to her face. 'What are you reading?'

'Maria sent some stuff over for me to go through.' She sighed deeply. 'Potential projects, if I can ever get past this scandal.'

Nick frowned. 'Do designers, or whoever you usually work for, really take any notice of that sort of gossip? I mean, any publicity is good publicity, right?'

'I'm not sure that holds true with sex scandals. At least not when you've made your career from being a supposedly pure, angelic English rose.' She smiled sadly. 'Remember I told you I'd just signed to promote a perfume called Innocence? Well, they wriggled out of that contract pretty sharply. God knows what I'll be considered to promote when this all blows over. I doubt they make fragrances called Whore or Hooker.'

'Stop it.' His voice was sharper than he'd intended, but it had the desired result. She shut up, gaping at him, clearly surprised he'd shouted. So was he, but he hated to think she had so little respect for herself.

'Sorry.' She bit into her lip and looked away.

In a flash he realised just how selfish he'd been over the last week. He'd brought her back to England to support her through this ordeal, then proceeded to bury himself in his work and avoid her. Some knight in shining armour he'd turned out to be.

'No, I'm the one who's sorry. Sorry I've not been around much this week. I've been working,' he added lamely.

'I didn't expect you to be around all the time. You have your own life to live. And I really appreciate what you've done for me, truly.'

'Forget it.' She was far too kind to say it, but as her friend he could have done a heck of a lot more. 'How do you fancy going out on the river today?' he asked after a short while. 'We could take a picnic. You could relax in the back with your shades and a good book, and I could put my macho captain's hat on and steer?'

'Macho captain's hat, eh?' Her delicious lips curved. 'Now that I have to see. Have you got a boat then?'

'Well, it's not one of your celebrity style fancy yachts, but it does for messing about on the river round here.' He stood and took her hand, pulling her up with him. 'Come on, shipmate.'

The afternoon was heaven. Not least because Nick had come back to her. Gone was the diffident, elusive man Lizzie had shared a house with the last few days. Back was the friend of old. She glanced over at him, unable to resist a smile at his baseball cap, proudly sporting the word *Captain*. Given to him, so he claimed, by a friend. Had it been Sally?

The swift flare of jealousy was too painful to be ignored so she acknowledged it with a grimace but pushed it to one side. Nothing was going to ruin today for her. She glanced back at Nick, enjoying a quiet study of him while he wasn't looking. What with his carelessly placed cap, casual polo shirt and dark sunglasses, he looked pretty cool – and, because he didn't realise it, sexier than any of the models she'd ever worked with.

They stopped for a picnic, Nick surprising her by slipping out a bottle of champagne. It was almost surreal to be sitting by the riverbank on a blanket, sipping champagne and eating strawberries.

'This setting couldn't be more English,' she murmured dreamily as she refilled her glass. How many was that now? Certainly enough to make her very aware of every inch of his long, lean body stretched out beside her.

'Oh, I don't know. We could do with a cricket match going on behind us. And perhaps a brass band playing.' He lay his head down on the blanket and gazed up at the sky. 'Do you ever miss England?'

'No, not really,' she replied honestly, glancing over at him as he turned his head to face her. She saw something flicker in his eyes but it was gone too fast for her to read it. 'Of course there are some things I miss. Fish and chips, proper football, marmite on toast, queuing.'

He gave her a small smile, one that didn't reach his eyes. 'If that's all you miss, it's no wonder you haven't been back since—'

'The funeral,' she finished for him. 'I haven't thought of it like that. To me it's not the country you miss, but the people. With Robert and my parents no longer here—'

'There wasn't any reason to come back.'

This time he finished the sentence for her. And this time she recognised the look in his eyes. Hurt, plain and simple. 'That's not quite what I meant.' And it wasn't. If only he knew. 'Of course, it would be great to come back and see you.'

Another smile that didn't reach his eyes. 'Sure.' Immediately he started to clear away the picnic things.

Thoughtfully Lizzie got to her feet, the champagne sloshing around her bloodstream quite nicely. Her words had been ill-chosen, but his reaction to them seemed out of proportion.

She shot him another glance, but he avoided her eyes.

'I'm bound to come to London with work at some point. When I do, I'll give you a call. And with more notice than the day before,' she told him pointedly, though she smiled to take some of the edge off her words.

He stiffened, then acknowledged her dig with a nod of his head. 'Touché.'

They walked back to the boat in silence, but it wasn't as comfortable as it had been before the picnic. Briefly she wished she hadn't drunk so much. It was hard enough to read Nick when she was sober, but being mildly pissed made it almost impossible.

On the journey back down the river Nick cranked up the stereo, hoping the calm of the classical music would hide his lack of conversation. It was high time he learnt not to ask questions he didn't want to know the answer to. What had he expected her to say? *Yes, of course I miss England, because I really miss you.* Furtively he glanced over his shoulder at her. Glass of champagne in her hand – she'd not wanted to waste it and he was driving them home so couldn't drink any more – she was absorbed in her book. It gave him another chance to study her. She'd tied back her hair with a multi-coloured scarf and hidden both beneath a wide-brimmed straw hat. Large designer sunglasses hid most of her face. Despite this, it was impossible to hide her sex appeal. From the brim of her hat to the delicate sandals on her feet, she oozed a poise and glamour that other women simply didn't have. She'd casually knotted her shirt at the waist, exposing a hint of tanned, flat stomach. Her shorts were pink and very … well, short.

He gritted his teeth and looked away. There was a limit to the number of long runs and cold showers a man could take. Spending all this time with her was slowly driving him crazy.

As he helped her off the boat, Lizzie swayed a little.

'Oops, I think I might be the teeniest bit piddled.'

'Piddled?'

'You know, slightly sloshed. Not quite three sheets to the wind, but definitely two.' She lost her footing and giggled. 'Maybe two and a half.'

'You're a lightweight.'

She arched him a look. 'No way. I could drink you under a table.' Another laugh bubbled out of her. 'Oh, that sounds a bit funny, doesn't it? As if I can drink you, which I can't. Well, not all of you. There are bits of you I could drink, maybe.'

'We need to get you into the car,' he interrupted quickly. Saints alive, his overactive imagination had no problem thinking of the bits of him she could drink. No problem at all.

Once he'd bundled her in, Lizzie turned on the radio and proceeded to sing every song the station played, whether she knew the words or not.

'Come on. I shhhouldn't sing alone,' she slurred. 'My voice is bad. Very bad.'

'Mine is superb,' he lied, 'but I prefer to keep it under wraps. You know, British reserve and all that.'

Lizzie stuck out her tongue, turned the volume up even higher. And carried on singing.

When they arrived back at the barn, she was still raring to

go. 'Come on outside, Nick, and bring another bottle. I want to party.'

He took one look at her soft, slightly unfocussed blue eyes and knew he was heading for trouble. It didn't stop him from pulling a bottle of white wine out of the fridge, grabbing two glasses and going to join her.

'What a stupendous day,' she said with a sigh, leaning back against the wooden steamer chair. Squeezing his arm, she winked at him, sending his blood pressure through the roof. 'You know, it's been lovely to spend time with you again. I missed you these last few days.'

'Yes, well, as I already explained ... I was busy.'

She laughed, the sound husky and deliciously sexy. 'Come on, Nick. Wasn't it you who told me I may be blonde, but I'm not dumb? You stayed away because you were embarrassed we kissed.'

He felt his face heat and belatedly realised there wasn't enough alcohol in his system for this conversation. 'That probably had something to do with it, yes,' he admitted.

'Such a shame.' She let out a long, wistful sounding sigh. 'But it's probably just as well we stopped,' she continued, running a finger lazily across the rim of her glass. It didn't take much to imagine that finger running over his body. 'Sex with me would have been a real let down.'

He almost choked on the large swallow of wine he'd taken. 'Pardon?'

She shrugged, sipping at her own glass. Clearly drink made her gloriously, frighteningly, uninhibited. 'I've never been any good at it. Sex, I mean.'

This time he couldn't stop himself from spluttering.

She gave him a hard stare. 'It's not funny, you know.'

'I'm not laughing, believe me.' He took a deep breath, both to clear the wine from his lungs and to gather his wits. 'What you're saying is rubbish,' he ventured finally. 'It's not a question of being good or not. Just whether you're doing it with the right person.' He cringed. 'And I didn't mean that as a come on.'

She giggled. 'I know. I thought maybe after all that business with Charles I'd never want a man near me ever again, but, well … that kiss was pretty hot.'

His heart hammered wildly in his chest. 'That's good to know.'

'Would it have got hotter? You know, if we'd carried on.'

Hell's teeth. How was his heart not exploding? 'I've not had any complaints so far.'

Somewhere in the back of Lizzie's mind there was a voice telling her to shut up, but she was in too much of an alcohol induced high to listen. 'I remember asking you to make love to me once. You turned me down.'

'Of course I turned you down. You didn't want me, just a willing male body.'

'Why do you say that?' Her fogged brain tried to grasp both what he'd said, and what he hadn't.

'It doesn't matter.'

Even her pickled brain registered his closed off, *I'm not discussing this*, expression. 'Most men wouldn't have said no.'

'I'm not most men.'

'No, you're certainly not.' For a few heartbeats their eyes clashed. Unspoken emotions swirled in his and she regretted being so drunk she couldn't fathom them. When he broke the connection, staring down at his hands, it only encouraged the devil in her to goad him more. 'You'll be pleased to know I did manage to find someone willing to … what's the term they use? Debunk … oops, no, deflower me. Such a stupid phrase. I mean, it's not like I was a pansy and he came along and pulled my head off.' She giggled at her description. 'Mind you, his technique wasn't all that much better …'

Nick's hand shot up. 'Stop right there, please. This conversation has gone way beyond my comfort zone.'

'Really?' He was looking pretty uncomfortable, but she was on a roll. 'So you're not interested in who got the job you turned down?' His face paled even further and even drunk

Lizzie realised she'd gone too far. That was the trouble when a pissed extrovert tried talking to a sober introvert.

'No, I'm not,' he replied tightly, shooting up to his feet. 'I don't know about you, but I'm shattered. I'm off to bed.'

'Is that an invitation?' Oh God. Please, someone, stop her mouth coming out with words her mind hadn't sanctioned.

'You know it's not.'

He looked so stiff and awkward, the drunk side of her wanted to giggle again. 'Well, for the record, that's the second time you've turned me down.'

Hands on hips, he raised his eyes heavenwards. When he finally lowered them again – he must have been counting to ten – his voice was slow and almost eerily calm. 'Just to be clear. I'm not turning you down. We're not having this conversation. You're drunk and you don't know what you're saying.'

'Maybe.' She reached for her drink, the party girl in her not ready to stop. 'Or maybe I still remember how hot it felt when you kissed me.'

She watched as Nick's gaze travelled down from her eyes and rested on her lips. Automatically they parted, wanting to feel not just the heat of his gaze, but of his mouth, his tongue. His breath against her neck.

'Exactly how drunk are you?' he asked roughly, reaching to pull her to her feet.

'A teeny bit.' She started to sway and her fingers clutched at his arm, wrapping them round his hard bicep. Arousal rushed through her. 'Oops, maybe a tiny bit more than a teeny bit, if you know what I mean.'

He didn't reply, just stood watching her, a tight expression on his face. As her fingers pressed against his hot skin to feel the hard muscle of his arm, Nick's eyes flared. Even she, a tiny bit more than a teeny bit drunk, recognised the heat she saw there.

'You can kiss me again,' she told him softly. 'You know, if you want to.'

\* \* \*

Her husky voice wrapped round his balls and tugged at them. How many years had he loved this woman? How many years had he wanted her? So why wasn't he forgetting all his principles and sweeping her into his arms? Into his bed? He'd taken other women to bed on far less invitation.

He watched, spellbound, as she tucked a strand of silky blonde hair behind her ear, her tongue darting across her full bottom lip. Another bolt of desire shot through him.

'Do you want me to?' His voice was thick, his arousal an aching throb between his legs.

She seemed surprised at his question. 'Of course.'

He bent his head, a heartbeat away from taking her up on her offer. From touching his mouth to those soft, inviting lips and plundering the sweet depths he knew he'd find behind them. But then instead of gazing at her eyes, he stared into them. Still large and blue, they were alarmingly unfocussed.

As if he'd stepped into an ice cold shower, sanity returned. She wasn't a teeny bit drunk. She was out of her head drunk. If he took her to bed now, he'd be no better than that blasted son of a bitch, Charles. Worse, when she woke up in the morning, their friendship would be over.

So instead of kissing her until they both couldn't stand, he clutched at the last dredges of his restraint and drew back, sliding his arm around her waist. 'It's time you were in bed. Come on.'

She didn't complain when he almost hauled her up the stairs, but giggled every now and again when she lost her footing. When he stopped at her bed and gave her a slight shove, she collapsed onto it, smiling dreamily. He debated helping her undress, but there wasn't a huge gap between clutching at restraint, and saying to hell with everything and just taking what he wanted.

'Goodnight, Lizzie.'

He doubted she heard the words. She curled onto her side, closed her eyes and fell sound asleep.

# Chapter Fourteen

When she woke the next morning, Lizzie was convinced a herd of buffalo were stampeding through her head. There couldn't be any other explanation for the incessant pounding. Clutching at her temple, she lay back against the pillow and sighed deeply. She was twenty-six, not sixteen. Old enough to have learnt when to stop drinking. Experienced enough to know if she didn't, she paid for it the next day, in spades. Staggering off the bed, which brought a whole new dimension of dizziness and nausea to the uproar in her head, she fumbled around in her handbag for the paracetamol tablets she had the sense to keep there. It was just a shame she hadn't had the sense to take the flipping things last night. After swallowing a couple, she snuggled under the duvet and drifted back to sleep.

When she woke again an hour later, the herd of buffalo had slowed to a walk and she felt strong enough to risk getting out of bed. As she peeled off last night's clothes – nice, who said models today didn't have standards – she saw a note that had been pushed under her door. *Hope your head survived. Give me a call when you surface, Nick.*

Smug bastard. Scrunching up the paper, she called him all kinds of names under her breath. Why wasn't he suffering, like she was? Weren't they both meant to have been drinking? Wasn't that the point of sharing a bottle? Clearly not when you shared one with Nick Templeton. He obviously preferred to ease back and watch while his companion made a fool of herself. Charming.

Slowly she made her way down the stairs, thanking all those painful lessons in deportment that enabled her to keep her head reasonably still. When she reached the kitchen she grabbed at the phone and dialled Nick's number.

'Templeton.'

'Why did you let me drink so much, you bastard?'

A deep chuckle echoed down the line. 'The mood you were in, there was no stopping you. I certainly wasn't prepared to risk a punch in the ribs trying. Anyway, it probably did you good to let your hair down.'

'That's not what my head is saying right now.'

Again he laughed. 'Drink lots of water, take some headache tablets and go for a long walk. You'll feel right as rain in a few hours.'

'Yeah, well, I've done the first two already and I still feel lousy.' She hesitated. 'Did I say or do anything embarrassing last night?'

'You mean other than inviting yourself into my bed?'

She swore, and was rewarded with more rich laughter. 'If you were a decent man you'd have got drunk with me. At least then neither of us would remember what we said the next morning.'

'I think it's a good job I stayed sober.'

She had a burning memory of the feel of his lips on hers. 'Perhaps.'

Silence hung between them for a few seconds. 'Well, enjoy your day, Lizzie. I'll try not to be late back.'

With a heavy heart she put down the phone. So, it seemed she'd propositioned Nick twice now. Sure, both times she'd been the worse for drink. But both times he'd turned her down.

And now he was back in the office where his sometime lover also worked. Her heart twisted. God, she hated this feeling. Unrequited love. What a romantic phrase for a really shitty feeling.

She took Nick's advice and went for a long walk in the fresh air. Maybe it was the walk, or the tablets finally kicking in, but she felt better for it as she strode back towards the barn. That was until she was accosted by two men, one carrying a camera with a giant zoom lens.

'Miss Donavue, how would you describe your relationship with Nicholas Templeton?'

She glared at him and continued to walk.

'Is he your new lover?'

She was used to dealing with the press, especially speculation about her love life, so this shouldn't be fazing her, but it was. She didn't feel like Elizabeth Donavue any more. She felt like Lizzie. And Lizzie didn't want to discuss her personal life with this man. Nor did she want that prying camera lens shoved at her face.

'Does he mind that you were recently photographed in bed with two other men?' The journalist continued, keeping pace with her. 'Are you planning on making it a foursome?'

'Leave me the hell alone,' she bit out angrily, immediately breaking her first rule of dealing with the press. Never let them see they've upset you. She ran the remaining way, opening the door with shaking hands and slamming it shut behind her. Then she slumped to the floor, wrapped her arms around her legs and began to cry.

The sound of a ringing phone cut into her misery. After wiping crossly at her wet cheeks, she stumbled to her feet to answer it.

'Hello?'

'There you are. I've been trying to get hold of you. How's the head now?'

How did Nick seem to know when she needed him? Was he psychic? 'It's much better, thanks.'

There was a pause. 'Are you okay?'

'Yes, yes, I'm fine.' Despite her best efforts, she heard her voice crack.

'No you're not. What's happened?'

She opened her mouth to speak, then shut it again. She couldn't go moaning to Nick every time she had a minor crisis.

'You can't fool me, Lizzie. I can tell you're upset.'

A lump lodged in her throat and she suddenly forgot all

about trying to be strong and independent. 'There was another reporter here this morning, asking about our relationship. Wondering if you're my latest lover.'

'Damn.' She could almost hear his brain ticking. 'What did you say?'

'I lost it and told him to leave me alone. I should have stuck to no comment. Or simply put them straight.'

'Hey, don't worry. They're just trying to needle you into admitting something that will give them a story. Though I hardly think the supermodel dating an accountant qualifies as one.' He let out a short, sharp breath. 'Or maybe it does, because it's so unbelievable.'

'Why? Because supermodels aren't bright enough?'

He snorted with disbelief. 'Yeah, that's exactly what I was thinking.' This time the breath he let out was deeper and longer. 'Look, stay inside. I'll be back as soon as I can.'

'You don't need to rush back on my account,' she muttered, still not sure what he meant by his previous comment. 'I'm fine.'

'Of course you are. You always cry when you're doing okay.' He paused and when he spoke again his tone was much softer. 'It's okay to feel upset, Lizzie. Having people prying into your private life is bound to be distressing. Go and take a bath, read a book, or do whatever you usually do to chill out.'

'Eat chocolate. Though most of the time I have to make do with thinking about eating it.'

He laughed, breaking the tension. 'Okay then, go and stuff your face with a bar of Dairy Milk. I'll see you later.'

Unsettled, Lizzie stared at the phone. Men. They were nothing but trouble. Even the good ones, like Nick, were capable of scrambling a woman's mind, tearing at her emotions. What she needed more than anything was a chat with a member of her own sex.

Knowing just the woman, she dashed up the stairs to her bedroom and plucked her mobile phone from her handbag.

The phone she'd kept turned off ever since the scandal had broken. After waiting for it to find a signal she watched with trepidation as it bleeped and buzzed, updating with all her messages. There were hundreds. Missed calls, voice messages, texts. It looked like everyone she'd ever worked with had been in contact with her. Lizzie ignored the lot of them and went into her contacts. She had one really good friend in LA – an actress she'd met at a charity event. Though she was a fair bit older than Lizzie, they'd hit it off immediately. She was the one woman Lizzie felt able to talk to about things other than fashion and make-up.

'Catherine, it's me, Elizabeth.'

The lady on the other end of the phone screeched with pleasure and immediately began to bombard her with questions in her slight Californian drawl. How was she holding up? Why hadn't she returned any of her calls? And finally – when those were answered and apologies made – where was she?

'I'm in England, staying with an old friend.' Lizzie wondered if her careful reply had sounded casual enough.

'What sort of friend are we talking, my dear? Friend as in purely platonic, or friend as in you want to jump his bones?'

'A bit of both?' she replied on a laugh, appreciating Catherine's directness as it was so similar to her own.

'Umm. So you haven't slept with this friend yet?'

'We've shared one kiss, that's all.' Her mind went back to that moment after she'd woken from the nightmare. 'One breathtaking, hotter than hot, kiss. Apparently I also propositioned him, only I was the worse for alcohol and don't remember. Needless to say, he turned me down.'

'Do you *want* to sleep with him?'

'Yes.' The word slipped out quickly, instinctively – bypassing her brain and coming straight from her heart.

'And what about him? Do you think he feels the same way?'

Her mind replayed conflicting images. Nick's eyes when they rested on her when he thought she wasn't looking. Nick pushing her away after their kiss, promising he would keep his hands to himself. 'I don't know.'

'Then, my dear, I know exactly what you need to do. Take him out of England and into the sun for a few days. I'll email you the details of my villa. Use it. A little holiday will do you good, and if you lie round the pool in one of those tiny bikinis of yours, the man won't be able to resist.'

It sounded heavenly, but was it really that simple? 'I'm not sure.'

'About which part? The holiday or the sex?'

A giggle exploded out of her. 'Oh, Catherine, it's so good to talk to you. I'm sure the holiday will do me the power of good, and I'm equally sure the sex would be great, too.' For a moment she halted, aware of how odd that sounded. 'Funny, I guess I should be scared off it for life after what I've just been through.'

'Perhaps you would be, if you could remember any of what happened.'

'It certainly helps that I don't.' A small shudder ran through her. 'I felt violated looking at the photos, I still do, but then Nick came along and ...' Snippets of the night before came back to her. The feel of his muscular arm beneath her fingers. The warmth from his body as it had stood so close to hers. The heat in his eyes. 'Let's just say it's no longer the sex I'm unsure about. It's what will happen after it.'

'Hopefully, my dear, it will be so good you'll do it again. And again.'

The image of her and Nick stretched out on a bed, their limbs entwined, was enough to make her toes curl. 'But then what? Won't it just make coming back to LA even more difficult?'

'Elizabeth Donavue, I thought you were a live for the moment kind of gal. Go, have fun. The future will work itself out.'

Lizzie wanted to take that advice so much that she could

almost feel the sand between her toes. 'You know what? I might just take you up on that offer of the villa after all.'

Back in his London office, Nick finally gave up and saved the document he'd been working on. It was doomed to not get finished today. First he'd had Sally, and their not-quite-as-easy-as-it-should-have-been catch-up lunch. Then the call from Lizzie.

As he closed down his computer he thought back to his talk with Sally. Although he'd been in the office several times since Lizzie had turned up, Sally had been busy visiting clients. Today had been the first time they'd been able to meet up. For a woman who'd reassured him she was fine about Lizzie, her eyes had suggested something different. While he had no doubt her heart wasn't involved, her ego was another matter.

'You know if the situation was reversed,' he'd told her when the stilted conversation had got too much for him, 'and you were sharing a home with a man you'd been in love with for years, I'd feel put out.'

She'd smiled sadly at him. 'Okay, you're right. I'm not finding this as easy as I thought I would. Or as easy as I want it to feel,' she added with emphasis.

He'd realised then that no relationship involving something as intimate as sex was ever uncomplicated. 'I think we should call time while we're still friends,' he'd told her, very aware of the irony of his statement. It was exactly what he feared with Lizzie, that loss of friendship should either of them act on the sexual chemistry now simmering between them.

Only with Lizzie, his heart would be shattered, too.

Sally had seemed surprised, and a little … annoyed, perhaps even upset, at his statement. As they'd stood to leave she'd given him a lingering kiss on the mouth, as if trying to prove something to him. He'd spent the next few hours wondering if her heart had been more involved in their relationship than he'd thought.

Then Lizzie had called, and Sally had immediately slipped from his mind.

Now he was anxious to leave.

He was halfway out of the door when the sound of the phone ringing on his desk halted him.

In two minds whether to answer it or not, he glanced at his watch – only 4.30 pm. For a man renowned for religiously working a minimum of ten hours a day, his recent coming and going on a whim was starting to raise a few eyebrows. He might be a partner, but he wasn't unsackable. 'Templeton,' he barked into the receiver.

'Ah, so you do go to work occasionally.' The sweetly sarcastic voice of his sister.

'I'm nearly always working.'

'That used to be true, until a certain model appeared on the scene again. Now when I try your office, you're hardly ever there.'

With a sigh of resignation, he sat back down at his desk. 'Was there a purpose to this call, or is it *wind up my brother* time?'

'I see having a glamorous house guest hasn't improved your manners. I was phoning, darling brother, to see how you and Lizzie were getting on. I'd have phoned your mobile, but I wasn't sure if she'd be with you. This way I can ask all the questions I want to ask.'

A sliver of panic rippled through him. 'We're getting on fine.'

'Are you sleeping with her yet?'

Good God. He eased open the top button of his shirt and slid his tie down enough so he could breathe again. 'Of course I'm not.' It was hard to know which was the more far-fetched. The idea of him sleeping with a glamorous supermodel, or the truth. The idea of him sharing the same roof as the woman he loved and *not* sleeping with her.

'Why not? You've had a thing for her for ages, and now

she's living with you. Blimey, Nick, you'll never get a better opportunity than this.'

'I'm not sure I need relationship advice from my baby sister, thank you very much.' Was it him, or was his office suddenly uncomfortably hot?

'That same baby sister is happily living with the man she loves. She wasn't too scared to go after what she wanted.'

'I'm not scared.' *Liar. You're terrified Lizzie will laugh at you and never be able to look you in the eye ever again.* 'But it's … well … complicated.'

'All relationships are. What's so complex about this one?'

'She thinks of me as a brother. She lives in America. She's recovering from a sex ordeal.' The barriers slipped easily off his tongue. 'Do I need to go on, because I can. She's way out of my league, she loves parties and the limelight—'

'Enough,' Charlotte stopped him in mid-flow. 'That sounds like a list of excuses, not a list of genuine reasons that might keep you from getting together, even if it's only for a passionate, romantic, short-term fling.' When he didn't reply, just huffed into the silence, she sighed. 'I can tell you're anxious to rush back to your cosy life in the country, so I won't keep you. Just do yourself a favour, Nick. Don't analyse this too much. Relationships aren't something you can work out on a spreadsheet.'

She put the phone down before he could muster up a suitable, pithy reply. Sisters. Sometimes they thought they knew everything. Yanking his tie further down, he picked up his briefcase and walked out to his car. As he drove the long commute back to the barn, he couldn't help but think what an odd existence he had at the moment, caught between two lives. Between country dweller and city lawyer. Between friend and lover.

# Chapter Fifteen

When Nick finally arrived at the barn he found Lizzie curled up on the sofa watching an American soap opera with half an eye.

'If you're watching that, you must be feeling rough.'

Unfurling her long legs from the sofa, she moved towards him with her arms outstretched. 'Nick, I'm so sorry.'

As she easily settled into his arms, his chest tightened. He was going to miss this when she'd gone. Not just someone to come home to, but Lizzie to come home to. 'I'll take the hug, but what are you sorry about?'

'Dragging you into all this mess.'

'Dragging *me* in? If I recall correctly, I was the one who hauled you back to England with me. And I don't regret a single minute.'

'Tell me that tomorrow when you find yourself plastered all over the papers as my latest love interest.'

He laughed incredulously. 'Yeah, that's really going to harm my reputation, people thinking I'm having an affair with Elizabeth Donavue.'

'It might do, if Sally believes it.'

He recalled Sally's face as she'd drawn back from kissing him and felt a wave of misgiving. Sally probably would put two and two together and believe he'd ended things because he'd started sleeping with Lizzie. While he didn't care too much about the dint to his reputation, he was annoyed that a couple of bastards, out to make money from Lizzie's misfortune, might end up hurting Sally, too. 'We've already established Sally and I aren't in a relationship.' He shifted away from Lizzie slightly, enough so he could keep his equilibrium vaguely intact. 'You know, you've got to stop worrying so much. In a few months' time nobody will remember any of this. I'm going up to call

Dan now, see if he's filed the lawsuit yet. Do you want to listen in?'

She nodded. 'I'll be there in a minute.'

While Nick strode upstairs to his office to make the call, Lizzie hunted down the printout of the email Catherine had sent through – the details of her villa by the sea. She'd spent all afternoon eyeing it longingly, but now she wasn't sure. Nick had looked so tired when he'd come in. Obviously travelling between the barn and his office in London was really taking its toll. How could she now ask him to drop everything and go on *holiday* with her?

Plus there was Sally to consider. Sally, who she conveniently kept forgetting. No matter how much he continued to deny they were serious, what sort of woman did it make her that she was considering tempting Nick into an affair, when he was already sleeping with someone else?

Sighing wistfully, she scrunched the picture into the palm of her hand and climbed the stairs to join him.

'That's great news, Dan,' she heard him saying on the phone when she quietly eased the study door open. 'Damages for rape, blackmail, defamation of character ... yes, we'll take whatever we can. By the time he's had his lawyer read through that, Charles will rue the day he ever hurt her.' He smiled when he noticed Lizzie and put Dan onto speakerphone. 'I've got Lizzie with me now, Dan.' He glanced at her. 'Dan was just saying he's filed the lawsuit. Charles has a week to answer the charges.'

'So soon?' She'd assumed this would drag on for months.

Nick grinned. 'I think Dan's pulled strings we're not allowed to ask him about. You'd have to take the fifth on that, hey buddie?'

The American chuckled. 'Sure thing. Suffice to say there's a ground swell of support for you here, Elizabeth. Seeing what you've gone through, and how you're standing up to him

134

rather than letting him get away with his shameful behaviour, has encouraged more and more women to come forward with their own experiences. I'm quietly confident.'

Nick laughed. 'Dan and the word *quiet* do not go together in the same sentence. Seriously though Dan, we appreciate all you've done on this. I owe you.'

'You don't owe me a damn thing,' Dan's voice boomed back. 'Consider us even. Now, you folks relax and leave it in the capable hands of your American friends. I'll keep you updated.'

Nick said goodbye and cut the call.

Perching on the edge of his desk, Lizzie felt dazed. 'Wow, I can't believe this is all happening so fast.'

'Dan's a good man with a lot of important connections. He'll get us the right verdict, trust me.' He pulled his chair out slightly so he could look at her properly. 'It's a crying shame we can't put Charles in jail, where he belongs, but at least this way he'll be ruined and your reputation back in order.'

Lizzie chewed her bottom lip. 'I'm not so sure it will be that easy. Restoring my reputation, I mean.'

'It will,' he asserted, his voice allowing no argument. 'When the outcome of this civil case hits the media, everyone will know who is the victim here. It will work out, Lizzie. Trust me.'

She nodded, on the verge of tears again. Two weeks ago she'd been staring down a cold, dark tunnel, with no exit in sight. Now one was being dangled, teasingly, in front of her nose.

'What's that?' he asked, noticing the sheet of paper balled up in her hand.

Quickly she glanced down, feeling foolish. 'Nothing really.'

'What does *nothing really* mean? Is it something, or isn't it?'

She rolled her eyes at him. 'Okay, it's *something* that seemed like a good idea earlier, after the altercation with the journalist.' Feeling oddly nervous, she attempted to smooth out the printout. 'The other night, you asked me to picture something to make me relax. A beach you said, with sand and warm turquoise water. Well, I could really do with a bit of that right now. I mean, staying here has been terrific, exactly what I needed, but now the press know I'm here.' Her mouth ran out of words and she ended up shrugging awkwardly.

'You want to go on holiday for a while?' he asked softly.

'Yes,' she admitted. 'It occurred to me I haven't had a break for years. Now seems like a good time.' She glanced up at him. 'Just a few days, you know. Maybe a week? If you can't take the time off, I'll understand, I know how busy you've been.'

'You want me to go with you?' he blurted, looking totally shocked.

'Well, yes, obviously. I mean it wouldn't be much fun on my own.' Heck, she couldn't think of anything worse. Leave Nick when, by the sound of things, she only had a short time left with him? The thought knotted her stomach. 'Of course if you don't want to come ...' She let the sentence hang.

He shook his head. 'No, I mean, yes.' A rueful grin spread across his face. 'I've never been good at double negatives. Yes, of course, if you'd like me to come, I'd love to join you.' He frowned slightly. 'When were you planning on going?'

Oops. She tried to look shamefaced. 'I was thinking, maybe tomorrow?' His eyebrows shot skywards. 'I know it's short notice,' she added quickly, 'and I can wait if you need to sort stuff out, but ...'

'You really want to get away?'

Her mouth felt dry and her heart was thumping away like the clappers. All she could do was nod. This was more than just a break in the sun. It was her and Nick and a romantic hideaway. It was a fantasy, a pipedream, but one she so desperately wanted to come true.

'You don't muck around when you set your mind on something, do you?' He ran a hand through his hair, which she now understood was his way of taking time out, pausing to think. 'I should be okay, as long as I can work wherever we're going. Where is that, by the way?'

Joy swept through her, exploding out in a bubble of laughter. 'Sardinia. I've got a friend who has a villa there.' She waved the picture under his nose, but he barely glanced at it.

'Okay then, good.' A bemused smile spread across his face. 'It looks like we're going on holiday then.'

'Yes, it does. I'm off to pack.' Feeling almost giddy with delight, she almost skipped towards the door. 'By the way, what did Dan mean by you being even now?'

'Nothing, really. He practiced law in the UK for a while and got into trouble with his accounts.' He smiled. 'I guess I saved his financial ass a few times.'

'You're good at that, you know, saving people's asses. You're saving mine now.'

'Well, it's nice to get the credit, but it's Dan who's doing the hard work.' He deliberately looked her over. 'Mind you, as asses go, yours is high on the list of ones I would like to save.'

He was teasing, she knew it, but it didn't stop her almost gliding down the corridor. She was going to a Mediterranean island with Nick. Sun, sea, sand and ... Raising her eyes to the ceiling, she pushed open her bedroom door. She was supposed to have convinced herself having an affair with Nick was the wrong thing to do. But she was tired of being sensible, especially when her body was crying out for her to be naughty.

# Chapter Sixteen

The journey to Sardinia had been blissfully uneventful, no doubt because Lizzie had booked them on a private plane. At first it had rankled with Nick, a painful reminder of their different lifestyles. After a few glasses of champagne though, he'd decided to ditch his pride and enjoy the ride. It was her money, after all.

She hadn't told him the name of the friend who'd loaned her the use of the villa, and he'd been careful not to ask. As he gazed now at the magnificent five-bedroom whitewashed property, overlooking a private beach, it didn't take a genius to figure out whoever she was, she was loaded. Loaded and with superb taste. It wasn't going to be a hardship spending a few days here, especially as he got to see Lizzie looking so happy. And in a bikini.

Almost the moment they'd arrived, Lizzie had shrugged into the tiny black number and dived into the pool, leaving her suitcase untouched. He, on the other hand, had carefully unpacked all his things and placed them into drawers, which pretty much summed up how different they were. One spontaneous, the other methodical. He tried to tell himself that methodical, or practical, as he preferred to think, didn't automatically translate into boring.

They'd chosen to spend the balmy late afternoon sitting by the pool, looking out over the sea. It was idyllic, certainly. Or, it would be, if he weren't so uncomfortably aware of the person sitting beside him. A quick glance in her direction confirmed she still had her nose in a trashy novel, so once again he played with fire and allowed his eyes to hover hungrily over her. Three small triangles of black and a couple of bits of string were all that prevented him from seeing her full naked beauty. He'd heard it said blondes looked good in black. He wasn't going to argue.

She stretched and he stifled a groan, totally unable to stop staring at her. She wasn't as skinny as some models. More toned than bony, with curves that definitely went in and out in all the right places. Smooth and lightly tanned, her legs went on forever, but her waist was tiny. He reckoned he could probably circle it with both of his hands. And after he'd done that, he'd stroke his fingers lazily across her soft skin. The colour of caramel, it looked good enough to run his tongue along.

Abruptly he jumped up from the lounger. 'I'm going to fetch a drink,' he announced, his voice sounding alarmingly rough. 'Do you want anything?'

Tipping her sunglasses onto the top of her head, she smiled, clearly oblivious to the havoc she was causing him. She was so damned beautiful it almost hurt to look at her. 'If you can find some, a gin and tonic would go down a treat. But go easy on the gin. I don't want another hangover like the last one.'

Nodding, he escaped quickly into the cool of the villa. How in God's name was he going to get through the next few days with her wearing nothing but that itsy bitsy bikini? He'd barely coped living with her in England, but at least then she'd been wearing clothes.

With a deep sigh he found two glasses and poured enough gin into his to hopefully take the edge off his lust. After adding a splash of tonic, ice and a slice of lemon, he took a hefty swig from his glass before joining her outside again. Perhaps he would become immune to the sight of her in a day or two.

Either that or he'd turn into an alcoholic.

Warily he settled back into his recliner, carefully placing the drinks on the small table between them. Lizzie smiled her thanks and leant forward to take a sip, giving him an eyeful of glorious cleavage. Hastily he reached for his own drink. Become immune to her? Yeah, right. It hadn't happened in the last eight years or so, it was hardly going to start on a ruddy beach holiday.

He sought refuge in his reading. And another mouthful of gin.

'Why don't you take your shirt off, Nick?' Lizzie asked him

after a while, eyeing him over the top of her sunglasses. A hint of a smile on her lips.

'Because I'm English.' He looked down at his unremarkable blue T-shirt. Admittedly it was hot, but there was no way he was going to strip off in front of a woman who made a living out of posing with male models. And whose list of past lovers included a hot-shot baseball star and several muscle bound actors.

She grinned. 'Come on, England hasn't changed that much over the last few years. I've seen Englishmen taking their shirts off on the beach lots of times. Admittedly it's usually the ones with the large pot belly.' She prodded his stomach. 'You've not got one of those, have you?'

His body twitched at what had been only the lightest touch of her fingers. Nervously he crossed his legs. 'No.'

'So, what's stopping you?'

'Maybe I don't want to get burnt.'

'Or maybe you're shy?'

Now she was teasing him. 'Maybe I am.' It was easier to agree.

She let out an exasperated hiss. 'For goodness sake, Nick. I'm sitting by your side in next to nothing. In fact, as you've seen the photographs of me in the papers recently, you've already seen me in absolutely nothing. The least you can do is strip down, too. You're making me feel uncomfortable.'

He sighed and yanked off his shirt. 'There. Happy?' He stuck his nose back into the report he was reading before he had the chance to catch the amusement on her face.

Lizzie slid him a sideways glance. He looked so adorable, all stiff and awkward without his T-shirt. In Los Angeles men took their shirts off at the drop of a hat, only too ready to impress the ladies with their rippling, tanned physiques. Sure, Nick's chest could do with a bit of sun, but it was hard and well defined. The lean muscles of an athlete, rather than the heavy muscles of a bodybuilder.

'All you need now is a hankie on your head,' she remarked lightly.

He snorted. 'I said I was English, not an English stereotype.' Threading a hand through his thick dark hair, he smiled smugly. 'Look, no bald patch. I believe that's why they put the hankie on the head. To prevent a burnt scalp.'

Because he looked so adorable, and because she ached to kiss his dimpled smile off his face, Lizzie had to turn away. She tried to concentrate on her book again, but it was impossible with Nick sitting next to her, his chest muscles glinting in the sun. A sexy trail of dark hair running down from his navel and disappearing into his plain black trunks.

'I'm heading in for another drink. Do you want one?'

He looked surprised. 'I thought you didn't want a hangover?'

'What, after two weak gins? I'm hardier than that. Besides,' she nodded in the direction of the view, 'it's sinful to sit here and not drink a G&T.'

He laughed and her insides somersaulted. Heaven help her, it wasn't the weak gin making her feel all fluttery. It was him.

As she made the drinks, she acknowledged what she'd known for years. Nick was special, and she was falling for him, hard. Was she deluding herself to think he felt the same way? She didn't think so. That look he'd given her by the pool sure as heck hadn't come from the eyes of a friend or a brother. Catherine's bikini test had been right.

But even if he did feel the same way, was she right to encourage it? He was the closest thing she had to family left in the world. More than that, these last two weeks had shown her he was the most important person in her life, full stop. Was it worth risking losing him for a holiday fling? Because there would be no happy ever after, not for them. A long distance relationship, carried out under the curse of the media spotlight? She couldn't see Nick enjoying either. When he settled down, it wasn't going to be with a needy, limelight grabbing model with a sordid sexual past. No, it would be with someone like himself: smart, unselfish and self-reliant. Suddenly she thought of Sally again. A partner at his firm, so he'd said. A woman who appeared unclingy, secure enough to let him lead his own life independently from hers. Yet there when he needed her.

Shoving the gin bottle down with more force than necessary, Lizzie clutched the glasses and strode back outside.

'What does Sally think of you coming away with me?' she asked as she sat back down beside him.

He gave her a sharp look. 'I've told you already—'

'You aren't serious, aren't an item, just use each other for sex, blah, blah.' His eyes narrowed and she realised the gin was making her tongue loose. 'Sorry. I just don't want to be the cause of any problems between you.'

His jaw tightened. 'You think I'd have kissed you like I did the other evening if there was anything remotely serious going on between me and Sally?'

Of course he wouldn't have. Nick was as honest, as straight, as decent as they came. 'You're right. Forget I said anything. It's none of my business.'

If anything, his face tightened further. 'We're friends. It is your business. But you don't need to worry about upsetting her. Our ...' He hesitated, as if unsure of the right words. 'Our agreement is over.'

Nick cringed, and the look of bemusement on Lizzie's face racked his embarrassment up a further notch. Had he seriously called his 'thing' with Sally an agreement? It sounded like a bloody business transaction.

'I'm sure she'd be delighted to hear your description,' Lizzie murmured, her eyes alive with amusement. There was something else there, too. Was he deluding himself to think it was relief? Maybe even delight?

'Piss off,' he muttered back at her and she laughed, a rich, spontaneous, joyful noise that wrenched all the angst out of him. He was left feeling only pleasure at how happy she looked.

And a deep, aching, pulsing lust at how damn gorgeous she looked.

'I'm going inside for a bit,' he announced, standing quickly, something he regretted instantly as the combination of alcohol and sun nearly unbalanced him.

'Whoa, steady there.' Giggling, she stood and clutched at his arm.

He looked down at her hand. 'Is that to help steady me or you?'

She bit at the underside of her lip. 'A little of both. I should go in, too. I don't want to get sunstroke on our first day. Do you want to see if there's a movie on?'

A film? Awkwardly he moved away from her grip. He'd just spent two hours next to her in a bikini. Now she expected him to spend two hours curled up beside her on a sofa? God help him, he didn't have that sort of control. 'Lizzie, I need to work. You might be on holiday, but I'm not.' Desperation made his words far too sharp, and she flinched.

'Fine. Maybe I'll see you later.' She slumped back onto the lounger and pretended to read.

'It's upside down.'

She frowned, followed the direction of his eyes, and, huffing, spun the book the right way up.

Sighing, he shrugged on his T-shirt. 'Look, I'm sorry, I didn't mean to snap.' He picked up his papers and empty glass. 'I'll be done in a couple of hours. How about I cook us a meal?' Her eyes remained firmly in her book. 'Peace offering?'

'I'd rather stay mad at you.'

'Prawn linguine?' He knew Catherine's fridge held all the ingredients – it had been thoughtfully stocked by a local couple who looked after the place for her.

Her lips twitched. 'Okay. And I guess I should apologise, too. I know you've got to work. How about I set the table? We can sit out on the terrace. Enjoy the view while we can.'

Nodding, Nick wandered back inside the villa. He might have managed to escape bikini-clad Lizzie for a few hours, but he wasn't sure Lizzie on the terrace in the moonlight was going to be any easier to resist.

A few hours later Nick studied Lizzie against the backdrop of the night sky as they ate on the terrace overlooking the bay. Just as the moon cast a soft glow on the calm sea below them, so Lizzie's beauty seemed to have a luminescent quality about it. It made it hard to breathe, hard to swallow. He felt like a man who'd gone twenty rounds with Muhammad Ali and didn't have the energy for another bout. For years he'd fought his attraction to her, bitten his tongue and kept his feelings to himself. But after two weeks of being with her almost 24/7, sharing his home with her, sharing meals with her – now under a star-filled sky, for crying out loud – he simply couldn't handle it any longer. The mental and physical exhaustion of keeping his feelings to himself now outweighed the risk of humiliation and loss of her friendship. He wanted, no he needed, more.

Please God, let him not make a total arse of himself.

As she finished her meal, he reached across the table and clasped her hand. When she looked up, startled, he tightened his grip. 'I was wondering, what's the etiquette for finding out if a friend wants to become a lover?'

She flushed. As she slowly put down the glass she'd just picked up, her eyes evaded his, and his heart froze. He'd got it spectacularly wrong. She didn't think of him that way at all, of course she didn't. What had he been thinking? And now he'd embarrassed the hell out of both of them. Scalded, he quickly withdrew his hand. 'Shit, sorry. I must have had too much to drink. Forget I said that.'

Finally she looked at him, blue eyes large in the moonlight. 'I have to admit, I've never had a chat up line quite like that before.'

She was laughing at him. The one thing he'd been certain

she'd never do. What a bloody fool he was. 'Yeah, well, they don't call me Smooth Nick for nothing.' He drew back his chair, uncaring that it scraped against the marble tiles. He was desperate to escape, to go and lick his wounds somewhere dark and private. 'If you'll excuse me, I need to …' He couldn't even think of a reasonable excuse. His mind was too full of humiliation and crashing dreams.

Livid with herself, Lizzie flung her hand across Nick's arm, stopping him in his tracks. She often resorted to humour when she felt uncertain or scared, and right now she was definitely scared. But that was no excuse. Making a crass joke when Nick was putting his pride on the line was unforgivable. 'Please, slow down,' she whispered. 'I'm sorry. You took me by surprise.'

'I find that hard to believe.' His jaw was so tense she was afraid it might snap.

'Why? Twice I've propositioned you, and twice you've turned me down.'

'Twice when you were drunk.'

She took hold of his hand, gently prising apart the rigidly held fingers. 'Well, I'm not drunk now. Why don't you ask me to dance? Perhaps then you can find the answer to your question.'

He hesitated, searching her eyes. She hoped he could read her plea. *Please don't let my stupid joke put you off.*

'Okay,' he said finally, and as her shoulders sagged in relief, her heart started a little jig. 'But there's a fundamental flaw in your plan.'

Her breath caught. 'Oh?'

'You seem to have forgotten, I can't dance to save my life.' Relief washed through her for the second time as he helped her to her feet. 'Perhaps we can sway to the non-existent music.'

'Swaying sounds wonderful.' Her heart felt like it had wings as she moved into his arms.

# Chapter Seventeen

Lizzie melted against him. His embrace was everything Nick was; warm, solid, infinitely strong. She clasped her arms around his neck, running her hands through his short hair, nuzzling up against his neck, filling her nostrils with his natural masculine smell. Her mind emptied of everything but the feel of the hard muscles of his chest against her breasts, the caress of his hands as they gently smoothed over her back. The press of his thigh muscles on hers.

It hadn't been that many days ago when the thought of having a man press against her, his hands on her body, had filled her with revulsion. Then Nick had come back into her life. Carefully he'd begun to fix not just the outside pieces of her life, but the insides, too. Here was a man she trusted with all her heart. He didn't want to make love to her for the headlines she could generate him, or the money he could extort from her. No, this strong, sexy, kind man wanted her only for herself. Reaching up, she took his face in her hands and kissed him softly on the lips.

He responded instantly, his mouth moving gently against hers as his tongue started a slow caress, tenderly pushing her lips apart. Drawing her more fully against him, he deepened the kiss, his mouth becoming more urgent as he slid his hands down her body, moving unerringly towards her breasts. With exquisite slowness, he brushed his palms across her nipples, releasing a moan from her. His fingers continued to tease, drifting back and forth over her nipples until they stood out prominently against the silk of her top.

Finally he broke away, but only to burrow his face in her hair. 'I want you, Lizzie,' he whispered huskily against her ear. 'Now is the time for you to push me away. Because if you don't …'

'If I don't?'

'God help me, if you don't I'll pick you up and carry you upstairs to bed.'

She laughed gently. 'That sounds rather exciting.'

To her astonishment he proceeded to place one arm underneath her thighs and lift her into his arms. She found herself giggling helplessly as he walked towards the stairs. Perhaps it wasn't the most romantic response she could have mustered, but she was fast discovering humour was a powerful aphrodisiac.

'Crikey, you're not as light as you look, are you?' he complained as they finally approached the landing.

She swatted him. 'I don't think Rhett ever said that to Scarlett.'

'Yeah well, maybe Scarlett ate like a sparrow. You, on the other hand ...' He kicked open the door to the main bedroom and almost threw her onto the bed. '... haven't been able to get enough of my cooking.'

When he sat down on the bed next to her, panting slightly with the effort of carrying her up the stairs, Lizzie couldn't stop herself. She burst out laughing. Any remaining doubts she'd harboured – whether memories of what Charles had done would haunt her, ruining this moment – vanished. She'd never felt so totally sure, or so totally relaxed, about making love with a man. 'I have to say, sex has never been like this before,' she told him, wrapping her arms around him.

He looked at her quizzically. 'Err, in case you haven't noticed, we've not started yet.'

'Well, maybe technically not, but ...' She smiled. 'So far I like your style, Nick Templeton.'

'What style would that be?' he asked, pushing her down onto the bed. 'The *make them laugh so they don't notice when you pull their knickers down* style?'

Giggling again, she reached up to stroke his cheek. 'Umm, works for me.'

Slowly, with the utmost care, Nick began to undo the buttons of her silk top. 'You're beautiful, Lizzie. So unbelievably, stunningly beautiful.' He kissed her shoulders, leaving a burning trail in his wake, then started to peel away the rest of her clothes. 'Thank goodness for warm climates.'

'No socks?'

His chuckle against her skin was like a caress. 'Amongst other things, yes.'

She sighed as he covered one of her breasts with his mouth, teasing and delighting. But she wanted to play, too. 'Nick, you need to undress.'

'Umm,' he murmured, moving on to the other nipple.

'Ahh, that feels, oh ...'

With his mouth still occupied on her breast, he trailed his hand over her waist and down between her legs.

She gave up trying to get him to take off his shirt and gave in to the sheer wonder of being pleasured. Of having a man focus totally on her needs and not his own. As his movements gathered pace, within seconds she was crying out in satisfaction.

'That was incredible,' she managed finally, taking hold of his hand and bringing it up to her lips. 'Thank you.'

He gazed down at her, eyes so dark they were almost black. 'My pleasure.'

She smiled ruefully at his still clothed body. 'You're wearing far too many clothes for this party.'

'We can soon solve that.' Instantly he stood and quickly stripped. After slipping on a condom he nestled his large frame between her legs. 'Ready for act two?'

She took his face in her hands and brought it towards her. 'Bring it on.'

Whether it was his technique, or whether it was because she was so relaxed in his presence, or whether it was just Nick, she didn't know. Whatever it was, the pleasure she felt as he entered her, as he thrust his powerful hips deeply inside her, filling her until she almost cried with ecstasy, was more than anything she'd ever known. She wanted to tell him how amazing he felt, but her mind couldn't work out the words. It was too full of him, and the glorious sensations he was creating inside her. Her orgasm, when it came, was deep, long and powerful. She was just about aware enough to notice when Nick allowed himself to let go, too.

Taking care not to squash her, he moved onto his back, pulling her with him.

'So how does act three go?' she asked dreamily, finding a comfortable position wrapped tight against his chest.

His chest rumbled with laughter. 'Well, first there's a long interval.' She pouted. 'During which you're welcome to get yourself and your partner a drink.'

She pretended to consider his words. 'I guess I could do that. It all depends whether act three is up to the standard of acts one and two.'

Moving slightly, he gazed into her eyes. Her heart squeezed at the desire she saw swirling there. 'Lizzie, I could perform an entire symphony with you, and each time it would be better than the last.' Then, as if aware that he was being too heavy, he patted her on the bottom. 'Now, about those interval drinks.'

When she was gone, Nick collapsed back onto the bed and covered his head with his hands. What had he done? How was he going to go on from here? Making love to her had been so ... words failed him. It had been more than even he'd dreamed, and his dreams had been pretty damn amazing. In them he'd managed to imagine his own pleasure fairly accurately, but he hadn't factored in how phenomenal it was to feel Lizzie's uninhibited response to him, too. It had blown his mind, not to mention his ego.

But what now? How could he possibly go back to simply being friends?

'Nick?' He flung his hands from his face and sat up quickly,

149

though clearly not quickly enough. 'Regretting it already?' Her words were sharp, but he read the hurt lying at the heart of them.

'No, of course not.' He tried a reassuring smile.

Setting down the drinks, she perched on the bed, as far away from him as she could. Then, pulling her knees up to her chin, she wrapped her arms tightly around her legs. 'I wouldn't blame you if you were regretting it,' she said flatly, staring straight ahead, all joy completely removed from her face. 'You're probably already wondering how you could have made love to the same woman who let Charles and that other man ...' Her words faltered as they caught in her throat.

Love for her tore through him. In a flash he was beside her, ignoring her body language and enfolding her in his arms. 'Of course I'm not. How can you even think that?'

'What then?'

She was so stiff in his arms, he ached for her. 'I'm terrified we're going to lose what we have,' he admitted finally. 'We both know an affair between us can only be short lived. Soon you'll be back in America, getting on with your life. Will you still count me as a friend, even now we've slept together?'

He felt her sag against him. 'Oh, Nick, I'll always want you in my life. After the experience with Charles ...' She shuddered. 'I didn't think I'd want to get involved with another man ever again. I mean, what if I picked another loser? Someone who only wanted to make love to me so he could use me?' She turned and nestled back against him. 'With you, I don't have any worries. I trust you implicitly.'

'I see.' His voice sounded so tight, she couldn't fail to pick up on it.

'What's wrong? What have I said?'

It was his chance to tell her the truth; that they both yearned for different things. She wanted a holiday fling, a way to get back into the swing of dating men again. He wanted forever. But if he told her that, she'd scuttle back to America in the blink of an eye. Probably before the case was even over, definitely before he was ready to let her go. So he settled for humour, though laced with more than a grain of truth. 'A man likes to think a woman wants him for his body, not just because she trusts him,' he replied lightly, kissing her on the shoulder.

The worry banished from her eyes. 'I presumed you'd take that for granted.'

'Sure, why wouldn't I?' The list of her ex boyfriends flashed through his mind and he cringed.

'You might not think it, but you've got a very sexy body.' As if to prove what she thought, Lizzie pushed him down onto the bed and traced her fingers delicately across his chest. 'Look at those pecs, and your hard, flat stomach.' She gazed up at him beneath a curtain of blonde hair and smiled. 'Of course you could do with a bit of a tan, but we can work on that over the next few days.'

'And that's where we're ending this conversation.' He caught her fingers and brought them to his lips. 'Are you ready for act three?'

Laughing, she crawled up the bed so her mouth was aligned with his. 'I've always been in favour of short intervals.'

# Chapter Eighteen

Nick woke early, doing a quick double take when he caught sight of Lizzie sprawled out next to him. He had to smile. In sleep, she looked nothing like the ultra glamorous, elegant model. Sexy, certainly, with her usually smooth hair tumbling in a mass of confusion around her face and across the pillow. Elegant, no, not at that moment. He leant over to kiss her on the nape of her neck, but pulled back at the last minute, flipping onto his back and staring at the ceiling.

In the cold light of day, would she regret what they'd done? He cast an eye over her sleeping form, remembering her wholehearted response to him last night. No, he didn't think she was the type to regret. But it still begged the question. Would she have leapt so easily into bed with him if she hadn't had a court case hanging over her head, or the horrors of her experience with Charles still fresh in her mind?

'Good morning, lover.' He turned to find Lizzie on her side, smiling up at him with sleepy blue eyes. 'Hey, why are you looking so pensive?'

He rolled so he could face her. 'How can you possibly look more beautiful now, without make-up, and with tangled bed hair?' Slowly he trailed a finger down the side of her face, tracing its soft lines. He ached to kiss her again, but was unsure of his moves, frightened to assume anything.

'Nick?' Her eyes grew troubled. 'What is it?'

Letting out a sigh, he flipped onto his back again. 'Honestly? I'm hoping to God I haven't taken advantage of you. If Charles hadn't blackmailed you, we would never have ended up in bed together.'

Lizzie sat up and glared at him. 'What a stupid thing to say. How do you know that? Maybe this was always destined to happen.'

'And what exactly is this, Lizzie? One night of unforgettable but never to be repeated bliss, or something more?'

'What do you want it to be?'

He smiled wryly at the clever way she turned the conversation. 'I want to make love to you this morning, this afternoon, tonight, and every other chance I get before you go back to America.' *And for the rest of my life*, he added in his head.

Chuckling softly, she moved to lie across him, her breasts teasing his chest. 'That's good, because that's exactly what I want, too.' She bent her head to capture his mouth. 'Here's to a few more days of the four s's.'

They had breakfast on the balcony and made love once more before hunting down some snorkels and wandering down the steps to the beach. It was as if her life in Los Angeles didn't exist. Lizzie had finally found relaxation, peace and a man she not only had amazing sex with, but she could be herself with. A man who was not only a great friend, but who she was seriously falling in love with. She ignored the voices in her head telling her this wasn't going to last – that it wasn't real life. They could take a running jump for a while.

'How is your swimming these days? Progressed from the doggy paddle?'

His eyes teased and she slanted him a look. 'I think you'll find I'm no longer that six-year-old girl you tried to teach to swim.'

The glance he shot back was hot and heavy. 'I know.'

Instantly her pulse rocketed and her insides liquidised. Incredible. She even felt herself blush. He might have a deceptively calm, quiet exterior but beneath it lurked a positive sex God. He looked ready to take her again, this time on the beach steps. A shiver ran through her, but she didn't feel cold. On the contrary, she felt hot. Extremely hot.

'Last one in the sea cooks dinner,' she announced, jumping off the last step and onto the beach.

'Hey, that's not fair,' she heard Nick yell after her. Racing across the sand, she risked a quick peek over her shoulder and smiled at the sight of him struggling to run with flippers in his hands and assorted masks and snorkels dangling from the rucksack on his back.

Arriving at the sea, she splashed straight into it.

'Yikes, that's cold,' Nick exclaimed a moment later as he hit the water.

She ducked her head into the waves, loving the feel of the spray on her face. 'You always were a big chicken when it came to cold water.'

'Who, me?' He shook his head at her. 'I think you're confusing me with Robert. I've just got a healthy respect for the temperature of the sea. Probably because I don't have the luxury of the layers of blubber you females enjoy.'

With one sharp pull she tugged him, very efficiently, into the cold water. 'Blubber my arse.' When he reared up and deliberately looked at her bum, she pushed him under again. 'I have it on good authority that my bottom is perfect.' She wriggled that part of her anatomy suggestively in his face. 'I was signed by Calvin Klein to be their swimwear model, I'll have you know.'

Standing up, he reached out and pinched her rear. 'Umm, maybe I can see why, but to be sure I'll have to take these down.'

She swatted away the hand that tugged at her bikini bottoms and went to fetch the mask and snorkel he'd abandoned on the beach. 'You know, I haven't been snorkelling since ...' Abruptly she stopped. A family holiday in the Greek islands. She must have been about ten, Robert a much older fifteen. He'd begged their parents to allow Nick to come too, successfully arguing there was no way he could be expected to put up with his kid sister for a whole week. With a pang of remorse and a heavy dose of guilt she thought of Robert now, lying on his bed in LA, staring unseeing at the ceiling. It was a sharp reminder of why the life she was living with Nick could only ever be a temporary escape.

Nick gave her hand a light squeeze, gently bringing her attention back to him. 'It was Greece,' he supplied softly. 'I thought I'd died and gone to heaven. A holiday abroad, with my substitute parents and best friend.' He flashed her a smile. 'Just a shame this annoying brat followed us round all the time.'

She pushed him again, hard, but this time he was ready for her, laughing as he captured her hands. It was only later, as she was snorkelling, that she realised he'd known exactly what to say to lift her mood.

They snorkelled for half an hour before falling, dripping wet, onto their towels. Nick leant on his elbow, watching Lizzie as she stretched out in front of him. She had the grace of a cat and the body of a siren. It was no wonder he couldn't get enough of her. Of its own volition, his hand reached out and began to trace the skin at her slender waist.

'All those people who gaze at this body in magazines; the women with envy, the men with desire.' His fingers smoothed across her toned stomach. 'They have no idea that what they're seeing is only a pale copy of the real thing.'

'I'll have you know I'm lightly tanned.' Her face smiled up at him.

He ignored her self-effacing comment and carried on his study. 'Your skin is amazingly soft.' He wished he knew how to describe it to do it justice. Saying it was like silk was too clichéd, yet he couldn't think of any other description. He was a numbers man, not a words man. Deciding he was better letting his actions do the talking, he dropped light kisses across her stomach, his face erupting in a satisfied smirk as her nipples hardened.

'Lizzie.' She turned to meet his eyes and whatever he was going to say stuck in his throat. Unable to resist, he bent to capture her mouth, kissing her with the intensity of a man starved of female company. It was how he felt around her. For years he'd made do with loving her in his dreams. Now, for these few precious days, she was a reality. He intended to make the most it.

His hands crept under her bikini top, palming her breasts, but suddenly the answering warmth wasn't there. Worse, she was pushing him away.

'Nick, no.' Sitting up, she crossed her arms over her chest. 'God, what if someone's out here, taking photographs? I've had enough of people watching me have sex to last me a lifetime.'

Her words sliced through him and he rolled away, feeling every inch the horny teenager accused of pawing a girl out of his league. 'You're right, sorry,' he replied tightly, turning his eyes towards the sea, hurt and annoyed with his lack of control. The trouble was, they were coming at this affair from two very different directions. She was a touch of paradise he'd never be able to get enough of. He was a pleasant distraction from her troubles back at home.

Lizzie reached out a hand to touch his leg. 'Nick, sorry, that sounded harsher than I meant it to.'

Cutting off her attempt to placate him, he scrambled to his feet. 'I'm going for a swim.' With a bit of luck the cold water would dampen his flaming ardour, something he couldn't seem to keep in check when he was with her.

Calling herself all kinds of names, Lizzie levered herself onto her elbows and watched anxiously as Nick swam up and down the small bay. She'd panicked, pure and simple. A sudden flashback to the photographs of herself on a bed, Charles licking her breasts, another man looking on with a leer on his face. For a fleeting moment she'd felt the awareness of a camera with a long telephoto lens. By the time she'd realised her fear was irrational, that the private, secluded bay was totally deserted, it was too late. She'd pushed Nick away, denting his pride.

Huffing out a breath, she sat up and rested her head on her knees, her eyes on the lone swimmer. She might have gone about things like a charging bull, but Nick had the sensitivity of flipping litmus paper. How could he possibly think she didn't want him? Couldn't he tell that every time he touched her, her body leapt into flames?

Perhaps he was finding the transition from friend to lover too weird. Funny, because she was finding it exactly the opposite. Having a lover who was also a friend was so incredibly … natural. One minute he'd make her laugh, the next she'd be breathless and giddy with desire. He didn't seek to control her, only to pleasure her. And when the passion was temporarily spent, there were no uncomfortable silences. Instead there was cuddling, warmth, teasing. It was all so new to her, but she could so easily get used to it. Too easily.

Finally he strode out of the sea and walked towards her. Unabashed, she stared at him, watching the streams of water running off his hard body. A body usually quietly hidden beneath conservative clothes. That was Nick. Understated, but actually quite magnificent.

'Feel better?' she asked as he drew closer.

Her heart sank as he avoided her eyes, instead reaching down for his towel. 'If you mean have I got my libido in check, then, yes.'

'Nick, come on, don't be like this.' She shook her head, frustrated with him. 'It wasn't a rejection. You know that.' Standing up she ran her hands over his chest, kissing him lightly on the lips. He remained rigid, unmoving. Swearing under her breath she gave up and went to sit back on the towel. 'In case you haven't noticed, I'm currently the paparazzi's number one dream target. The last thing I need right now is to give them more ammunition.' She pleaded with him to understand. 'I'm a famous figure. I have to be extremely careful about my privacy.'

'Yeah, I noticed.' With vigorous strokes, he rubbed himself down with the towel. He still hadn't looked at her.

'So that's it, is it? You're going to have a strop all day just because I declined your offer of sex on the beach?'

'I wanted to make love to you,' he corrected softly. 'But I hear what you're saying. I'll restrict my amorous overtures to the safety of indoors in future.'

She let out a sigh of pure, unbridled frustration. 'God, you can be so bloody infuriating.'

'No doubt.' He picked up the snorkel equipment and hoisted it over his shoulder. 'I'll see you back at the villa. I need to catch up on some work.'

As Nick made his way off the beach, he didn't dare to look behind in case he was caught by one of the daggers he knew Lizzie must be mentally flinging at him. Okay, he was being petty, and it sure as hell wasn't pretty, but it summed up exactly how he felt. As if he needed her to remind him she was a famous figure. Angrily he shoved the towel around his neck. He knew she was, damn it. Just as he knew she was not only out of his league, she was playing in an entirely different division.

And now he was feeling good and sorry for himself, which pissed him off even more.

Dumping the snorkels back in the pool hut, Nick acknowledged Lizzie had a right to be concerned about being photographed again. The scars from the last ordeal were still very fresh, something he of all people should know. So what he should have done was cut her some slack. Shown some understanding. Not stormed off like a truculent teenager.

The trouble was, he reflected as he strode through the villa to the bathroom, it was hard enough handling the fact he was having an affair with Lizzie, the beautiful girl he'd fallen in love with all those years ago. When he was reminded he was also sleeping with Elizabeth Donavue, dazzling supermodel and pin up to millions of men around the globe, it sent him into free fall.

He was attractive and successful. He believed that. But next to Elizabeth Donavue, he wondered if he'd ever be attractive or successful enough.

# Chapter Nineteen

When Nick finally surfaced, Lizzie was in her least favourite room of any house, the kitchen. She was attempting to make a chicken and mushroom pasta dish, the best peace offering she could dream up on the spur of the moment.

'Are you planning on adding sliced finger to the dish?' he asked from the doorway, watching her attempting to chop up the mushrooms.

'I thought it might make a new twist on humble pie,' she retorted, throwing down the knife in despair. Maybe this wasn't such a good idea, after all. 'Well, don't just stand there laughing. Help me.' He raised an eyebrow. 'Please.'

Seemingly satisfied, he manoeuvred her gently out of the way and started to expertly slice through the mushrooms. 'Show off,' she muttered under her breath.

'Well, practice does tend to make perfect.' He glanced at her as he eased the mushrooms into the waiting frying pan. 'I can't imagine the LA set do much of their own cooking.'

She didn't want to talk about the culinary habits of her American friends. 'Are you still annoyed with me?' she asked instead, needing to know where she stood.

He took his time to answer her blunt question, turning on the gas, adding butter to the mushrooms. All with a meticulousness that made her want to shake him. 'No,' he replied finally. 'I guess I just felt ... brushed off.' He shrugged and stared broodily into the sizzling pan.

She couldn't bear to watch him hurting. Walking up behind him, she placed her arms around his waist. 'Whatever I made you feel, I'm sorry. I didn't mean to.'

He turned and two deep brown pools stared back at her. 'And I'm sorry for being so sensitive.' Lightly he kissed the tip of her nose. 'I'm feeling my way here. I'm not sure of my moves any more. The role of sensible older brother came easily to me. I seem to have gone overboard on the lover part.'

Of all the stupid things he could say. 'You're joking, right? Just because I don't want to make love in the potential glare of a paparazzi lens, doesn't mean I want us to slow down.' Putting her hands on either side of his face, she kissed him long and hard. 'I want you, Nick Templeton. If you're willing to come with me, right now, I'll show you just how much.'

Finally he laughed. 'Well, that's an offer I can't refuse.' He turned round to eye up the mushrooms. 'But what about your pasta dish?'

She turned off the gas and dragged him out of the kitchen. 'It would have been rubbish anyway.'

The next few days went more quickly than either of them wanted. Lizzie was enjoying reacquainting herself with the girl who loved to laugh, to drink, and tell rude stories until the small hours. The one who went around without make-up, in the most casual of clothes. The girl who couldn't stop smiling. Under Nick's gentle, caring wing she'd come back.

As for Nick, he knew that any day now Dan would phone with news from Charles's lawyers, and his time with Lizzie would be over. The friend in him waited anxiously for that call, knowing it would mean Lizzie could leave this mess behind her.

The lover in him prayed for the phone not to ring. Because it was the lover who'd have to say goodbye to her as she boarded the plane back to America.

That evening, the call he'd been both dreading and anticipating came through.

'Lizzie,' he shouted up at her, hoping she wasn't still in the shower. 'I've got Dan on the phone.'

She appeared on the landing, a giant white fluffy towel wrapped around her body. 'What's he said?' she asked breathlessly, running down the stairs at a pace far too fast for the hard marble tiles.

Relaxing only when she careered to a stop next to him, Nick put Dan onto loudspeaker. 'She's here now, Dan. Better give the lady the news before she passes out with the suspense.'

'Hey, Lizzie.' Dan's laid-back voice echoed across the room. 'It seems your friend Charles hasn't got the stomach for a public court fight. His attorney's been in touch and they want to settle. Now I need to know what's acceptable to you.'

Nick watched as joy and hope spread across her gorgeous face. Even the selfish lover in him, the one who'd wanted the case, and thus his time with Lizzie, to stretch out indefinitely, found he couldn't be anything other than happy for her. She'd been through hell. It was only right she could finally start to look forward.

'That's fantastic,' she whispered hoarsely.

Before Nick knew it, she'd thrown herself at him, wrapping her still damp legs around his hips and her arms around his neck. Not content with that, she proceeded to kiss the very life from him. Momentarily stunned, it didn't take long for his body to recover from the shock and respond in an equally eager fashion. Within nanoseconds he was kissing her back, notching up the intensity even further. When his legs started to buckle, he headed for the wall, pushing her against it so he could get more leverage. Damn, he was wearing too many clothes.

'Err, I'm waiting for an answer.' Dan's voice cut into the fog of desire.

With a monumental effort Nick dragged his mouth from Lizzie's, only to see her blue eyes laughing at him. 'We're just thinking on that, Dan,' he finally croaked out, sounding like a man who'd run two marathons, then smoked a pack of cigars. 'Can we get back to you in a little while?'

'Sure. You guys enjoy your celebration. I'll be here when you're ready to talk.'

Lizzie giggled as Nick ended the call. 'In a little while?' She hoisted her legs more firmly round his and dropped her towel. 'I was rather hoping it would take longer than that.'

Kicking the phone away, Nick began to pull at his clothing. 'It can take as long you like,' he finally ground out before his mouth descended on her breast.

It was a long while later when Nick finally returned Dan's call. Lizzie left them to talk. As she told Nick, all she wanted was for Charles to publicly admit what he'd done. She didn't want his tainted money. Just her reputation restored.

With Nick's deep voice humming in the background, Lizzie picked up the glass of champagne he'd insisted on opening and went to sit on the terrace. She could finally see her career opening up again. The light was clearly there now, at the end of that tunnel she'd been stuck in. Perhaps before long her agent would be on the phone with a flood of new offers. Her life could begin again.

So why, after the initial rush of happiness at the thought of being vindicated, was she now feeling so, well, flat? Wasn't it time to go back to her career, her apartment overlooking the beach in Santa Monica? Catch up with some of her friends? She sighed, clutching at her drink. Much as she tried, she couldn't summon up the enthusiasm for any of it.

'For a woman who should be celebrating, you're looking far too sad.' Nick walked out towards her, carrying a half-filled glass. He'd thrown on some old shorts and a faded T-shirt. His face was in need of a shave. Yet it was this very realness that was so attractive to her.

In a flash she realised she wasn't ready to let him go. She wasn't sure she'd ever be ready.

Attempting a smile, she took another sip of champagne. 'I was just thinking about when I should go home.'

'Ahh.' Slowly he sat down next to her. 'Well, that's up to you.'

She sensed a tenseness in him, and wondered if he, too, hated the thought of her leaving.

'Could I stay with you a little longer? Until the dust settles?' Oh God, she was weak. Drawing out the inevitable.

Putting down his glass, he leaned across and took hold of her hands in his. 'Having you stay with me hasn't exactly been torture, you know, though sometimes the meals have been slightly ropey.' She tried to smile, but it was impossible when her throat was clogged with emotion and her heart so full. 'You can stay with me as long as you want.'

What would he say if she told him she wanted forever? Even if she dared ask, it wasn't possible. It might be what she wanted, but it wasn't what she could have. She'd already ruined three lives. She couldn't, wouldn't, ruin his, too.

'Lizzie?' Nick's warm voice interrupted her anguished thoughts.

'Sorry, I was miles away.'

'Already back in LA, eh?'

'Yes.'

His jaw tightened. 'Well, you'll be there for real soon enough.'

'Too soon,' she whispered, causing him to frown in confusion. Clearly he believed she wanted to go back, when in reality the thought filled her with dread.

'This is a night for celebration, not sadness,' he remarked suddenly, springing up and hauling her to her feet. 'Come and sway with me on the terrace. Then, if you're really lucky, I'll let you take me to bed.'

Pushing away her sombre thoughts, she remembered her favourite motto. *Live for now*. Today wasn't the time to change it.

# Chapter Twenty

Following Charles's confession, it didn't take long for the media sympathy to swing straight back in Lizzie's favour. Just, Nick reminded her rather smugly, as he'd predicted. In fact, since they'd arrived back in England, she'd been inundated with new offers sent over by her agent. Apparently she was now flavour of the month. What a crazy world she inhabited.

Almost as crazy as the life they were living in England. They'd been back three days and each of those mornings Nick had woken with her in his arms and wondered if it would be his last.

'Lizzie,' he called out as he returned from his first day back in the office since they'd come back. 'I'm home.' Wincing at the glib phrase – heck, he sounded like the returning husband – he went to hunt her down. They might be playing at being married, but the clock was ticking on their time together. Sooner or later she'd find the perfect job, and she'd be gone.

'I'm out on the patio.'

Squinting through the glass doors, he made out her slender figure sitting cross-legged on the lounger, sunglasses perched on her head, papers in her hand. She waved, and held up a glass. He knew the signal. Diving into the fridge, he pulled out the bottle of Sauvignon and went to join her.

'What are you reading?'

She looked at him sombrely and his heart almost stopped. 'A contract. Maria phoned to warn she was emailing it through. It's the perfume again, Innocence. And this time they don't just want me to front the campaign for the fragrance, they want me to represent the whole company brand. It seems they're jumping up and down, desperate for me to sign and get started.'

'Which company?' he asked quietly, his heart a heavy weight in his chest.

'Astella.'

His hand gripped at the wine glass. Astella was *the* fashion house. Even he'd heard of it. Famous for its iconic perfume, chic make-up and cutting edge fashion, it was a label models and film stars clamoured to be associated with. And they wanted Lizzie.

Feeling as though he'd had the stuffing knocked out of him, Nick slowly pulled the cork out of the bottle and poured them both a drink. 'That's good, isn't it?' he said eventually.

'Yes, I guess it is.'

He clung gratefully to the fact that she looked no happier than he was. 'When do they want you to start?'

He watched her swallow, then take in a deep breath. 'As soon as possible.'

His world caved in. The dread, the sickening anticipation he'd experienced for days all came to a head and he almost couldn't breathe. It was really happening. Lizzie was going to leave him.

'You don't have to do it,' he told her, his voice sounding as unravelled as he felt. 'Stay here with me, instead.'

He saw the answer in her eyes, and his heart crumpled. 'I can't,' she replied brokenly.

A lone tear slid down her cheek but he was too focussed on his own misery to take much notice of hers. 'No, sorry, of course you can't. You need to go back to your career, don't you?'

The venom in his tone made her flinch. 'Yes.'

'Well, that put me firmly in my place, didn't it?' He let out a low, humourless laugh. 'Then again, why am I so surprised? Your career has always been the most important thing in your world, hasn't it?' He wondered how many rungs he was below it. Or even if he was on the damn ladder at all.

Lizzie longed to deny his statement, then slap his face. Or slap first, deny afterwards. But what he was saying was true,

166

wasn't it? She'd put her career before her parents' happiness, first insisting on going to America, then whining when she was lonely, forcing them to go out and see her. So no, she deserved his cruel words, though it didn't mean she had to take them sitting down.

'Would you be so scathing of my career if I were a doctor? A lawyer?' She didn't let him answer. 'Besides, it's my career that helps to pay for Robert's medical needs. You seem to have conveniently forgotten I have a brother in a coma in LA, but I can't. There isn't a day goes by without me remembering where my brother is.' *Or who put him there.*

For a moment he said nothing. Just put his face in his hands and rubbed at his forehead. When he finally sat back up, he looked strained and so terribly sad. 'I don't mean to be scathing of your career. Truth is, I admire the hell out of what you've achieved. I lashed out because I don't want you to go back, though I know you have to.' He gave her a forlorn smile. 'How does that saying go? All good things must come to an end.'

'We were a good thing, weren't we?'

Tenderly he trailed a finger down her cheek. 'Better than good.'

She couldn't handle the anguish in his eyes, or the way her heart was falling apart inside her chest. Jerkily she got to her feet. 'I'll go and phone Maria.' Picking up the contract, she walked inside.

When she'd finished on the phone to her agent – at least someone was happy about all this – she found Nick still on the patio, staring morosely at the hills as the night grew dark around him. 'I told Maria I'd fly back tomorrow.'

'So soon?'

His voice sounded strangled and Lizzie felt her eyes prick. Hurting herself was bad enough, but hurting Nick? That was agony. 'I might as well,' she replied numbly. 'I mean, if I've got to go, there's no point putting it off. It's just I'm not really ready to go yet ...' Her voice broke as her mind swirled with images of the time they'd spent together. The walks across the hills, the day on the river, the time at the villa. She didn't want all that to end.

Before she knew it, Nick's arms were around her, bringing with them the feeling of security, the sense of a strong warm haven she longed for. She burst into tears.

Nick held her, his heart breaking. He wanted to tell her they could fly Robert to England. That he'd help pay the medical bills, but somehow he knew she'd say no to that, too. Her life was in America now, and he had no right to expect her to give it up for him.

'Will you come and visit me?' Her big blue eyes glistened with tears as she stared up at him.

'Hell, Lizzie, I don't know.' He wasn't sure he was up for the torture of a slow transatlantic relationship death. 'Isn't it better to have a clean break? Not see each other for a while?'

She clutched at him, shaking her head. 'I don't think I can get on that plane if I know it's the last time I'll see you for a long time.'

He didn't think he could put her on the plane, period.

'Please?'

He studied her reddened nose and swollen eyes, and knew it would take a stronger man than him to refuse her. 'Okay.'

'Promise?'

He mustered the strength to smile. 'Promise.' Using his thumb, he wiped the tears from her eyes. 'Though by the time you've become the face of Astella, you might not want to know me any more.'

She put a hand on either side of his face, clutching at him almost violently. 'I will always want to see you, Nick. Always.'

'Good.' Taking her hand, he led her into the barn and into his bedroom.

He took his time undressing her, wondering if this would be

the last time. The modelling world would soon captivate her again, as would another hunky male celebrity. It was unlikely she'd keep him to his promise when the world's sexiest men were back on her doorstep.

'Nick?'

He glanced down to find his hands clenching at her bra straps. 'Sorry.' Forcing them to relax, he gently tugged off her bra. Tonight he'd give her something to remember him by. And give the next man she took to her bed one hell of a lot to live up to.

Once again Lizzie found herself at the airport, saying goodbye to Nick. The last time she'd been too dazed with grief to remember much about it. This time she knew the pain of leaving Nick would stay in her memory for a long, long time.

Standing in the sterile departure lounge, all she could see around her were happy faces. Families preparing to go on holiday, lovers checking in for a romantic weekend break. God, what was she doing, leaving this man she loved so much? She flung her arms around him.

'I've changed my mind. I want to stay. Please, let me stay.'

Briefly his arms tightened, but then he drew away. 'You don't mean that. You've just been handed a dream contract. Go home. Take up the Astella offer. You'll live to regret it otherwise.'

She wouldn't. For all the prestige it represented, it wasn't the Astella contract pushing her onto that plane. It was her pride, her need to return to the place she'd left in shame with her head held high. Mostly though, it was Robert. She'd caused irrevocable damage to her family and somehow she had to try and make amends. The reasons didn't matter though. She still had to get on the ruddy plane.

'When will you come out and see me?'

'When you invite me.'

'Tomorrow?'

His smile didn't reach his eyes. 'I sense delaying tactics. Go and get on the plane, Lizzie. When you touch down in LA you'll feel a whole lot better. If nothing else, at least you'll have had a long sleep.'

The memory of that journey to England made her heart ache. 'I don't usually sleep on a plane. Not like I did coming over here. I must have been shattered.'

'As long as it wasn't the company.'

She tried to smile, but when tears flooded down her cheeks she knew it was no use. If she didn't go now, she'd never go. Giving him a final quick kiss, she turned and walked away.

Staying might be what she wanted, but for too long she'd had what she wanted. Now it was time for what she deserved.

# Chapter Twenty-One

It had been four weeks since she'd last seen Nick. Four seemingly endless weeks since he'd looked down at her with those expressive brown eyes and told her if she didn't take up the Astella offer, she'd regret it.

Right now, exhausted from a 5 a.m. start and roasting under hot camera lights, Lizzie was pretty sure he was wrong. The desire to model had been in her head and her heart from an early age, but a lot had happened in the eight years since she'd left England, all starry eyed, to model in New York. Sure she'd made a steady rise to the top, but on the journey up there she'd lost everything that was really important to her. Her family, her dignity and her sense of identity.

Somewhere along the line she also seemed to have lost her love for modelling. Where once it had been fun, an opportunity to travel and mingle with people she'd never otherwise have a chance of meeting, now she could only see it as a way to be near Robert and pay for his care. She had no skills other than her ability to pose in front of the camera, so while she could, she had to make the most of the one asset she had. In her heart though, she wasn't modelling in LA. She was back in England, living in the country. With Nick.

She'd finally fallen head over heels in love, and it had to be with a man who lived thousands of miles away from her. But if living with him was pie in the sky, surely it wasn't too much to ask to see him now and again? Despite a fair degree of prodding though, so far Nick hadn't committed to a date to fly over. If she had any sense she'd know he was being evasive, and leave it.

Instead she found herself dialling his number after the shoot.

'Hello, Nick Templeton's phone.'

Expecting to hear Nick's deep voice, Lizzie was nonplussed

to hear the voice of a woman. A young, breathy sounding woman. It left her totally wrong-footed.

'Where's Nick?'

'He's just popped out. He'll be back any minute. Can I tell him who's called?' The woman on the other end of the phone was composure itself.

'Could you ask him to phone Lizzie?' In her daze, she nearly forgot her manners. 'Please.'

Of course there were dozens of perfectly logical explanations for why a woman was answering his personal mobile phone at nine o'clock at night, and none of them required either party to be naked. So why couldn't she think of any of them right now? Why could she only remember his hesitancy about coming out to see her?

Lost in her dark thoughts, she almost missed hearing her phone ring.

'Hi, Lizzie, it's Nick.'

She'd been dying to talk to him, but now she was, she didn't know what to say. 'Thank you for phoning back.' Formal and polite – very different from how she'd have been if he'd answered his own stupid phone.

'No problem. How are things in the hotbed of LA?'

It was no use. She couldn't have a casual conversation with him when her mind was screaming *who was the woman who answered your phone?* 'Where are you, Nick?' she asked sharply.

'Still at work. Why? Are you okay? You sound a bit odd.'

'Why did that woman answer your mobile?'

'Who, Sally? I guess she must have heard it ringing on my desk when I dashed out to buy a sandwich.'

Her heart went into free fall. 'The same Sally you were seeing?'

'Yes.'

There was a humming silence while she worked out what to say that wouldn't make her sound like a paranoid, jealous bitch. 'I assumed ... I mean, I thought ...' *We were still in a relationship*. God, had she been totally stupid? Was it out of sight, out of mind for him?

'Lizzie, what's wrong? Surely you don't believe ...' She heard him exhale sharply. 'I'm not seeing her again, if that's what you're thinking. We're both in the office. Working.'

Slowly she let out the breath she'd been holding. Okay, now he'd explained, maybe she did sound paranoid. But it was easy to be paranoid when you were thousands of miles away from the man you loved. 'So I don't need to get on a plane and challenge her to a duel at dawn?'

A soft huff. 'You don't need to get on a plane for that reason, no.' Before she could ask him if he wanted her to get on a plane for a different reason – to see him – he was talking again. 'You seem to have forgotten I'm a workaholic accountant. You, on the other hand, have been draping yourself over hot male models. I've far more grounds to be jealous than you.'

Her heart thumped. 'And are you?'

'What, of those handsome male models? Of course I am.'

For the first time since she'd answered the phone, the hand holding it relaxed. 'Good, then we're even.'

Not by a long way, he thought grimly. Still, the fact that she'd been jealous at the thought of him going back to Sally was a welcome massage to his ego. Even if it was well off the mark. Sally had been interested enough, but there was no way he could go back to the hollow relationship he had with her. Not after getting a taste of what a real relationship would feel like. One with the woman he loved totally. Absolutely. Hopelessly. 'Back to my original question. How's the world of modelling?'

'There have been some good days. I've just come back from a shoot in Mauritius.'

He whistled. 'I'm starting to regret asking you now.'

'It wasn't a patch on our few days in Sardinia.'

'That's more like it.'

He heard a soft sigh. 'I hate to sound like a broken record, but when are you coming to see me?'

Time for his stock response. 'Well, I've got quite a lot on at the moment.'

'So you keep telling me. I'm beginning to think you don't want to see me.'

How wrong could she be? At the airport he'd barely managed to stop himself from blurting out *yes* to her plea to stay with him. Only the knowledge that the quiet pace of life with him would soon become a noose around her neck, slowly strangling the sparkle and vitality from her, had made him see sense. She was like a stunning, rare butterfly. He could enjoy her when she fluttered into his life occasionally, but there was no way he could keep her caged.

'Nick? Are you still there?'

He shook himself. 'Yes, I'm here. Sorry, I'm a bit distracted at the moment. I really do have a lot of work lined up, which is why I'm still at the office at nine o'clock at night.' Though if he'd thought for one moment there was a chance for them, he'd have dumped the work on a junior colleague weeks ago and dashed across to see her.

'Okay, I hear how busy you are. Message received, loud and clear.'

The hurt in her voice was unmistakable, even across thousands of miles. 'Lizzie, if it helps any, I miss you. A lot.'

'Good. I miss you, too.'

Her voice sounded so fragile, as if she was trying not to cry. God he hated this. Being so far from her was agony. Where once he'd been strong, keeping his feelings hidden, keeping his distance, now he was so flipping weak, it was pitiful. 'How about in a week's time?' he blurted. 'I can probably take a few days.'

'Oh, yes, please. Stay as long as you can.'

His dumb heart lifted at her words. It didn't care that she was a supermodel, living in the glitz of LA and he was an

English accountant who fled to the quiet of the countryside at weekends. No, his heart figured while she still wanted to see him, it still had a chance with her. 'Well, I'd better go back to putting together my spreadsheet on accelerated depreciation. I guess you'd better go back to wrapping yourself around those male models.'

'See you soon,' she whispered softly.

A few evenings later, feeling better than she had done in weeks now she had the promise of seeing Nick, Lizzie put on her best public face and attended the launch party of the new fragrance she was promoting. Innocence. The irony of the name, after what she'd been through, wasn't lost on the thousands of people who flocked to see the launch. Nor was it lost on Hank, the broodingly handsome, annoyingly temperamental, model who'd been chosen as the face of Astella's latest fragrance for men. Sin. It was an essence that oozed from him as he swaggered up to her.

'At last, Elizabeth has come out to play.' With a proprietary air, he tugged at a lock of her hair.

'I've come out to do my job,' she corrected stiffly. 'Not to play.' On the previous occasions they'd met he'd left her in no doubt she was on his list of potential targets. Women he'd zero in on, capture and spit out when he'd had enough. Several months ago there had been a moment, a wild scary moment, when she'd nearly let herself be caught. Instead she'd started dating Charles. Out of the frying pan ... into a raging inferno.

'Come on, don't disappoint me. I've seen how good you are at playing,' he murmured silkily. 'Thanks to those recent photographs we all have.'

His dark words were a sickening reminder of how, despite the statement of admission from Charles, the memories of that sordid episode would be hard to exorcise. Most people she'd mixed with since her return had been sympathetic and kind, but there would always be the Hanks of this world. Ready to bait and needle her. 'I'll do my job with you, Hank. Nothing more.'

He laughed, his black eyes glittering. 'What's wrong? One man no longer enough for you? I can assure you, I'm all the man you'll ever need.'

Her stomach churned and a cold sweat pricked at her skin. What type of woman had she turned into that she'd nearly slept with Hank? Had actually slept with the cold-blooded blackmailer, Charles? The Lizzie of old – secure, bristling with confidence, happy, albeit with the occasional bouts of loneliness – wouldn't have given men like Hank and Charles the time of day. But the woman who'd emerged from the agony of her parents' death was chillingly different. Not outwardly, perhaps, but inside, in her head. She was riddled with such heavy guilt it was like a poison, eating away at her mind. It didn't matter that she couldn't have known the tragic consequences of her simple plea for her family to visit her. In her head, their deaths were her fault. Since then she'd started to punish herself, dangerously associating with men she knew would treat her badly. Back in England, her time with Nick had been a special treat. Something she hadn't deserved but had snatched at greedily, hoping his goodness would rub off on her. Now she was in LA again, and terrified of falling back into her old ways.

'Elizabeth, Hank, we need you for the photo call.'

Hank arched his eyebrow and smiled cynically, holding out his arm for her to take. 'Come along, sugar. It's time to drape adoringly over me for the cameras. Later I might let you do it for real.'

Gritting her teeth, Lizzie took his arm, knowing it was what the company needed from her, and what the media were expecting. Innocence and Sin. Two new faces for Astella's two new perfumes. As Innocence she had to stand and smile sweetly, looking coy while Sin tried to tempt her down a different path.

The cameras flashed as Hank smouldered down at her, draping his arm possessively round her shoulders, his grip biting into her skin. Next to him she stood tensely, trying to imagine it was Nick, not Hank, who was holding her. But the arrogance of Hank's tight hold, the cruel, knowing smile that played across his lips as she flinched, was so far removed from the quiet, gentle intensity of Nick it made her want to weep.

As soon as she was able to escape, Lizzie excused herself and dashed off to the Ladies'. There she stood, hands braced against the sink, trying to quell the nausea swirling around in her stomach. It wasn't the first time she'd had to pretend to like a man for the cameras. It was part of her job, part of the fantasy she was paid to create. So why now was it such an ordeal? Was it because it was Hank? Or would she have felt the same revulsion towards any man who held her in such a possessive way? Any man who wasn't Nick.

# Chapter Twenty-Two

Nick couldn't get the images he'd seen in yesterday's paper out of his head. Lizzie with a tall, dark, dangerous-looking man, holding her as if he owned her. The quintessential brooding hero. Bronte's Rochester. Austen's Darcy. Involuntarily his hands clenched and he tried to remind himself that it was simply a carefully posed photograph to launch two new perfumes. Any sexual chemistry between the models was created purely for the cameras.

Wasn't it?

He let out a deep, long breath and forced his fists to unclench. He'd know soon enough. Just as he'd know whether he was making this trip as her friend, or her lover. He was damned if he knew what he was supposed to be any more.

The taxi dropped him off outside her apartment block. The same one he'd found her hiding away in only a couple of months ago. He felt he'd lived a lifetime in the intervening weeks.

After checking in with the downstairs security, he called for the lift, his mind still back on the last time he'd been here.

'Nick.' He'd barely set foot in her corridor before she flung herself at him, hugging him in a vice-like grip. Silky blonde hair brushed against his cheek. 'I can't believe you're finally here.'

He sighed with pleasure as her familiar scent swept through his nostrils. She felt wonderful. More than wonderful. Bloody, amazingly, magnificent. 'Lizzie.' There were so many things he longed to say, but he could only just manage her name.

Taking hold of his hand, she led him into her apartment. 'I'm so sorry I couldn't come to the airport to greet you. The media interest isn't as bad as it was – they've found another target for a while, thank God – but I didn't want to risk being noticed and dragging you into this crazy world. Well, not any more than you might have to be, because, you know, if they see you with me while you're here, they're bound to start taking photos and asking questions ...' She trailed off, obviously realising she was babbling. Was it possible she was *nervous*?

He shot out an arm and grabbed her round the waist. 'Are you going to stop talking long enough so I can kiss you?'

'Yes,' she whispered softly. 'Most definitely, yes.'

And then he did what he'd imagined doing all those nights they'd been apart. He placed his hands on either side of her gorgeous face, lowered his lips to hers and planted a tender kiss there. 'Hello.'

Her arms wrapped round his neck and she pushed her mouth more firmly against his. 'Hello back.'

She didn't seem to be letting him go. In fact she was opening her mouth now, her tongue darting out to dance with his. To hell with it. He angled his head and kissed her deeper, longer. With more heat. Women who wanted to be just friends didn't put their tongues down a man's throat.

Lizzie's fears that Nick would be distant, that he'd only come because she'd pestered him to, just as she'd pestered her parents two years ago, vanished as his hands rested on her hips, drawing her against his very obvious arousal.

'I think the unpacking can wait,' she announced huskily.

'Too damn right.' His mouth descended once more, devouring her with a hunger that took her breath away.

He'd gone from achingly tender, to scorchingly passionate, in the blink of an eye. Dazzled by the change of pace, Lizzie clung to him, moaning with delight as his hands crept under her blouse and teased their way over her breasts. Undone by his touch, she reached for his shirt, desperate to feel his skin and the tight, hard muscles underneath. When the small buttons started driving her mad, she opted to rip the thing off instead. It was much harder than she'd bargained for. 'In the movies, these stupid buttons fly off,' she mumbled in frustration, resorting to undoing each one in turn.

'In the movies, I'd be the one ripping your clothes off,' he countered, ignoring the buttons on her blouse and pulling it over her head. 'There, at least I've got further than you.'

She undid the final button and had the satisfaction of pushing back his shirt and burrowing into the warm, hard chest. 'Did I tell you how much I've missed you?'

He reached down and lifted her up into his arms. 'I think you might have done, once or twice. Now it's my turn to show you how much I've missed you.' With that he strode purposefully towards the bedroom.

'I think perhaps you did miss me, after all.' Full of a warm, fuzzy contentment she traced circles on his chest with her index finger. 'But maybe you could show me again, just so I'm sure.'

'Always happy to oblige.' He started to kiss her collarbone – who knew that was so sexy? – but the mood was interrupted by a ringing phone. 'You could let it ring,' he suggested, running his fingers down her sides.

The fact that she was tempted said a lot about the wonder of his touch. 'But then I'd never know what I was missing out on. I'm far too nosey to do that.'

Smiling, she eased herself up and fumbled around for the phone on her bedside table. 'Hey, Catherine.'

They exchanged the usual greetings, but Catherine being Catherine, soon got down to business.

'Has that man of yours finally arrived then?'

'He's lying right next to me now.' Oops, maybe she should have said sitting …

'Oh dear, am I interrupting?'

'No, no, you're fine.' Clearly bored of waiting, Nick eased himself behind her and began to kiss the nape of her neck. Her skin tingled. 'Perhaps we could speed this conversation up a bit though?'

An amused chuckle sounded down the phone. 'I'm having a party at my house tomorrow. Nothing formal, just a small gathering. I'd love you to come.'

'A party tomorrow?' she repeated, turning to glance questioningly at Nick. Head bent, poised to kiss her shoulder, he paused and looked up. The smile he gave her was so forced, it almost made her giggle. 'Yes, we'd love to come. Thank you.'

'You should have left it ringing,' he mumbled when she came off the phone.

Smiling sweetly, she crawled back under the duvet. 'Come on, cheer up, it won't be that bad. A party, in Beverly Hills? Some people would give their eye teeth for an invite.' She traced the corners of his mouth with her tongue. 'You never know, you might even enjoy it.'

'Perhaps.'

He still wasn't smiling, so she planted a kiss on his nose. 'When was the last party you went to?'

He wrinkled his brow. 'Your eighteenth?'

'You're kidding.' When he didn't refute his answer, she shook her head in disgust. 'Well, I'm not going to apologise for accepting then. Two parties in eight years isn't much to ask of you, is it?'

Finally he crooked her a smile. 'I guess I can manage it. Once every four years is about the right average.'

They spent the following morning visiting Robert and then driving along the coast to Malibu, dropping down onto the beach when Lizzie felt sure they were away from prying eyes. It was a stunning coastline and Nick could tell Lizzie was enjoying showing it to him, much as he'd loved showing her the countryside around his barn. Which did she prefer, he wondered, then stopped himself. Now wasn't the time to go down that route.

They slipped off their shoes and walked along the sand, their footprints looking slightly incongruous. Hers so slender and dainty next to his hulking size thirteens.

'When do we have to be at the party?' He winced.

'We don't *have* to go anywhere.' Ah, she'd picked up on his lack of enthusiasm then. 'Seriously, I can phone and cancel. I don't care what we do, as long as I'm with you.'

As he had done yesterday, when she'd greeted him so wholeheartedly, Nick felt another fluttering of hope. Could he dare to believe she was growing to love him? That they did have a future together? Sure her place was here, so he'd have to be the one to move, but if she really did love him, he could do that, couldn't he? There were differences between accounting in the US and Britain, but he had a brain. He could learn. There was still the fact that the life she led, filled with parties and celebrity friends, would slowly drive him crazy, but again, he could try to like it. He wasn't completely socially inept. 'I'm fine with going,' he replied, and it was almost the truth.

Her expression told him she doubted his words.

'I'd have to be a fool to miss out on the opportunity of mingling with LA's finest,' he added in an attempt to reinforce his statement. 'I presume I will see some stars?'

'Well, Tom Cruise won't be flying in, if that's what you mean, but, yes, you'll probably recognise a few faces.'

'And the dress code? I'm not sure I packed the tuxedo.' He'd intended the words to be tongue in cheek, but suddenly realised it could actually be a posh affair, for all he knew. His face must have registered his horror, because she laughed.

'Don't fret. It's an informal do at Catherine's house – she's the friend who lent us the villa. You can keep the tux in your case.' She took his hand and tugged. 'It's probably time we were heading back. If we go now, we might manage a little siesta before we need to get ready.'

Her eyes burned back at him, and desire kicked in, fast

and hot. Lizzie knew exactly which buttons to press to get a reaction from him. She always had. 'Sounds good,' he croaked.

The siesta had come and gone – with no sleeping involved – and Nick found himself getting ready for a party. A phrase he didn't use very often. Lizzie had said casual, but to Nick's mind casual meant jogging bottoms and somehow he couldn't see this LA set turning up in a bunch of shell suits. Instead he opted to wear a blue linen shirt, chino trousers and the one jacket he'd brought with him. It was part determination not to be under dressed and part armour. In a jacket, or even better, a suit, he became Nicholas Templeton, partner in a thriving accountancy firm. That man was self-assured and assertive. Confident of his place at the business table. Nick Templeton, sometime boyfriend of the glamorous supermodel Elizabeth Donavue, was an entirely different matter. It was a role he'd only ever played in his dreams before now. And in his dreams, he thought despairingly as he surveyed himself in the mirror, he didn't look like a flaming stuffed shirt.

He let out a resigned sigh. To hell with it. There was no time to change now. Even if there was, his small holdall was hardly crammed full of hot party gear – whatever that was. Her crowd would have to accept him as he was. It wasn't as if they'd be regularly running in to each other. Unless he moved here ...

He gave his hair a final cursory comb and went to hunt down some Dutch courage in the kitchen.

Delving into the fridge, he smiled with relief when he found a bottle of cold beer. Easing off the top, he settled against the counter and waited for Lizzie to make her entrance. He wasn't disappointed. Five minutes later she positively floated into the room in a soft, ice blue, silk number. He wondered why he'd wasted his energy worrying about what to wear. No one, absolutely no one, was going to give him a second glance when he turned up with that vision by his side.

'You look …' His mind fumbled for the words. Why was he so useless when it came to complimenting a woman? No, that wasn't true. Complimenting *this* woman.

'Ravishing? Amazing? Glorious?' she supplied, giving him a twirl, eyes alight with amusement.

'Yeah, all of those things,' he agreed, taking her hand and pulling her towards him. 'Add breathtaking, too.' He nibbled the soft lobe of her ear. 'And good enough to eat.'

Giggling, she wriggled out of his grasp. 'Oh no, you don't. I can see your ploy, distract her with flattery and kisses and we'll end up in bed and miss the party.'

'Sounds like a good plan to me.'

'Only because you've not spent an hour doing your hair and make-up.'

He planted some teasing kisses along her neck. Wow, she smelt as fantastic as she looked. 'I can be careful.'

'I bet you can, but you'll have to wait till later.' Her neck was no longer in striking distance. She'd moved ahead and was pulling at his arm. 'Come on, it's time to party.'

Nick gave in to the inevitable and followed her out. Perhaps the evening wouldn't be as bad as he feared.

# Chapter Twenty-Three

Lizzie was looking forward to the evening almost as much as she knew the man sitting next to her in the limo wasn't. She wanted Nick to meet some of her friends and if it meant him being uncomfortable, she was sorry, but this was important to her. He was important to her. She glanced over at him as the chauffeur drove them through the exclusive tree-lined streets of Beverly Hills, and had to smother a smile. He was resolutely staring out of the window, no doubt psyching himself up. She could never understand why parties weren't his thing. When he was one on one, he was sharp and very funny. In smaller gatherings he'd hold his own, articulating his thoughts when he considered the conversation important enough. In a party though, he faded into the background, choosing the quiet corner. As someone drawn to the dance floor and the glittering lights, it was hard for her to understand his preference, though it didn't mean she didn't respect it. The very fact that he wasn't a swaggering, arrogant extrovert was part of his charm. Part of what she'd fallen in love with. That and his strength, his desire to give rather than take. His innate goodness.

She bit her lip, looking back out of the window. God, he was so different to her. So much better. She was the one always on the take. Self-centred and demanding, she pushed people into doing what she wanted them to do, irrespective of their wishes. She hadn't even learnt from her last monumentally selfish act, despite the tragic consequences. Oh no, what she'd done to her family, now she was doing to Nick. Pestering him to come over and see her, ignoring the fact that he'd kept telling her he was busy. Heck, she was even dragging him to a party he didn't want to go to. Because he was kind, because he cared, he was doing what she'd asked. Instinctively she reached across and squeezed his hand, her heart feeling uncomfortably tight in her chest.

'What was that for?'

'Does there have to be a reason?'

'Well, no, I guess not.' He looked so adorable, his eyes like those of a Labrador who wasn't sure what its master was trying to tell him.

Unable to resist, she leant over and planted a soft kiss on his mouth. 'It was just to thank you for being you.'

'By the end of tonight you might be wishing I was someone else.'

She had no time to wonder what he meant by that because security were waving them through Catherine's gates and up the sweeping driveway towards the white mansion at the top of the hill. A typical Hollywood style grand villa, it boasted ornate balustrades, a sweeping marble staircase, tall, Roman style columns and an immaculate lawn. Oh, and the compulsory swimming pool.

'Just your average house in Beverly Hills then,' Nick remarked as he helped her out of the limousine. Suddenly his attention was caught by a vision in vivid purple. 'Oh my God, isn't that ...' He didn't have time to finish his sentence before Lizzie was swept into a full on embrace by the woman in question.

'Catherine, I'd like you to meet Nick.' It was quite obvious Nick knew who the glamorous brunette was.

'Nick, a pleasure to meet you.' Catherine extended her hand, and Nick gallantly kissed it.

'I rather think the pleasure is all mine.'

Catherine let out an amused chuckle. 'Oh, you Englishmen have such manners. Delightful.' She clasped both of them by the hand and walked with them up the steps. 'Now, come on in and make yourselves at home.' On reaching the top, she turned and smiled at Nick. 'Don't be a stranger, Nick. Before the evening's over I want to find out exactly what it is about you that's put such a huge smile on Elizabeth's face.' She reached up and placed a hand on his cheek, studying him. 'Though I think I can probably work some of that out for myself.'

Catherine wandered off to greet more guests and Lizzie glanced slyly over at Nick. 'Glad you came now?'

His breath came out in a rush. 'Hell's teeth, you could have warned me. I mean, she's one of my all time favourite pin-ups.' Lizzie raised her eyebrows at him and he grinned. 'Along with you, of course.' His eyes swung back to Catherine's tall, elegant figure. 'But I mean, wow. She doesn't disappoint in the flesh, does she?'

Lizzie put a hand on the side of his face and pulled his attention back to her. 'No, she doesn't.' She raised her mouth and kissed him hard on the lips. 'And that's just to remind you who you came with.'

She was drawing back when he circled her waist with his arm and pulled her more firmly against him. 'How could I ever forget that?' he whispered before deepening the kiss.

The man could kiss. There was no doubt about it. In fact his kisses should carry a health warning. In particular, they shouldn't be allowed in a public place because when she was kissing him, she became totally unaware, and dangerously uncaring, of where she was.

'Hey, lovebirds. What's the phrase the kids use? You need to get a room.'

With her mind still full of Nick's kiss, it took a moment for Lizzie to take in who was speaking. 'Siobhan,' she managed as her and Nick drew apart. 'Good to see you.'

Lizzie turned to Nick and made the introductions. Siobhan was a fellow model. Poor Nick would be totally fed up with meeting models by the end of the evening. On the other hand – she took in his slightly gaping mouth, the glazed expression – perhaps he'd quite enjoy it.

'Is everyone at this party going to be an actress or a model?' Nick asked as she guided them towards the bar.

'Are you hoping the answer will be yes or no?'

His boyish grin spoke volumes. 'I've got to admit, as parties go, this one certainly has its advantages.'

Shaking her head at him, she surveyed the partygoers. 'Well, I hate to disappoint, but I can also spot a few actors, a couple of directors, some photographers.'

'Any accountants?'

'Only you so far.' Clasping his jacket lapels, she drew him towards her and kissed him again. 'But the night is young.'

They found a table and were soon joined by a few more models from the agency. Nick looked in his element, so much so he didn't bat an eyelid when she told him she needed another drink. Typical. Give a man a pretty face and he forgot everything else around him. Even those he'd come to the party with, apparently. Huffing out a breath she rose to her feet and wandered over to the bar. She was almost there when she was accosted by Catherine and dragged over to a quiet corner.

'Darling, he's adorable,' she gushed. 'Lean, athletic body topped by puppy dog eyes in an intelligent face. Please tell me this man is it.'

Lizzie found she couldn't speak. Biting at her lip, she sadly shook her head.

'Why ever not? You know I've been worried for you lately, my darling. Your taste in men has taken a real nosedive and that was even before that toerag Charles. This one though.' Her eyes zeroed in on Nick, who was grinning at Siobhan and making her laugh. 'This one is a keeper.'

'I want to keep him,' Lizzie replied quietly. 'But I'm very much afraid I can't.'

'Can't?'

Watching Nick made her heart ache, so Lizzie turned her focus back to Catherine. 'I know this sounds melodramatic, but he's too good, Catherine. Certainly for someone like me.'

'What utter nonsense. He sounds exactly right for someone like you. Much more so than those awful types you've been cavorting with recently.'

Lizzie swallowed and wished she had a drink in her hands. She needed it right now. 'Maybe, but Nick lives in England.

I need to live out here. He loves the peace and quiet. I need limelight and attention.'

Catherine narrowed her eyes and stared at her. 'You don't need the limelight. It just comes with your job.'

'True, but I do need the job. Besides, I think you get the partner you deserve in life. And I've got a terrible feeling that for me, it isn't Nick.'

'I've never heard anything so ridiculous.'

Catherine would have said more, but Lizzie decided it was high time she changed the subject. 'Sorry, ignore me. I'm being sentimental because he goes back home tomorrow. You know what will cheer me up?'

'It wouldn't be a turn on the dance floor by any chance?'

'Exactly.' She linked her arm through that of her friend. 'Come on. Let's show this crowd some real moves.'

As the party became more raucous, Nick grew more restless. He could honestly say he'd enjoyed the first few hours. There were definite benefits of being introduced to some of Lizzie's friends. At times he'd had to blink to remind himself this was real. He wasn't just experiencing some hot fantasy where he was surrounded by the world's most gorgeous women. He'd even managed to make a reasonable impression. Apparently his stereotypical English appearance was *cute*. Given a choice, he'd have gone with something more macho, but frankly beggars couldn't be choosers and Hugh Grant seemed to have done all right out of it.

It was the men he'd struggled with. At first he'd stuck to asking the typical outsider's questions of the modelling and film industry. Interspersed with a few occasional nods, the conversation, well monologue he supposed would be more accurate, had flowed reasonably well. When he'd run out of the obvious questions, though, it had all become a bit stilted. They weren't interested in what he did, so he held off discussing the finer points of cash flow forecasting. He did have a go at other subjects, but they seemed to be interested in only one. Baseball.

'Isn't that just rounders with a helmet?' he'd asked innocently.

The looks he'd been given had been sufficient to quell his next conversational gambit – a discussion on the English cricket season.

So he chose to excuse himself and retreat to a quiet corner where he could watch Lizzie, who was dancing with a few of her friends. In a room teeming full of beautiful women, she still managed to shine more vibrantly than the rest. Her beauty was part of it, but she also seemed to have this inner glow. It took him back to her eighteenth birthday party and how he'd watched her dance there, too. Her vivacity seemed to emphasise how very much she belonged here. While he, sitting alone and nursing a beer, clearly didn't.

His body tensed as he watched the model from the perfume ad, Hank somebody, slither towards Lizzie, like some giant reptile. A hunter towards its prey. Now he was right in front of her. Too damn close. Jealousy threaded its sharp claws round his heart and instinctively Nick stood, his body poised to march over and insert himself firmly and clearly between them. But as his feet started to move, he stopped himself. How would Lizzie feel if he strode over there like the petulant, jealous boyfriend, embarrassing her in front of the man she was currently working with?

He sat back down again and made himself look away.

Lizzie tried to push Hank away, but he was having none of it.

'Come on. Stop trying to fight the inevitable,' he whispered into her ear as his arms wrapped round her in a vice-like grip.

'There is nothing inevitable about you and me,' she tossed back, straining to break away. 'If you haven't already noticed, I've got a boyfriend.'

Hank turned and glanced over at where Nick was sitting

at the back of the room, quietly drinking his beer. 'What, the English twat?'

Lizzie stiffened, fighting to get her hands between them so she could shove him away. 'He's a damn sight more man that you'll ever be.'

Hank just shrugged off the insult. 'He looks like a bloke who prefers the quiet life. Not the type to want a woman whose tawdry sex life has been splashed across the papers.'

'That's where you're wrong.'

He raised a dark eyebrow. 'Am I? You really think that man hiding himself in the corner is going to want to hang round with a woman like you for too long? Hell, you've been in the spotlight so much these last few months you've even pushed me off the front pages of the gossip columns.'

She had a child like desire to shove her fingers in her ears and block out what Hank was saying. Awful as it was to listen to his words though, it was even more terrifying to realise their truth. All he was doing was repeating back her own fears.

With a strength born of despair and anger, Lizzie finally extracted herself from Hank's arms and dashed away from the rowdy dance floor to the relative peace of the poolside. Finding herself thankfully alone, she lay back on one of the loungers and stared, agonised, at the glass-like surface of the turquoise pool. What had she been thinking, forcing Nick out here? If she'd had any decency left in her at all, she would have said goodbye to him in England, like he'd suggested. But she hadn't. Desperate to hold onto him for as long as she could, she'd pleaded with him to come out, even though his reluctance had been obvious. The least she could do now was put him out of his misery. Give him back the quiet life he craved. She was a complication he didn't need and certainly didn't deserve, but he was too bloody nice to tell her.

She'd have to be the one to cut him loose. And while she was at it, she might as well cut out her heart.

\* \* \*

'What are you doing over here, all alone?'

From his seat in the corner, Nick turned and gave her a sheepish smile. 'Jet lag catching up with me.'

'Really? So if it weren't for that you'd have been right up there with me, strutting your stuff like Travolta?'

'Well, maybe not like Travolta. Isn't that style old hat now anyway?'

Lizzie sighed and slipped in next to him. 'Jet lag, my foot. We both know that's just an excuse, Nick.'

He flinched. 'Sorry. I didn't realise dancing was a compulsory part of the evening.'

'It isn't, but it might have been a gesture on your part to at least have a go, instead of sitting here like a boring sod.' Hurt flashed across his face and inside Lizzie recoiled at her harsh description. She was the sod, but somehow she had to find a way to provoke him. To make him angry. It was the only way she'd have a hope of doing what she needed to do, and ending the beautiful thing that had grown between them. She'd never manage it if he was kind to her.

'I'm not *like* a boring sod, I am a boring sod,' he replied tightly.

'You're not, but you could make more of an effort to mix.'

'Why, am I making you look bad?'

'Yes,' she replied quietly, before turning on her heel and walking away. Her eyes filled with tears and she briskly wiped them away. How it broke her heart to be so cruel to him. But she had to be cruel to be kind, didn't she? What a bloody stupid saying.

Nick sat back and kicked himself. Now he'd thoroughly pissed off the one person he'd craved to talk to all night. Disgusted with himself, he swallowed down his beer. He might not be having a great evening, but really, did he have to spoil hers as well? One minute she was dancing without a care in the world, the next she was obviously upset, and all because of him. He was acting like a blinking wet weekend. Reluctantly he rose to his feet. Time to bite the bullet and get on that ruddy dance floor.

He was loitering on the edge, toying whether to wait for the next song or just barge straight on in there, when a soft Californian drawl came from behind him.

'Are you ever going to ask me to dance?'

Nick didn't realise the words were meant for him until a slim hand grasped him round the arm and started to move him towards the floor. Catherine.

'Dancing isn't one of my strong points,' he blurted as she wriggled her way through the gyrating throng and into some space. Christ, dancing was bad enough. The thought of dancing with his Hollywood pin-up drained away any dregs of co-ordination he might have had.

She laughed and eased her arms around his shoulders. 'Don't look so worried. I'm not going to eat you.'

They started to move. Nick knew he was holding himself too stiffly, too formally, but he couldn't seem to relax. He had a gorgeous woman in his arms, but he was praying for the music to finish.

'You'll take care of Elizabeth, won't you?' Catherine whispered into his ear as they skirted round the outside of the dance floor.

Her question took him by surprise. 'Yes. Always.'

'Good, because whatever else she might tell you, she needs you in her life, Nick. She really does.'

As he contemplated her words, the music changed to a slow beat and, miraculously, he found Lizzie beside him. 'You've got no idea how grateful I am to see you,' he told her, gathering her into his arms.

She raised an eyebrow. 'But you were dancing with your favourite actress.'

He shook his head. 'No, I was humiliating myself in front of her. But now I'm going to shuffle with my all-time favourite model while subtly plastering my body indecently against hers.'

For a second, just the briefest of moments, he felt her hesitate, as if she was coming to a decision. He held his breath, terrified, but then she relaxed against him and he breathed again.

Later though, as they got ready for bed, Nick felt Lizzie withdrawing from him. It wasn't anything she said, rather the things she didn't say. He was used to her chatting away ten to the dozen, laughing about what she'd seen, giggling over the antics of the people she'd met. Tonight she was eerily quiet. When she did speak, it was only to answer a specific question, and even then her replies were monosyllabic.

'Are you still angry with me?' he asked finally as he pulled off his boxers and slipped into the bed.

She turned away from him and slipped on a nightdress. 'No.'

'It sure as hell doesn't feel that way. Look, let me apologise again for being a miserable git.'

'You've done enough apologising, Nick,' she interrupted, pulling back the sheet and sliding underneath it. 'I know you don't like parties. I shouldn't have taken you. The matter's over.'

Then she did something she'd never done before. She turned on her side, away from him. He was left staring at her long, slender back. A beautiful sight, but not one he wanted to be faced with. Tentatively he draped an arm around her waist. 'Lizzie.'

'I'm tired, Nick. Good night.'

Ouch. Her message was cuttingly clear. Smarting from the rejection he rolled onto his back and stared up at the immaculate white ceiling. Long into the night, long after he felt her fall asleep, he still stared. Only inches separated them, but he might as well have been back in England for all the closeness he felt.

# Chapter Twenty-Four

Nick woke from a restless sleep to find the bed beside him empty. In the short time they'd been together, he'd always woken with his arms wrapped around her. Then again, they'd never gone to sleep without making love, either. The sense of foreboding he'd experienced last night came back in full force. It wasn't something he'd imagined, as he'd tried to kid himself during those dark, lonely hours. Now she'd seen him try to mix in her world, seen how embarrassing he'd been, how stiff, how awkward, how bloody *dull*, Lizzie didn't want him any more.

Had Catherine, who'd seemed so warm, so welcoming, laughed quietly with Lizzie behind his back while she'd told Lizzie how he'd stepped on her toes while they were dancing? He shook off the thought. No. Catherine had been the one to point out how much she believed Lizzie needed him in her life.

It must have been Hank, who Nick knew damn well had stared pointedly over at him sitting in the corner while he'd been dancing with Lizzie. Had seeing the comparison between them, Hank so bold, brash, broodingly handsome, him so ... opposite in every way ... had that been what had convinced her?

Sitting up, Nick hung his head in his hands and tried to quell the feeling of fear. This outcome shouldn't come as a surprise – he'd always known it was coming. It was why he'd wanted the clean break. Yet he'd still foolishly persisted in keeping a small kernel of hope alive. Sure she hadn't chosen to stay in England when he'd asked, but she'd kept phoning him, hadn't she? Kept asking him to come over. It had to have been his pathetic performance last night that had brought her hurtling back to her senses, because it was now pretty damn clear she wanted to get back on with her life. One that didn't involve him.

\* \* \*

Down the hallway, in the kitchen, Lizzie splashed cold water into the kettle and tried not to cry. The sooner she got this over and done with, the better. Drawing it out was just prolonging the agony. And if Nick put his arms around her once more, like he had done last night, she knew she wasn't going to be able to have the strength to carry it through. She had to, for both their sakes. He didn't deserve to be drawn any further into a world he didn't want anything to do with. She needed to stop living a fantasy and face up to life without him.

She looked up with a start as Nick's tall frame filled the doorway, clad in a rumpled T-shirt and boxers. 'Here you are.'

'Clearly.' Her arms ached to hug him, to kiss the tiredness from his face, but instead she forced herself to put teabags into mugs. 'I was going to bring you breakfast in bed.'

'Looks like I've saved you the bother.' He cocked his head to the side and studied her. 'What's wrong, Lizzie?'

'Nothing.' She kicked herself at her instinctive response. It was just the opening she'd needed, and she'd ducked it.

'Last night you didn't want to talk.' He paused, his eyes searching hers. 'Or make love. This morning you couldn't leave my side fast enough. I think I'm entitled to know what's going on.'

'I ...' Words she'd carefully rehearsed as she'd watched the sun rise suddenly stuck in her throat.

Slowly he walked towards her. Taking hold of her hands, he brought them to rest against his warm chest. 'Since when have you not been able to talk to me?'

Her eyes filled. She didn't want him to be kind, or sweet. She wanted him angry with her. Cold and distant. Anything but the gentle concern she was staring at now.

'This is so hard,' she whispered, dropping her eyes to look at their entwined hands. Hers small and pale. His strong and capable.

'Shall I make it easier?' Abruptly he let go of her and stared out of the window where the waves were splashing onto the beach. 'You want us to finish.'

She swallowed her surprise. Of course he knew. His sensitivity was a big part of who he was. 'Yes,' she replied, her voice catching in her throat. 'I think it's for the best.'

Nick spun round sharply. 'For the best?' He sounded as raw and as hurt as she felt. 'Best for who?'

'Best for both of us.' A part of her died with each lie she spoke.

'I can see why it's best for you, but don't bloody kid yourself this is best for me.'

She gripped at the back of the kitchen chair, desperately trying to control the anguish churning inside her. 'Of course it is. We can't carry on a relationship across the Atlantic. I can't stay in England and you hate it here.'

Nick felt his heart turn in on itself, shrivelling into a burnt out husk in his chest. 'This is about last night, isn't it?' With an anger born of fear, he shoved at the chair, causing it to wobble dangerously. 'Just because I'm not prepared to make a total prick of myself on the dance floor, you suddenly think we're not compatible?' It didn't matter he'd thought those very same sentiments himself. Faced with losing the woman he loved, logic flew out of the window. He wasn't going to give in without a fight.

'We're not,' she replied bluntly. 'I'm a model, for God's sake. I'm extrovert, love to be the centre of attention, often selfish, very needy. You're—'

'Quiet. Dull,' he supplied coldly.

'No,' she threw back. 'You're anything but dull. You're funny, smart, generous, warm.'

'But that isn't what you want.'

'Of course it's what I want. It's what every woman wants.'

Her voice wobbled and he stared at her sharply, wondering why she looked so cut up when she was the one doing this to them. 'Then what's the problem?' he asked quietly.

'The problem?' She sucked in a breath and let it out slowly. 'The problem is, you're too damn nice.'

'Too *nice*?' He rocked back, stunned. Whatever he'd been expecting, it hadn't been that. 'And that's a bad thing?' As soon as the words were out, he wanted to withdraw them. Of course it was a bad thing. How many romantic heroes were ever described as *nice*? It was a wishy-washy word. Tepid and uninspiring.

'Of course it isn't bad.' Refusing to look at him, she sunk down on the closest chair and wrapped her arms tightly around herself. Tears streamed down her face.

'But nice isn't what you want, is it? You like your men mean, moody and exciting,' he supplied, fighting the urge to go over and hold her. She was clearly upset, but damn it, so was he. 'I know, I've seen the list of your past lovers.' He shook his head, forcing his shoulders to loosen from their rigid set, his hands to relax. 'You know I should feel insulted. The fact that you prefer the likes of a bastard like Charles, to someone who wants to take care of you. Instead, I almost feel sorry for you.'

Her head jerked up. 'How can you throw that man's name in my face, after all I've been through?'

'I'll tell you how.' Vibrating with anger, sliced to the core that she didn't want him any more, Nick strode towards her. 'I ... care for you, that's how.' Hell, he'd almost told her he loved her. Almost spilt his guts and got down on one knee, ready to beg. Thank God he'd stopped himself. He didn't want her pity, he wanted her love. But damn it, if he couldn't have that, he'd take desire. She might not want him any more, but that hadn't been the case twenty-four hours ago. He'd make her feel it again.

With a desperate lunge he grabbed her hand and pulled her up from her chair, yanking her towards him. Teetering on the brink of control, he brought his head down and savaged her mouth. As he plundered her soft lips with his tongue, rasping her bottom lip with his teeth, he allowed the burning, savage emotions coiling inside him to run free. When he finally lifted his head it was to drag her away from the kitchen and into the hallway. There he pushed her against the wall and pulled off her robe, shoving it onto the floor. For once his mind wasn't on tenderness, on giving pleasure. It clawed with a need he couldn't control. A need to bind her to him forever and never let her go.

Lizzie felt a moan escape her lips and she dug her fingers into Nick's hair, securing his mouth exactly where she wanted it. Against hers. It didn't matter that he was kissing her with anger and hurt. It didn't matter that when this was over he'd walk away, hating himself almost as much as he'd hate her for what she'd done to him. She needed to make love to him one last time before he disappeared. And he would disappear for good this time. She knew that. His pride wouldn't allow anything else. Soon he'd realise it was the image of her he'd come to care for, not the real person. Because that person wouldn't be able to hold onto a man like him.

Nick lifted her up, pushing her legs either side of his waist. Then, without warning, he plunged into her, driving her back against the wall. She'd never been taken with such hunger, such raw passion. It snatched the oxygen from her blood and the breath from her lungs. For all that she loved the gentle way he'd made love to her before, there was something so elemental about the way he loved her now, so primitive. She was allowing herself to be dominated, but this time it wasn't because she wanted to punish herself. It was because she wanted one last chance to be with the man she loved.

His thrusts increased in pace, increased in intensity. Harder and harder he drove into her, jamming her back up against the wall. Just when she thought she couldn't survive it, that she'd black out with pleasure, she felt her body let go and an orgasm rip through her. With a cry of pure female satisfaction, she collapsed against him. Nick gave an agonised groan and with one final thrust of his hips he came inside her.

As she slowly came back to earth, Nick swore harshly and

stepped away. Immediately missing his warmth, his support, she swayed, her legs feeling unsteady.

She watched as he yanked up his boxers with quick, jerky movements.

'Still think I'm too nice?' he asked, his voice brutally hard and filled with disgust.

'Nick, I—'

'I didn't use a condom,' he interrupted rudely.

'It's okay. It's nowhere near the right time in my cycle.'

He nodded grimly. 'At least you won't be forced to stay with me for the sake of our unborn child then.'

While she began slowly dying inside, he started off towards the bedroom. 'I'm going to take a shower.' He didn't bother to look back at her.

The drive back to the airport was undertaken in silence. He'd wanted to take a cab. She'd insisted on dropping him off. Something she bitterly regretted as tension filled the car, crackling between them. Finally she pulled up outside the airport terminal.

'Is this goodbye?' She heard the tremble in her voice. Pushing Nick away was one of the hardest things she'd ever done. But as hard as it was, losing his friendship would be even worse.

He sighed, his voice no longer sounding angry but resigned. And achingly sad. 'That's up to you.'

'I don't want it to be,' she whispered.

'Then you know where to find me.' He climbed out of the car and grabbed his holdall from the back seat.

Tears welled and she tried not to think about the fact that this could be it. That he'd walk into the airport terminal and never see her again. A sob escaped her.

Instantly he dropped the holdall and bent back inside the car. Gently he placed a hand on her cheek, using his thumb to wipe away the tears. 'I'll always be there for you, Lizzie.

No matter what,' he told her roughly. 'If you need me, for anything at all, call me. Don't let me have to come and find you like that again.'

Her breath caught on another sob as he withdrew his hand and then, with a final wave, disappeared into the terminal building. For a long while she simply sat in her car, staring at the doors, willing him to reappear. To tell her he wasn't going to accept that they were over. That he loved her so much he didn't care about her faults, about what she'd done to her family. He was going to drag her back to England with him and wouldn't take no for an answer.

But he didn't come back.

A couple of hours later Nick was on his way back to England. As he reclined the back of his seat in the vain hope of getting some sleep, he couldn't help but wonder what he'd done in life to be fated to always love what he couldn't have.

# Chapter Twenty-Five

Lizzie threw herself back into her work, just as she had the last time her heart had been shattered. At least this time nobody had died. Nick was still there, even if he was thousands of miles away. And even if she hadn't heard from him since she'd dropped him off at the airport four months ago. During the day she plastered a smile on her face and pranced about in the latest lines of designer fashion. During the nights she cuddled a pillow, drank shots of whiskey, watched late night films and devoured supposedly low calorie chocolate. Inside she ached with the pain of loss.

Tonight she was in New York to attend a gala to celebrate a hundred years of the Astella fashion house. It was the largest fashion event to be held in the Big Apple in recent memory and was expected to be attended by a host of celebrities. There were even rumours of royalty. None of it interested Lizzie, who'd never felt so disinclined to go to a party in her life. Partly due to the ache in her heart and partly because she'd be attending with Hank. Definitely not her choice. As Astella's newest stars, they were expected to make a suitably high profile entrance together, their faces reminders of the perfumes they were helping to sell.

With a long sigh, Lizzie squeezed into the silver gown laid out on the bed. The dress had been made especially for her, carefully crafted to follow the same fluid lines as the perfume bottle. It was demure and sophisticated at the front, just as *innocence* should be, but plunged daringly at the back, a hint of *sin*. Brushing briefly at blonde hair recently ironed straight by her favourite hairdresser, she gave herself a critical once over. It gave her little satisfaction to note she looked good. Hank was going to go crazy when he saw her in this dress. His overtures were becoming more and more insistent and she'd had to literally push him away on more than one occasion recently. The man had one hell of an ego, flatly refusing to believe she didn't want anything to do with him.

A large black limousine picked her up, with Hank already inside. He greeted her with a lascivious smile and a wink. She turned her head to stare out of the window.

Once they arrived Hank immediately climbed out and walked round to take her hand. As he helped her onto the red carpet, he wrapped his arm tightly around her waist. Too tightly.

'Come on, darlin', let's give them a show.'

The glint of amusement in his black eyes told her he knew exactly what he was doing, but Lizzie couldn't argue with him. Not in front of the waiting press. So instead of shoving his hands off and slapping him hard round the face, she turned to the cameras and prepared to do her job.

'Elizabeth, over here!' Reporters from all the major news channels were there, waving frantically at her. Lizzie gave them a beaming smile.

'Love your dress!' someone from the crowd yelled and again Lizzie smiled in the direction of the voice. It was a routine she'd perfected over the years. Walk slowly, smile, keep your head high and your shoulders back. Never let them know what you're thinking.

'I've got quite a fondness for that dress too,' Hank whispered in her ear as they made their way towards the entrance. 'I'll like it even more when it's lying on the floor of my bedroom.'

'The only bedroom floor it's going to be lying on is mine.'

He laughed darkly. 'Works for me.'

Nick settled down in front of the sixty inch plasma screen television he'd just had installed in his London flat. If he was lucky, he would catch the last fifteen minutes of the Chelsea match. Balancing his microwave meal for one on his lap – he'd lost interest in cooking for himself – he flicked through the channels to find the boys in blue. Hell, they were losing again. Obviously his crappy life was now overflowing onto the team he supported. When had Chelsea ever had such a bad start to a season? And when had he ever felt so damned miserable? He couldn't blame work, because at least that area of his life was going well. He kept some hellish hours, but the ever-increasing workload was the sign of a thriving practice. No, it was the part of his life outside work that was shitty. He found it hard enough to summon up the will to go out, the thought of dating again made his insides shrivel. At this rate, he was going to be a sad, lonely old bachelor. Fast forward thirty years, and he couldn't see much about his life changing. Except maybe Chelsea having a better season.

The match ended and the late night news began. Nick watched it idly as he finished his meal. He really should get himself off to bed, but he was too tired to contemplate moving from the sofa. The image of a silver-clad goddess on a red carpet flashed across the screen, snapping him out of his exhaustion. Fumbling around for the remote control, he zapped up the volume.

'English model Elizabeth Donovue, resplendent in silver, was just one of the big names greeted by thousands of cheers as she attended the hundredth anniversary party of the Astella fashion house in New York,' the entertainment correspondent reported.

Mesmerised, Nick stared at the screen. How had he forgotten how beautiful she was? How much her smile lit up everything around her? She looked stunning ... and happy. *And* on the arm of that bloody Hank. She wasn't sitting at home with a flat beer and a microwave meal. No, she was being squeezed by a hunky man, lapping up the attention of the world's media and having the time of her life. His chest felt painfully tight, and for one wild moment he thought he was having a heart attack. God, what he wouldn't do to hear her voice. To reassure himself he was still part of her life.

Automatically he began to dial her number, then caught himself. What was he now, a raving masochist? Even if she answered her phone, which he doubted she'd hear above the noise of the party she was obviously attending, what on earth could he possibly say to her?

'Nick?'

His phone echoed with the sound of her surprised voice, barely audible above a background noise of chatter and raucous laughter. He swore, crudely and succinctly. He hadn't cancelled the bloody call fast enough. 'Err, hi.'

'It's lovely to hear from you. Is everything okay?'

He could hear the worry in her voice and thumped his fist against his forehead. What the heck was he going to say now?

'Nick?' She was raising her voice, obviously trying to listen over the background din. 'I can't hear you very well. You'll have to speak up.'

So now he'd have to shout the words he hadn't yet worked out how to say. Closing his eyes, he went with the truth. 'I've just seen you on the news, attending the Astella party which I guess is what I can hear in the background. I ...' He sighed and lay back against the sofa, rubbing at his eyes. 'I just wanted to tell you how great you looked.' There was a pause, probably as she worked out what to say to his lame words.

'Thank you.'

'Hank didn't look too bad, either.' *And he should keep his bloody mouth shut.* Now she was going to think he was jealous. Bad enough that he was, that his heart felt pulverised at the sight of them together, but letting her know that was embarrassing her as much as it was him. 'Sorry, I shouldn't have said that.'

Another pause. 'It's okay. There isn't anything going on between Hank and me, you know. It's just hype to boost interest in the perfume.'

This was too hard. The pain of losing her still too raw. 'Well, I'll leave you to it.'

'What about you, Nick? Have you swept any women off their feet recently?'

A laugh tore out of him. 'You've seen my style. Sweeping hardly describes it.'

'That didn't answer my question.'

Nick laughed again, only this time it carried the edge of insanity. As if he could possibly contemplate seeing another woman now. Lizzie had absolutely no idea. Hardly surprising, as he'd never had the balls to tell her how he felt. Perhaps if he'd gone down on his knees and pleaded with her? Told her how much he loved her? He grimaced. A fat lot of difference that would have made. He wasn't her type. Apparently, he was too nice. 'No, there haven't been any women.'

'Does that include Sally?'

Part of him wanted to lie, to make it seem as if he'd put her behind him and was getting on with his life. But Lizzie was still, he hoped, his friend, and friends deserved honesty. 'It includes Sally.'

Once again a silence settled between them. Dimly he heard Hank in the background. 'Come on, sugar. Get off the phone, we're here to party.'

'Nick, I—'

'Have to go. I know. Well, have a good evening.'

Before she could say anything further, he pressed the disconnect button. Something he should have done the moment he'd first thought of dialling her ruddy number.

Acutely annoyed with himself, he picked up his dirty plate and rammed it into the dishwasher. Lizzie was off to party and he was off to bed, no doubt to spend another night tossing and turning and wishing with every fibre of his being that she was there beside him. In or out of that skintight silver dress.

While Nick was trying to get some sleep, Lizzie was trying to look like she was enjoying herself. Not easy when Hank seemed to follow her everywhere she went. Even to the Ladies'.

'Haven't you found some other woman to pester yet?' she asked him coldly as she walked out to find him leaning against the wall, legs nonchalantly crossed, waiting for her.

'Sure, but none of them are as beautiful as you.'

'Flattery won't get you anywhere.'

'No? What will then?' Suddenly he was grasping her hand by the wrist and yanking her towards him.

'Nothing you can say will get me into your bed.' She tried to pull her arm away but he held on firmly with one hand, while reaching out with the other. Within seconds he had her pinned against the wall, her hands above her head, gripped tightly by his strong fingers.

'How about what I might do?' he asked roughly. His breath was hot against her neck, a stale combination of whiskey and cigars.

'Have you resorted to forcing women now?' Despite the desire to escape, Lizzie stood still, knowing if she moved he'd probably enjoy it. A part of her, a very small one, was waiting for his kiss. Maybe this was what she needed to forget Nick. Maybe, if Hank kissed her, she would enjoy it. After all this was meant to be her type now, wasn't it? The mean bastard who took rather than asked. Who was rough rather than gentle. If Nick was too nice, this was what she was left with, wasn't it?

'I don't need to use force,' he replied smoothly. 'Women fall at my feet.'

'Well, this one isn't.'

'No?' He moved his head closer to her mouth, his dark eyes narrowing menacingly. 'I know what a woman like you needs. On the outside you pretend to be demure and sophisticated, but inside you're just one step up from a slut. One on one, two on one, you like it any way you can get it, don't you?'

Abruptly he shifted, grasping both her wrists in one large hand. With the other he began to paw at her, pulling at her dress, making a grab for her breast. As his hot palm touched her skin, she felt her flesh crawl. This wasn't what she needed. Not in a million years. There was no way she could stand to let this man touch her so roughly where Nick had touched her so gently. As if she was a prize to be cherished. Even at his most angry, the last time they'd made love, he'd been passionate, not cruel.

'Get off me,' she screamed.

Hank shot her a look of annoyance before darting his eyes up and down the corridor, obviously considering whether anyone was in earshot. Finally he pulled away, letting go of her wrists and revealing raw, red marks. A legacy of the powerful pinch of his fingers.

'Guess you'll have to come up with a clever explanation,' he remarked carelessly, following her eyes.

'And I guess, if you want to avoid a charge of harassment, you'll have to keep out of my way from now on,' she countered coldly.

'Touché.' With that he turned and sauntered back down the corridor.

Lizzie leant weakly against the wall, rubbing helplessly at the marks on her wrists. She'd never felt so ashamed of herself, or so alone. Since her parents' death she'd spent so much of her time fighting tooth and nail to keep her head above water. To not give in to the dark clutches of despair that sometimes threatened to drown her. But while outwardly she'd managed to maintain the appearance of a woman in control of her life, at the pinnacle of her career, inside she was still a girl who grieved for her family. A girl weighed down with guilt at their deaths.

A girl who'd driven away the one man capable of making her happy.

# Chapter Twenty-Six

The phone call, when it came, rocked Nick back on his heels. He wasn't sure what caused him more grief, the contents of the call, or the manner in which it was delivered. To hear of Robert's declining health was painfully hard. To hear of it from one of the nurses who'd been looking after him, rather than from Lizzie herself, was a double blow. Why hadn't *she* phoned him? Were they so estranged that she couldn't pick up the phone to tell him her brother was dying? His brother too, in all but blood. Hell, didn't he deserve to be told by Lizzie herself, rather than a stranger?

Anger, hurt and grief raged through his system as he made arrangements to get on the next flight to LA. She might not want him there, but he was going anyway. He sure as heck wasn't going to simply sit at home and wait for her to finally let him know his best friend was dead. If indeed, she'd even bother to do that.

In a matter of hours Nick was on board a flight to LA, his sister Charlotte by his side. When he'd phoned to let her know, she'd insisted on coming with him. As far as she was concerned, if her brother was like family to Robert and Lizzie, then so was she. Nick hadn't had the strength or heart to argue. Besides, he was happy for the moral support.

After the long, weary flight he checked them both into a hotel in Santa Monica and was contemplating when to call Lizzie when his mobile buzzed into life. Tired and emotionally strung out, he was ready to yell into the phone at her.

'Templeton,' he barked, even though he knew who it was from the caller ID.

'Nick.' Her voice, a broken whisper, sliced through his anger and left him aching to put his arms round her. 'I've been trying to call you. It's Robert. He's dying.' She'd barely got the words out before he heard a heart-wrenching sob.

'I know, Lizzie. One of the nurses called to tell me.'

He heard a sharp indrawn breath. 'Oh, I didn't realise they'd contacted you.'

'I called them every now and again to check on him. I guess they realised I'd want to know.' He let the subtle dig, that they'd told him straight away even though she hadn't, hang between them.

'I'm sorry,' she replied quietly. 'It should have been me who told you. It's just that since I heard the news ...' He heard a muffled sound, Lizzie trying to hide the fact that she was crying. 'For a while I wasn't thinking straight. Then I kept phoning you and there was no reply.'

God, she was killing him with her tears, but damn it, he was hurting too. Hurting that in the fog of her grief, she hadn't immediately, instinctively reached to call him. To share her pain. To ask for his help. 'What number am I on your list?' he asked abruptly.

That confused her. 'What list?'

'The mental one you must have in your head when tragedy strikes. Who did you call first? How far down was I?' That was when he saw Charlotte looking daggers at him and shaking her head. Shit, what was he doing? She was going through the agony of grief and he was taking her to task just because she didn't need him? 'Forget I said that. What I should be doing is telling you how sorry I am about Robert.'

'You're number one on my list, Nick. I phoned you as soon as I'd got my head on straight. As soon as the nursing staff told me Robert would hold out for a day or so yet. I knew you'd want the chance to see him before he ...' she trailed off and he heard her take a deep, shuddery breath. 'Before he goes.'

'I do.' He tried to ignore the fact that she'd been trying to contact him for his sake, not for hers. 'Charlotte and I have just landed.'

He heard her gasp. 'What? You mean you're here?'

'Of course we are. Charlotte's standing beside me as I speak, her eyes telling me quite clearly that I've made a total balls up of this phone call.'

'So that's why I couldn't contact you. You were already on the plane.' She was half laughing, half crying, but the joy in her voice was so evident it seeped through the cracks in his heart. 'Please, come as soon as you can. I'm sure Robert's hanging on for you.'

The last day had passed in a blur. She'd not been home long from the Astella party – just long enough to take a shower to rid herself of the lingering smell of Hank's aftershave – when Lizzie had received the call from the nurse. Robert had contracted pneumonia and wasn't expected to survive it. In a daze she'd rushed to his bedside and spent the night there, dozing on and off in between trying to phone Nick. She'd been distraught at not being able to contact him, distraught enough to phone his office and ask to speak to Sally. She'd sounded … depressingly lovely. Perhaps Sally had heard the anguish in her voice because she'd been full of sympathy when Lizzie had explained the situation, telling her Nick had left the office early but she'd let him know if she heard from him.

Meanwhile, unbeknown to her, Nick had already dropped everything and come over.

*He came to see his friend one more time*, she told herself firmly. And because he was her friend, too, and that's what friends did. Support each other.

As she looked down at the frail, lifeless body of her once vibrant brother, she didn't care why Nick had come. Only that any minute now he'd be here, with her.

'I love him,' she told Robert. 'But that probably doesn't surprise you. He was easy to let into our home, our hearts, wasn't he? The quiet to our storm. It was the perfect combination, wasn't it?'

The door creaked open and Lizzie leapt to her feet, barrelling into Nick the moment he stepped inside.

'Thank you so much for coming,' she told him, tears streaming down her face.

He squeezed her tightly, his body feeling as steady as a rock. 'Where else would I be?' His eyes strayed over to where Robert lay and she saw the pain cross his face. 'How much longer does he have?'

Lizzie grabbed hold of his hand and led him quickly out of the room. 'We don't know how much he can hear,' she explained at his confused expression. 'I know it seems unlikely he can hear anything, but if he can, I want it to be positive words. Happy words.'

'Of course.' He dragged a hand through his hair, something it looked like he'd done a lot on the journey over here. 'It might take me a while to get my game face on, but I can do that.'

She squeezed his hand. 'I know you can. And in answer to your question, they're not sure. Hours, perhaps a day.' Her eyes swept the corridor behind him. 'I thought you said Charlotte was with you?'

'She came over with me, yes, but didn't want to intrude. We'll see her back at the hotel when ... when ...'

'When he passes,' Lizzie filled in for him, feeling another rush of tears. 'I know it's for the best, I know he wouldn't want to be like this for any longer, but still. I'm going to miss him.'

The tears burst out of her again, and Nick held her silently, letting her cry. When she'd stopped, she blew her nose and put on a smile. 'Let's go and sit with Robert, shall we?'

She held her brother's hand while Nick and she caught up. For the first few minutes Nick was stilted, obviously finding it hard to include Robert in the conversation when he clearly believed Robert was dead to him already. But Lizzie wasn't ready to say goodbye to her brother yet – she'd never be ready – so she persevered and gradually Nick relaxed.

'I spoke to Sally, you know, when I was trying to get hold of you. She was very sweet. I liked her.'

Nick gave her a wry smile. 'Sally is a good person. Just not the person for me.' For the briefest of moments his eyes held hers and she read his sadness in them. Then he quickly looked away.

*I'm sorry*, she wanted to blurt. *I love you. I did what I did not to hurt you, but to protect you from me. I ruin everything.*

But she said none of those things. Now wasn't the time to pour out her heart. Not when her brother was slipping away.

Nick stared down at his friend, tears pricking his eyes. Lizzie had left to get them a drink and, he thought, to allow him some time to say his own goodbye.

The nurses had told them Robert's vital signs were worsening. It wouldn't be long now.

'So.' His voice croaked and he wished he didn't feel so horribly self-conscious. Wished he had Lizzie's ease when it came to talking to her dying brother. 'I guess it's about time I came clean about my feelings for your little sister.' He let out a strangled laugh. 'You probably already guessed though, didn't you, mate? You were always inviting me to every family event, making sure I was there whenever Lizzie came over from the States.'

A tear fell down his cheek, but Nick didn't wipe it away. His mind wasn't in the clinical looking room with the beeping monitors. It was back in England, with Robert. Back in the Donavue family home that Lizzie now owned, having officially bought it off him a few months ago. He didn't know what he'd have done without Robert growing up. He'd given him not just laughs and excitement, not just friendship, but a family, too. And, Nick realised with a start, he'd given him Lizzie. Sure Nick himself had then managed to cock everything up, but he'd like to bet Robert had known exactly what he'd been doing all those years ago.

'Thank you,' he whispered, reaching out to clutch Robert's thin hand. 'You were the best friend a guy could have. And don't you worry about your sister. I love her with everything I am. I'll always look out for her. Always.'

By the time Lizzie came in with the drinks, tears were rolling freely down Nick's face.

# Chapter Twenty-Seven

Lizzie liked to think that in the end, when he'd taken his final breath, Robert had known she and Nick were there with him. For all the times he'd been there for her, this was at least one thing she'd managed to do for him.

Now she was watching as the red velvet curtains in the crematorium were carefully pulled shut. The next time she would see Robert, he would be in an urn, his ashes ready to be taken back to England and scattered next to her parents' grave. Later she knew she'd feel some sort of relief that his terrible ordeal was finally over, but for now there was only grief. It wasn't the all-consuming agony she'd felt two years earlier, when she'd buried her parents. This time her grief was more hollow. Robert had gone, and with him the last remaining member of her once close, happy family. Even now, at his funeral, she couldn't help but think of what might have been if she hadn't insisted on going to America to model. If she'd gone to university in England instead, taken up a good, steady job like a teacher, would she still have them with her? Would Robert be alive, married, perhaps even a father? Anguish ripped through her and she had to shut her eyes against the pain.

A hand squeezed hers. 'Are you okay?'

Nick's kind eyes were filled with concern. She took in a shaky breath and nodded her head. With him by her side, she did almost feel okay. He'd been a tower of strength during the dark two days since Robert's death. It was Nick who'd listed out what needed to be done, made the phone calls, advised on the service, held her when she'd broken down. Charlotte had helped, too, perhaps in more ways than she could've guessed. Having her with them had been a welcome bridge between her and Nick. Without Charlotte it might have been awkward.

With her they were simply three close friends, coping as best they could through a difficult time.

After saying a final goodbye to Robert, they walked out into the sunlight.

'Come on, let's go out for lunch.' Nick tugged at her hand, pulling her towards the car he'd hired. 'Robert would have hated to see us so damned morose.'

He drove to a quiet place high in the hills. Lizzie put on her dark glasses, swept her blonde hair into her large black hat, and followed him and Charlotte into the restaurant. There, for a few precious hours, she relaxed. She'd even go as far as to say she had fun as they reminisced about their childhood. Nick made her laugh with tales of him and Robert, some of which she'd never heard before. But then, all too soon, it was time to leave.

'Nick, be a darling and drop me off first please?' Charlotte yawned as she climbed back into the car. 'I'm pooped.'

'Lightweight.' But he did as she asked and then it was just her and Nick arriving back at her apartment.

'Do you want to come in?' she asked as he parked in the underground car park.

'I wouldn't mind a coffee.'

Wordlessly they travelled up in the lift. Without the buffer of Charlotte, the tension rose steadily between them and Lizzie found it harder and harder to breathe.

By the time the lift opened, she almost ran out, hastily unlocking her front door and retreating into the kitchen. There she shrugged off her jacket and grabbed at the kettle. She was reaching out to turn on the tap when Nick put his hand on her wrist.

'When did these happen?' he asked in a low, controlled voice, looking down at her bruises.

Damn. She'd taken care to wear long sleeves and keep them covered these last few days. 'A while ago.'

A muscle in his jaw jumped. 'How?'

She snatched her arm away. 'It doesn't matter.'

'It matters,' he repeated with deceptive softness. 'Tell me how you got them, Lizzie.'

'I was held a little too roughly. I told him and he let go.' It was near enough to the truth.

'Who?'

His eyes weren't warm or kind any more. They were hard. 'None of your business,' she snapped, focussing on filling the kettle. She didn't want to have this conversation. Not now, not ever. And certainly not with Nick.

'When someone hurts a woman I care about, it is my business,' he told her quietly. When he could see she wasn't going to tell him, his jaw clenched. 'Was it Hank?'

Lizzie's head jerked, just a small movement, but enough to affirm Nick's suspicion. His gut twisted as he imagined what Hank must have been trying to do that required him to hold her so tightly it bruised her skin. With an oath he moved away and dragged a hand through his hair. 'Have you got any idea how hard it is to watch you demeaning yourself with this procession of arrogant pricks?'

She flinched from his words but looked at him squarely. 'It's my life,' she retorted, anger simmering in her big blue eyes.

'Yes, but don't expect me to sit back and watch you mess it up,' he asserted bluntly. 'You look like hell.'

'My brother's just died, how do you expect me to look?' Her anger was no longer simmering but boiling over.

'Robert effectively died a long time ago.' His sympathy was in short supply, now he'd seen the bruises. 'There's more to all this than his death. First there was Charles. Now Hank. Even before Charles, that list you gave me suggested a type, and it wasn't the kind you'd want to take home to your mother.'

Her eyes flared. 'Lucky I don't have a mother then.'

He ignored her. 'She'd be horrified, and you know it. You're letting these guys treat you like shit. Why?'

'Perhaps it's what I deserve,' she replied in a voice so quiet he almost couldn't hear it.

'What you *deserve*?' Incredulity had him almost shouting at her.

'Yes, what I deserve.' Her voice was stronger now and she was walking towards him, hands on her hips, eyes blazing. 'I killed Robert. I killed all of them. Now tell me I don't deserve to be punished.'

He stared at her open-mouthed. 'Is that really what you believe?'

'Yes.' It came out as a tortured cry. Then she shoved at him. 'Now go away and leave me alone.'

Nick couldn't believe what he was hearing, but Lizzie was glaring at him with such torment in her eyes, he knew she did. She believed every awful word she was saying. With his heart feeling like lead, he moved to put his arms around her, but she backed away.

'No, don't touch me.' Her voice started to break. 'Piss off.'

'Like hell.' More roughly than he'd have liked, because she was still trying to get away from him, Nick wrapped his arms around her and held her. Held her until she stopped trying to break free and finally started to cry.

Then he lifted her and carried her over to the sofa and held her again, just as he had all those months ago when he'd found her here.

'The driver of the other car killed them,' he told her firmly. 'Were you driving it?'

She glanced up, irritation written across her gorgeous tear-stained face. 'Don't try your fancy logic with me. I was the reason they were in that car. I was the one who phoned them, terribly homesick and pleaded with them to come and see me. If I hadn't begged them to come, they wouldn't have been anywhere near the damn car.'

'And why do you think they came running when you called them?'

'Because I asked them to.'

He shook his head, smoothing a hand down her soft blonde hair. 'No, Lizzie. Because they loved you. Do you seriously think they'd want to see you like this? Blaming yourself for their deaths? Is that truly what you believe?'

When she didn't answer he held his breath and hugged her closer. 'Have you ever talked to anyone else about this?' he asked.

Silently she shook her head.

'Then it's time you did. Bottling up this awful guilt for these last two years has made you unable to think straight. You've forgotten how much your mum and dad loved you. How much Robert loved you. They'd want you to be happy, not tormented by a totally misplaced sense of responsibility for what happened.'

Slowly Lizzie absorbed his words, feeling an incredible sense of relief that at last she'd voiced her anguish out loud. Nick hadn't done any of the things she'd feared – not condemned her, shouted at her stupidity or laughed at her. He'd simply come back at her with quiet understanding and reasoned argument. For the first time since the accident she took herself out of the equation and tried to see things as her parents would have. There was no doubt in her mind that seeing their beloved daughter riddled with guilt, punishing herself for her selfishness, wasn't what her family would have wanted. They'd done nothing but support her in her desire to become a model and in her move to America. Heck, how often had they told her how proud they were of what she'd achieved? How could she have forgotten that?

But would they still be proud of her now? Her career, yes. Her lapse with Charles, definitely not. Perhaps it was time for her to stop torturing herself. At the very least, it was time to try.

'When do you go back?' she asked after a while, aware she

was still nestled against his chest but far too secure to move away just yet.

'Tomorrow evening.'

'Have you any plans for the day?'

'No. Why?'

It felt silly to be this nervous about asking. 'Would you mind spending some of it with me?'

She felt his chest shake a little and looked up to find he was laughing softly. 'Who else do you think we'd planned to spend it with?'

And now she felt even more silly, though it was tempered with a bubble of happiness. She might have said goodbye to her own family, but for another day at least she'd still feel she belonged to someone.

The next day Nick said he didn't mind where they went, as long as it wasn't the places the tourists always went to. Charlotte said she wanted to do all the tourist favourites: the pier, the drive through Beverley Hills to see the actors' homes, the Hollywood walk of fame. The craziness of Venice beach. Lizzie laughed and went to get her wig. She knew who'd win out of that argument.

Later that afternoon, as she walked down the pier with her arms threaded through each of theirs, Lizzie felt lighter, more carefree than she could remember feeling for a long time. Even knowing they would later be getting on a plane didn't crush her like she thought it might. Following her confession to Nick she felt she'd turned a corner.

It didn't mean there weren't tears in her eyes when she dropped them off at the airport. She hugged Charlotte first, noticing how she then stood back, giving her and Nick some space.

'So.' He gazed at her, his dark eyes giving hers a careful study.

She smiled. 'So. Here we are again.'

'Will you promise to talk to someone? See a psychiatrist, or shrink as I believe you Yanks call them?'

'I might live over here but I'm English through and through.' His expression told her that she hadn't answered his question, so she touched a hand to his face and said the words she knew he wanted to hear. 'I promise.'

'I'm going to check up on you,' he warned.

'I hope so.'

Seemingly satisfied, he gave her one last hug before picking up both his and Charlotte's bags and disappearing into the terminal building.

It was only on the drive back that Lizzie began to realise that from this point on her life could change, if she wanted it to. With no more huge medical bills for Robert's care, the need to earn as much money as she could had disappeared. She could stop modelling; take a risk on a new career path. Perhaps try out acting.

And, she thought with a flutter of longing, she no longer had to stay in LA. She could even return to England.

There was a world of possibilities opening up for her, if she was brave enough to take them.

# Chapter Twenty-Eight

Nick kept to his threat and phoned Lizzie every couple of weeks. She didn't take up his offer to join him and Charlotte for Christmas, telling him she'd already agreed to spend it with Catherine. Knowing how hard it would have been to see her, Nick buried his disappointment and told himself it was for the best.

Each time they spoke, he was relieved to hear her sounding more and more positive. Yes, she'd found a great psychiatrist who was really helping her. Yes, she was eating properly.

No, she wasn't wallowing; she was getting on with her life.

No, she didn't have a man at the moment.

It was the last question he dreaded asking most. One day he wouldn't like the answer.

'I'm too busy for a man in my life,' she declared when he picked up the phone to her this time. 'I've been having acting lessons.'

He was delighted for her, he really was. It had been three months since Robert's death and Lizzie was beginning to sound like the Lizzie of old, bubbly, excited.

*Soon she won't need you any more*, a nasty voice niggled at him.

'Nick?'

He shook himself. 'Sorry, what did you say?'

She huffed. 'Forget it. It's not important.'

'It was clearly important enough for you to ask in the first place.'

'Yet not important enough for you to listen.'

'It's five thirty in the morning here. I've not had my first coffee yet, give me a break.'

He heard a gentle sigh. 'I'm over in London in February for London Fashion Week.'

'That's great.'

'And I wondered if you wanted to come.'

He froze, wishing to God he'd had that coffee.

'Okay, I get the message,' she said into the gaping silence he'd left. 'I didn't think you'd be interested.'

'I didn't say I wasn't interested.' He ached to see her, to take her out for a meal. To bring her back to the barn and just ... be with her, if that was all he could have. But watch a fashion show? 'Obviously it's not my type of thing, but I'm sure Charlotte would love to go.'

'Never mind. Forget I asked.' She sounded cooler now, more detached. 'I don't want your sister to feel as if she has to go.'

'Are you kidding? Charlotte would bust a gut to get to a fashion show.' He realised belatedly that he'd hurt her. If she'd asked him to go, it must have been important to her, yet because he knew he'd feel uncomfortable, he'd snubbed her invitation 'If you'd like me to be there too, then I'd like to go.'

He thought he could hear the smile in her voice. 'Liar.'

'Not a lie. Why wouldn't I want the chance to see a lot of gorgeous leggy women not wearing very much?'

His heart lifted as he heard her laughter. He hadn't realised how little she'd laughed since Robert had died. Since before that, if he was honest, at least compared to how often she'd laughed before her family's accident. 'Okay, if that's the only reason you want to come, I'll take it.'

'It's not the only reason. I'm quite looking forward to seeing you not wearing very much.' His remark was met with a silence that shrivelled his balls and punctured his heart. *She's your bloody friend, you dimwit.* Mortified at his slip from friend to lover, he cleared his throat. 'So, what are the dates, so I can block out my diary?'

'I'll email them to you.' Her voice was quieter now. Subdued? Horrified?

'Great.' His voice was too loud, as if he was trying too hard. 'I'll look forward to seeing you then.'

* * *

Lizzie put down the phone thoughtfully. Had Nick just flirted with her? In which case, was it too soon, too dangerous to hope that maybe, just maybe, there was still a chance for them?

Then again, he hadn't sounded keen to see the show. If the boot had been on the other foot, if he'd phoned to invite her to something that was important to him, she'd have jumped up and down with joy.

Of course it was early in the morning for him.

Before she could overthink it all, Catherine phoned.

'Hey there. How's things?'

Nick hadn't been the only one to keep an eye on her in the months since Robert's death. Catherine had taken to checking on her regularly too, insisting she join her for Christmas, making sure they had lunch every other week. 'Good, thank you. I've just been on the phone to Nick. I invited him to London Fashion Week.'

She didn't think it was possible to splutter elegantly, but that's what Catherine did. 'I bet he loved that.'

'You're right. He's agreed to go but I got the impression he'd rather go to a karaoke bar. Sober. And stand up to sing.'

Catherine's voice softened. 'And you're disappointed, aren't you?'

'Yes,' she admitted. 'I thought he might have understood how much I wanted to see a face in the crowd who was there to support, not critique. I always regret that since I moved here neither my parents or Robert saw me modelling.' She halted, forced herself to be truthful. 'I guess in all honesty I want him there for more than that. I want him there so he'll start to see me not as the beaten, battered woman I've become, but the woman I was before all that. Before the accident, before Charles. The model, doing what I do best.'

'And I'm sure if you'd explained it like that, the man who hates the limelight, hates being out of his comfort zone, would have agreed to come without a second's thought.'

Feeling immeasurably better, Lizzie smiled. 'How did you get to be so wise?'

'Age, my dear, just age. Now, my producer wants to meet you.'

Lizzie held a hand over her heart, feeling it thump. 'He does?'

'He does,' Catherine confirmed. 'He was thrilled to hear you were having acting lessons. Obviously there will be many other actresses he needs to consider, and you'd have to go through screening tests, but he did let slip he thought you'd be absolutely perfect for the role of Gretchen.'

It was a film Catherine was starring in. Gretchen was her daughter; a grieving widow who, wracked with guilt at surviving the accident her husband and child didn't, had begun to embark on a series of increasingly dangerous one-night stands. It wasn't hard to see why, at least on paper, she was perfect for it. 'I appreciate your note of caution. I won't get too excited,' she said breathlessly, her pulse racing.

Catherine chuckled. 'I hope you're a better actress in front of the camera than you are down the phone.'

'I'm a bloody awesome actress,' Lizzie replied, laughing. 'And I know that's not very English of me, but I can't help it. I think this is where my future lies.'

'And isn't it a wonderful coincidence that this film will be shot in England,' Catherine added. 'If you get the role, it might not just be your career this film will help to launch.'

As Lizzie ended the call, hope bloomed in her heart. Many months ago, after Sardinia, Nick had asked her to stay with him. Then, with Robert, with her modelling, she hadn't been able to.

Perhaps, if this role came off, if she came back to live in the same country as him again. If he could stop seeing her as the emotionally shaky shell of a woman she'd turned into. If all that could happen, perhaps there was a chance they could rekindle what they had.

# Chapter Twenty-Nine

To say he was bemused was an understatement. Nick couldn't believe he was sitting amongst this predominantly female audience, watching the most incredible, and to his mind incredulous, creations slide down the runway on models too thin and gaunt for his liking. Did designers really think women were going to buy this stuff? It was increasingly hard for him to believe as yet another model sashayed down the catwalk, spinning around on impossibly high heels and wearing an outfit surely put together by a child?

He stiffened automatically as Hank made his entrance, glowering at the audience as he strutted down the runway. The tanned, beautifully chiselled muscles of his chest were amply displayed by the open silk shirt he was almost wearing. If looks could kill, Nick thought grimly, the bastard would be dead.

Not wanting to waste any more of his energy on the prick, Nick glanced to his side. Charlotte was like a child at Christmas, round-eyed and open-mouthed. Well, at least someone was enjoying herself.

Then Lizzie appeared on the catwalk, and immediately his eyes wanted to look nowhere else. Totally unaware he was doing it, Nick straightened on his chair, his neck craning to get a better view. Whereas with the other models he'd noticed the clothes more than them, this time it was the other way round. Oh, he noticed enough of the wisps of silk that hung over her body to realise there wasn't much to them. Whatever she had on, it was the body beneath it that made it what it was. As she slowly glided down the catwalk, her hips swaying just a little, her head held high, her movements both graceful and sexy, he felt a burst of pride. He'd always known she was beautiful, with a face the camera adored. Only now did he realise how much more there was to what she did than simply smile. He wasn't the only male with a tongue hanging out of his mouth as she reached the end of the walk with a sensuous jiggle of her hips. She was smoking hot, sexy as hell. She owned the catwalk and nobody, nobody in that room looked anywhere else but at her.

A split second later her gaze sought out his and for one glorious instant, he felt the connection. It was as if they were alone in the room, just the two of them. Her lips curved in a half-smile and her eyes ... oh God, her eyes, what were they saying? But all too soon she was turning and moving away from him.

'You look like you want to gobble her up.'

His focus remained on Lizzie's retreating figure. He couldn't look away. 'She sure has a way of moving those long legs of hers.'

'Yes, she does.' Charlotte frowned. 'Nick, is there still something going on between you both? I know you used to have this crush on her, and that you had a short fling.'

'We did and it's over,' he replied shortly, the abruptness of his manner no doubt indicating to his highly perceptive sister that, for him, it was anything but over. Lizzie disappeared from the stage and he quickly changed the subject. 'So what do you think of all the frocks?'

Charlotte took a moment to scrutinise his face, but thankfully seemed to think better of launching into a long interrogation on his love life. At least for now. 'Frocks?' she replied instead, her voice signalling that it was possible for someone to sound both incredulous and disgusted at the same time. 'That's a word out of the Dark Ages. What you're looking at here, dear brother, is cutting edge design. Haute couture. If you're going to be hanging round fashion shows, you really have to use the right language.'

Nick didn't plan on ever going to another fashion show as long as he lived, but he kept his mouth firmly shut. All he wanted to do now was go home. Put some miles between him and Lizzie while he strapped his heart into some sort of order again. With distance, he could almost manage to forget her and what he'd lost. At least for some of the time.

After Lizzie had floated down the runway one last time, he turned to face his sister. Her eyes weren't on the catwalk. They were fixed unblinkingly on him. 'I'm going to get myself a drink,' he muttered. 'Do you want anything?'

Charlotte threaded her arm through his. 'Actually, yes, there is something I want,' she stated softly and very precisely. 'Come with me.'

Leading the way, she propelled him, very firmly, out of the main auditorium and into a small side room. There she pushed him, none too gently, onto a plush velvet settee. 'Does Lizzie know how you feel about her, Nick?'

He felt the blood drain from his face. Was he really that transparent? Please God let it only be his sister who was able to read him that closely, because if Lizzie knew it too ... he shuddered. It might work if they both believed they'd had a sweet affair that was now over. It wouldn't work if Lizzie thought he was still pining for her. Because then friendship would get confused with pity, and pity was something he couldn't live with.

Avoiding Charlotte's eyes, he looked down at his hands. 'I'm not sure what you mean,' he tried.

'Then I'll spell it out. Does she know you love her?'

He tried a casual shrug, though his acting had always been lousy. 'Of course she does. She's been like family. I suspect you love her, too. I mean, we've known each other forever.'

Charlotte pulled her armchair closer and hissed in frustration. 'Stop it. I'm not talking about love between friends, love between family. I'm talking love between man and woman. Love that should lead to marriage, children, and happy ever after.' Gently she patted his face. 'Why have you never told her you love her, Nick?' she asked more softly.

He shut his eyes and rubbed a hand across his forehead, feeling a build up of tension that would probably lead to one humdinger of a headache. 'What good would telling her serve? We tried being lovers; it didn't work out. I'm not about to start embarrassing her by spilling my feelings.'

'What if she feels the same way? Something passed between you both out there on the catwalk earlier. It wasn't just friendship.'

'Leave it,' he snapped. 'Yes, of course I love her, I always have, but the fact is, she doesn't feel the same way about me. That's why she ended it.'

'You *love* me?'

Suddenly, horror of horrors, he looked over his left shoulder to find Lizzie behind him, her face as pale as a sheet. Welcome to total humiliation. With an anguished groan he leant forward and hung his head in his hands, waiting for his frozen brain to come up with some totally rational, believable reason for why the words she'd just heard didn't actually mean what she thought they did. He couldn't think of any. All he *could* think of was how much he needed to get out of this damn place as quickly as possible; to hang on to any tiny shreds of dignity he still possessed.

'How long have you been listening?' He raised his head and dared to look at Lizzie.

'Long enough.' Her eyes were startlingly bright, her face still showing signs of shock. She moved towards him and he guessed she was wondering what to do, how to console him, how to help him out of the giant crater he'd just found himself in. He, too, was trying to work out how to escape, when salvation arrived in the unlikely form of Hank.

'Ah, there you are, babe,' he announced, striding up to Lizzie. 'They need us for the finale.' He placed a proprietary arm around Lizzie's waist, and Nick instantly saw red.

'Get your bloody hands off her,' he growled, shooting to his feet.

Hank raised a dark eyebrow, a sneer sliding across his handsome features. 'Who the hell are you?'

'I'm the man who's going to shove a fist in your face and ruin those perfect features of yours if you so much as touch her again.' Anger shimmered off him as he took a deliberate step forward, putting himself right in the model's personal space. He'd never been more grateful for his height.

Hank glared back for a few thumping moments, then dropped his arm from Lizzie's waist. 'Time to go, sweetheart. I'll be waiting for you.' He swaggered out the same way he'd entered.

'Nick.' He could see she didn't know what to do, what to say.

'Leave it.' Her eyes silently pleaded with him to talk to her, but Nick had had enough torture for one day. 'You know once there was a time I didn't think I was good enough for you,' he told her. 'God knows, my dear uncle was fond enough of telling me that, and in many ways it's still true. But when I look at the type of man you prefer, I realise I'm better than that. I would have been good for you, if you'd let me.' A wave of utter weariness descended on him and he slumped back onto the sofa. 'You'd better go.'

'But we need to talk about this—'

'No.' Nick spoke over her. Was she mad? Did she really think he wanted to *talk* about this? Sit down and pick over the bones of their relationship, friendship, whatever the hell it was, when he'd just opened up his heart and let her see right inside it? 'Don't keep them waiting. Go and do your job.'

He could see Lizzie was torn. In two minds whether to try and rescue their friendship or ensure she still had a career. Unsurprisingly, the career won. 'Okay, I can see you need some space, but don't think you're running away. I'll come and find you as soon as I'm done. There are things that need to be said.'

Perhaps, he thought. But he wasn't planning on saying anything for a while. At least not until he'd got his head together and didn't feel like dying with embarrassment every time he looked at her. Realising this was goodbye, he stood and gently kissed her cheek. 'Your parents would have been proud of you tonight. Robert would have been proud.' He paused and looked deep into her eyes. 'I'm really proud of you,' he added softly.

Tears spilt onto her cheeks. 'This conversation isn't over,' she warned, her voice thick with emotion.

But it was. Nick made sure of it. Although he had to drag Charlotte kicking and screaming, and flinging words like coward, numbskull and pig-headed at him, he was soon out in the cold London evening and flagging down a waiting taxi.

Lizzie should have been on cloud nine. The show had been incredibly well received. And so had she. Yet instead of enjoying the adulation of her peers, basking in the delight of the Astella design team, she was trying to find Nick. In her heart, she realised it was a fruitless exercise. As if he was really going to hang around, ready to put his heart on his sleeve and talk to her. In the end, pleading a headache, she escaped into a waiting limo and rang his mobile. He answered on the second ring.

'That's it then? You leave without saying goodbye?' Although she knew shouting at him wasn't likely to help, she couldn't stop herself. Her emotions were running far too high for a calm conversation.

'I did say goodbye,' he replied stiffly, immediately on the defensive.

She remembered his parting words, about how proud he was of her. His way of saying goodbye. 'And what about what I overheard?'

'That was a private conversation with my sister.'

'Private? You don't think I have a right to know how you feel?' When he didn't reply, she tried another angle. 'Were you ever going to tell me?'

His sigh was deep and heartfelt. 'No.'

She didn't know what answer she was expecting, but it wasn't that. '*No?*'

'What good would it have done?' His voice was quiet and steady, in direct contrast to hers. 'Listen to you now. You don't know what to say to me, how to deal with me. That's exactly what I was trying to avoid.'

Lizzie could think of plenty of things to say to him, but not now. Not on the phone and not when she was so cross with him, both for leaving without talking and for being so irritatingly calm. 'Damn you, Nick. I hate it when you speak to me in those careful, measured tones.'

There was a long pause. 'That's a shame, because this is who I am.'

'Nick …' This conversation was going all wrong, and she didn't know how to get it back on track.

'Take care. Have a safe flight back. Goodbye, Lizzie.'

She listened to the dial tone in a haze of confusion and utter frustration. Then she threw the phone on the limo floor, stretched out on the seat and screamed.

Thank heaven for the glass screen separating her and the driver.

It was only when she arrived at the hotel she'd been put up in that her brain finally started to make sense of everything she'd heard. Nick loved her. The person who knew her better than anyone else, who knew absolutely everything about her, including her God-awful mistakes, actually, hallelujah, jump with joy, shout from the rooftops, loved her.

A slow smile crept across her face, quickly followed by an ear to ear grin. If someone as rock steady as Nick still loved her, even after everything he'd seen, she couldn't be that much of a screw up, could she?

# Chapter Thirty

Lizzie knocked on the familiar rustic wooden door. It was ten o'clock on Sunday morning and she'd taken a punt on Nick being at the barn, rather than in London. After she'd finished the final show on Saturday she'd driven down to her parents' home. Her home, now she'd bought it from Nick.

There she'd spent the night trying to work out what she was going to say to him, which was a laugh really, because she knew even if she'd had a week, instead of a night, she still wouldn't know how to handle this meeting. It had been three days since Nick had admitted he loved her and then walked away. Three days during which she'd fretted about whether his version of love, and her version of love, meant the same thing.

The door creaked opened. 'Lizzie?'

She watched as a flash of pleasure came and went in his deep brown eyes, leaving only confusion. He had the look of a man who'd just woken up, only to find he had a giant hangover. She could almost see his mind trying to grasp what was going on. Whether she was real or not. As she peered at him more closely, she realised her hunch about the hangover probably wasn't far off the mark. His hair was mussed, his face drawn and badly in need of a shave. Those glorious brown eyes, on closer inspection, were bloodshot and exhausted.

'You look terrible,' she blurted. Instinctively she reached out to hug him, but he flinched, moving quickly into the hall.

'It's good to see you, too,' he replied stiffly, moving aside to let her in.

A night to consider what she was going to say to him and the best she'd managed was *you look terrible*? She was a flipping genius. 'Sorry, it's just you look kind of tired.' She let the sentence hang, knowing if she said anything further she was just going to dig herself an even bigger hole.

'I had a late night.'

She walked straight past him and into the lounge, hyper aware of his long, lean body following quietly, a few steps behind. It felt ridiculous, all this stiff formality, the tension. Why couldn't they just hug each other like they used to do? Like she so very much wanted to. 'So I see,' she replied instead, pointedly looking at the empty whiskey bottle and single glass. What was he trying to do? Drink himself to death?

Hastily he removed the evidence, throwing the bottle forcibly into the bin. 'So, what brings you here?' he asked, his restless eyes seeming to touch everywhere but her. 'I thought you'd be on your way back to LA by now.'

'I thought I'd take a break. Check up on the house.'

He nodded, thrusting a hand through his wayward hair, making it look even more dishevelled. 'I would have gone in and checked it for you. You only had to ask.'

'I know, but I'd already decided I was going to stay in England for a bit anyway.'

Silence hung between them. Lizzie wanted him to ask why, but he didn't. Instead he stared down at his grey tracksuit bottoms and creased T-shirt, as if suddenly realising what a mess he looked.

'Look, sorry, I wasn't expecting any visitors.' Finally he met her eyes, giving her a small, rueful smile. 'I'm not quite with it. Do you mind if I grab a quick shower? I may act a bit more human after that.' He indicated to the kitchen. 'Make yourself at home. You know where everything is.'

For a moment he held her gaze, his expression telling her quite clearly he remembered the time she'd spent here, when it had been her home, too. As his look burned into hers, Lizzie's shoulders relaxed. There, in his eloquent eyes, she'd seen all she needed to see. Her heart lifted and she started to smile, but he quickly turned and walked towards the stairs.

While Lizzie reacquainted herself with the kitchen, Nick tried to revive himself under the hot shower. Of all the times for her to pop in. She must think he was some heartbroken saddo, pining away for her. Which, okay, wasn't far from the truth. But, hell, it wasn't as if he broke into the whiskey *every* night. Just on those occasions after he'd accidentally blurted out his feelings to the woman he loved, only for her to stare back at him in shock.

Dragging on a pair of faded jeans and a navy polo shirt, he scrutinised himself in the mirror. It was bad enough she'd found out he was in love with her. He wasn't going to humiliate himself further by giving her the impression he couldn't live without her. Picking up his razor he shaved the stubble off his chin and then combed his damp hair into some sort of order. The face that stared back at him was still gaunt, bearing all the signs of a man who'd hardly slept the last three nights, but it was a definite improvement on fifteen minutes ago.

He took his time walking back downstairs, taking a few seconds to drink in the sight of his unexpected guest. She was curled up on his sofa, just where she used to sit. The last time she'd been here, they'd gone from friends to lovers. What were they now? Certainly not lovers, but not friends, either. Once more he cursed his weakness. He shouldn't have slept with her. He'd known it would complicate matters and end in heartbreak. Being able to say *I told you so* wasn't much of a consolation.

She looked up as she heard the stair creak and gave him a smile. One that reached into the depths of her stunning eyes and made his heart squeeze so painfully in his chest it pushed all the breath from his lungs. Transfixed, with every cell in his body crying out to him to run over and claim her, he stood on the final stair. She looked incredible. Unlike him, she definitely didn't have the appearance of a woman who hadn't been able to sleep. Quite the opposite, in fact. She was positively glowing with contentment, radiating happiness. 'You look well.' Inwardly he groaned. That was what you told an aged aunt, not a flaming supermodel.

Her eyebrows raised a fraction. 'You told me that on Thursday, but thank you. Again.'

The silence stretched and Nick felt like he was wading through a deep bog. Every step he took made him sink further.

'I made you a cup,' she told him, indicating the mug on the table.

'Thanks.' His voice sounded scratchy and he coughed to clear his throat, taking up a place on the sofa opposite her. 'So how long are you going to be in England?'

She smiled and took a sip of tea. 'That depends.'

Was it his imagination, or was she acting coy? 'On what?'

'On how long the man I'm in love with wants me to stay.'

For a few desperate seconds, time stood still. He wanted to be mistaken, to have misheard her somehow, but the soft look in her eyes told him he hadn't. 'Oh, I didn't realise you'd met someone new.' He struggled to sound normal, and not like a man whose heart was being trampled on. 'I thought you said you were too busy for men.'

'I haven't. Met anyone new, that is.'

'Oh.' This wasn't making any sense. His tired, dazed brain couldn't work it out. Then a cold shiver ran up his spine. 'Bloody hell, it's not Hank, is it?'

If Nick's face hadn't looked so anguished, Lizzie would have burst out laughing. 'Hank? God, no. Give me credit for having some sense.'

'Good. Because you deserve a damn sight better than a man like him.'

He said it with such utter conviction, her heart turned to goo and she couldn't seem to stop grinning. 'You know there was a time, not that long ago, when I wouldn't have believed that statement.'

He stared at her. 'What do you mean?'

'I mean that for a couple of years after the accident I didn't think I deserved love and happiness, or a man who could give me both.' She moved forward so she could perch on the edge of the sofa and look directly into his eyes. 'I didn't think I deserved you.'

'Me?' He gaped at her in open-mouthed astonishment. 'You didn't think you deserved me?' he repeated, clearly confused. 'How the hell did you work that one out?'

'I figured I wasn't allowed to be happy when my parents were dead. Especially when I was the one who—'

'Stop that,' he cut in forcefully. 'We've been through this. You didn't have anything to do with their deaths. You loved them. They knew that, just as they loved you.'

'I know.' She put the mug down on the table, her hands trembling too much to hold it. 'Thanks to you, and the lovely psychiatrist I've been talking to, I've finally begun to accept that. I'd been so wrapped up in my own thoughts, I'd forgotten to see things from their side. As you pointed out, they would have wanted me to be happy. I'm not just paying lip service when I say I know that now. I've always known it, but somewhere along the line I lost sight of it for a while.'

'And are you happy?' His voice was rough with the emotion he was clearly trying to keep contained. 'Does this man you love make you happy?'

His face was so earnest, his eyes blazing with a love he couldn't hide, but there was also anguish. He really didn't have a clue. 'He would make me happy, if he stopped staring at me and kissed me instead.'

For a second he looked baffled. Then she had the satisfaction of seeing the truth finally dawn. Anguish and confusion left his eyes, astonishment and wonder filling their place. 'Lizzie, I ... I don't know what to say.'

'You don't need to *say* anything.'

Before Nick had a chance to think, to work out the implications of what she'd just told him, she was sitting on his lap, her hands round his neck. His response was sharp and immediate. In a kind of mesmerised trance he watched her lips descend onto his and her hands drift under his shirt, running over his chest. He groaned out loud at their touch. Shifting so he could have better access to her, he pulled apart her blouse, revealing a sheer lace bra. Could she have worn anything sexier? Anything more capable of sending him hurtling into a frenzy of desire? But even as he fumbled for the clasp, a part of his brain was holding up a red flag, warning him to stop. As his body clamoured to get closer to her, to lose himself in her, his mind was dragging him back to reality.

'Ahh, Lizzie.' He gently pushed her back. 'I'm going to hate myself forever, but I can't do this.'

He felt her stiffen. 'What is it? At the fashion show you told your sister you loved me.' Pain clouded her eyes. 'Weren't you telling her the truth?'

'Are you out of your mind?' He gaped at her. 'Lizzie, I've loved you all my life. I was in love with you when you were too young to understand what love was all about.' He caught her face in his hands. 'I still love you. I will always love you.'

'Then what's the problem?'

'I can't do another fling,' he admitted brokenly. 'I love you so damn much, more than you'll ever know, but I'm sorry, I can't go there again. The last one nearly killed me.' Gently he smoothed at a stray lock of her hair, wondering how he could sit here and turn her down. But she'd made him greedy. Made him want more. 'I want forever, Lizzie, not just a few stolen weeks between your modelling commitments.'

Her eyes cleared and she beamed back at him. 'Blimey, is that all? Why on earth do you think I'm here? That's what I want, too. I'm not going back to LA. I'm moving back to England. I was rather hoping it was going to be with you.'

His hands were trembling so much he had to clasp them together. She'd finally said what he wanted to hear, but after all this time, he had trouble believing it. 'Lizzie, oh God.' He shook his head, hoping it would help him to think clearly. 'You know how I feel about you, but you need to think very hard about this. Your life is over there. I don't want you giving it up just to be with me.'

'Why not?'

'Because modelling has always been your dream. You love the drama, the excitement, the razzmatazz. If you gave all that up, in time you'd resent it. You'd resent me.'

'I've lived the dream, Nick. And, yes, for a while it was fun and I had a ball. But that part of my life is over now. I don't enjoy it any more. I haven't for quite a while now.'

He looked at her in surprise. 'Then why have you carried on?'

'Because it's all I knew. Robert's care was expensive and I couldn't see a way of me earning enough money from anything else. I don't have any qualifications. All I have is a photographic face.'

Gently he cradled her face in his hands. 'I've told you before, there's a damn sight more to you than just a face.'

Her eyes softened. 'You always did have faith in me.'

'Because I see you, Lizzie Donavue.' He fixed her with his gaze, hoping she could see his sincerity, his utter belief in her. 'Not just your beauty, but *you*.'

She gave him a tremulous smile, her hands reaching up to grip his. 'You know I told you about the acting lessons? Well, I've been given a role in a film being shot this summer. In England.'

His heart jumped. 'Seriously?'

'I've been lucky,' she added hastily. 'Catherine recommended me. She's starring in the film. I'm going to play her wayward daughter.'

'But that's fantastic.' He hoped she could hear the pride in his voice.

She must have done, because she beamed back at him. 'I'm yours forever, Nick, if you want me.'

He rained kisses down her nose, across her cheeks. 'You

238

need to be sure, Lizzie. I've let you disappear out of my life too many times already. Once I've got you, I'll never let you go.'

'I'm banking on it.'

'And what about the fact that I'm not your type? That I'm, what did you say back in LA, too nice?' *And why the hell wasn't he just taking her at her word and grabbing her with open arms? Why was he giving her this chance to doubt herself?*

She snuggled closer onto his lap and squeezed him tight. 'You've always been my type. You say you've loved me all your life, but I've loved you all my life, too.' When he was about to interrupt, she placed a finger on his lips, stopping him. 'I have. Why do you think I wanted you to be my first lover?'

'But, I thought—'

'I know. You were wrong. It wasn't just something I wanted to cross off my to-do list. I didn't just want any man. I wanted you. I may have been too young to really understand the concept, but I loved you, Nick.'

He cursed, loudly, at the wasted years, but Lizzie simply smiled. 'Perhaps I needed those years to experiment, to grow and work out what I really wanted in life. And now I know. I want a man who'll give, and not just take. Who'll be there for me, no matter what mess I might get myself into, and I get into quite a lot, as you've seen. One who'll tell me when I'm being stupid, who'll be calm when I'm being irrational. A strong, solid man who can see through the image of Elizabeth Donavue, right down to the real me. And who loves me anyway.'

She didn't let him speak, which was just as well. He was far too choked to say anything. Instead, still sitting astride his lap, she lowered her mouth to his. His mind was now so full, his head was in danger of exploding. Barely half an hour ago he'd been a broken man, wondering how he was going to pick up the pieces of his life without her. Now, here she was. Not just his friend, but his passionate, wonderful lover. One who wanted to spend the rest of her life here, with him.

He groaned as she rubbed her body against him.

'Can we do this now?' she whispered huskily in his ear.

'Hell, yes.' He would have loved to have lifted her gently into his arms and carried her manfully upstairs to his bed, but that wasn't going to happen. 'I'm afraid,' he muttered thickly as he struggled to undo her trousers, 'this is going to be over far too quickly.'

Making quick work of undoing his zipper, she laughed softly against his neck. 'That's okay. You have a lifetime to make it up to me.'

Lizzie was home and she'd never felt happier. Forget the adrenaline high of a fashion show or a perfume launch. Lying in bed, next to the man she loved, was a million times better. She smiled as she watched him sleep. He'd admitted, somewhere between the second and third time they'd made love, that he hadn't slept much since he'd left her in LA all those months ago. Thankfully his face looked less drawn now, more at peace. What a gorgeous face it was, she thought, as she traced the outline of his strong jaw and his lovely straight nose. But it was the man inside that was the most beautiful part of him. He gave her laughter, security, peace. If she had to sum it up in one word, it would be contentment. With him, she didn't feel the need to do anything. She was happy to just be. Coming back to England had been the easiest decision she'd ever had to make. Especially after she'd found the note in her mother's diary.

Suddenly realising she hadn't shown Nick yet, Lizzie scampered out of bed and rummaged round her handbag. Clasping the diary to her, she leapt back into bed.

'What on earth?' Nick opened an eye.

'Sorry, but I wanted to show you this.' She thrust the bookmarked page under his bleary eyes. 'I've been reading through all my mother's diaries. Please read out what she wrote on my twenty-first birthday.'

Nick struggled to sit up and focus his eyes. Frowning, he looked down at the neatly written page. 'My darling daughter looks stunning today,' he started, then grinned sideways at her. 'Obviously such a rare occasion she needed to mention it in her diary.'

Lizzie thumped him on the arm. 'Keep reading.'

'She seems really happy,' he continued, smirking slightly. 'I'm sure modelling is everything she dreamt it would be. If only she would stop cavorting with all these slick, young Americans. She's brought another one out with her tonight. He's all white teeth, square jaw, and boundless confidence.' Nick stopped to pull a face at her, but when his eyes skimmed over the next few sentences, the amusement left his eyes and his voice turned husky. 'I wish Lizzie could see how wrong this man is for her. I wish she could see the real gem that's right under her nose. Dear Nick, who is so clearly in love with her. I hope one day they will find each other.'

Listening to him read out her mother's words, tears welled once more in Lizzie's eyes.

'She called me a gem.' Nick looked like he was having trouble holding back the tears, too.

'Of course she did. She always knew a diamond was this girl's best friend.'

He let out a bark of laughter. 'That's a terrible pun.'

Lizzie reached to kiss him. 'I know, but it's also true. Best friend and lover. A girl can't ask for more.' She glanced down at her ring finger. 'Except perhaps a real diamond.'

Another burst of laughter rumbled through him as he carefully put the diary on the bedside table. 'Your subtlety is just one of the many things I love about you.' Before she could ask him to list some others, he placed a finger on her lips. 'I'll get you that diamond, Lizzie Donavue. But first, we have a lot of catching up to do.'

And with that, he pressed his mouth against hers, very effectively silencing her.

# Thank You

Thank you so much for taking the time to read *Too Damn Nice*. I get so much pleasure out of writing a book – spending months in a fantasy world with my perfect hero, what's not to love?! The greatest pleasure though, comes from hearing that others have enjoyed the fantasy I've created. I'm not alone in that. Authors love feedback – it can inspire, motivate, help us improve. It can also help spread the word. So if you feel inclined to leave a review on Amazon, Goodreads or any retail site where you purchased this book, I would be really grateful. And if you'd like to contact me (details are under my author profile) I'd be delighted to hear from you.

Kathryn x

# About the Author

Kathryn was born in Wallingford, England but has spent most of her life living in a village near Windsor. After studying pharmacy in Brighton she began her working life as a retail pharmacist. She quickly realised that trying to decipher doctor's handwriting wasn't for her and left to join the pharmaceutical industry where she spent twenty happy years working in medical communications. In 2011, backed by her family, she left the world of pharmaceutical science to begin life as a self-employed writer, juggling the two disciplines of medical writing and romance. Some days a racing heart is a medical condition, others it's the reaction to a hunky hero…

With two teenage boys and a husband who asks every Valentine's Day whether he has to bother buying a card again this year (yes, he does) the romance in her life is all in her head. Then again, her husband's unstinting support of her career change goes to prove that love isn't always about hearts and flowers – and heroes can come in many disguises.

*For more information on Kathryn:*
www.twitter.com/KathrynFreeman1
www.kathrynfreeman.co.uk

# More Choc Lit

*From Kathryn Freeman*

## Too Charming

**Does a girl ever really learn from her mistakes?**

Detective Sergeant Megan Taylor thinks so. She once lost her heart to a man who was too charming and she isn't about to make the same mistake again – especially not with sexy defence lawyer, Scott Armstrong. Aside from being far too sure of himself for his own good, Scott's major flaw is that he defends the very people that she works so hard to imprison.

But when Scott wants something he goes for it. And he wants Megan. One day she'll see him not as a lawyer, but as a man … and that's when she'll fall for him.

Yet just as Scott seems to be making inroads, a case presents itself that's far too close to home, throwing his life into chaos.

As Megan helps him pick up the pieces, can he persuade her that he isn't the careless charmer she thinks he is? Isn't a man innocent until proven guilty?

Available in paperback from all good bookshops and online stores. Visit www.choc-lit.com for details.

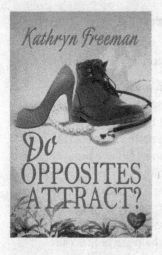

# Do Opposites Attract?

**There's no such thing as a class divide – until you're on separate sides**

Brianna Worthington has beauty, privilege and a very healthy trust fund. The only hardship she's ever witnessed has been on the television. Yet when she's invited to see how her mother's charity, Medic SOS, is dealing with the aftermath of a tornado in South America, even Brianna is surprised when she accepts.

Mitch McBride, Chief Medical Officer, doesn't need the patron's daughter disrupting his work. He's from the wrong side of the tracks and has led life on the edge, but he's not about to risk losing his job for a pretty face.

Poles apart, dynamite together, but can Brianna and Mitch ever bridge the gap separating them?

# Search for the Truth

**Sometimes the truth hurts ...**

When journalist Tess
Johnson takes a job at Helix
pharmaceuticals, she has a
very specific motive. Tess has
reason to believe the company
are knowingly producing a
potentially harmful drug and,
if her suspicions are confirmed,
she will stop at nothing to make
sure the truth comes out.

Jim Knight is the president of research and development at
Helix and is a force to be reckoned with. After a disastrous
office affair he's determined that nothing else will distract
him from his vision for the company. Failure is simply not an
option.

As Tess and Jim start working together, both have their
reasons for wanting to ignore the sexual chemistry that fires
between them. But chemistry, like most things in the world
of science, isn't always easy to control.

Available in paperback from all good
bookshops and online stores. Visit
www.choc-lit.com for details.

# Before You

## When life in the fast lane threatens to implode ...

Melanie Taylor's job working for the Delta racing team means she is constantly rubbing shoulders with Formula One superstars in glamorous locations like Monte Carlo. But she has already learned that keeping a professional distance is crucial if she doesn't want to get hurt.

New Delta team driver Aiden Foster lives his life like he drives his cars – fast and hard. But, no matter how successful he is, it seems he always falls short of his championship-winning father's legacy. If he could just stay focused, he could finally make that win.

Resolve begins to slip as Melanie and Aiden find themselves drawn to each other – with nowhere to hide as racing season begins. But certain risks are worth taking and, sometimes, there are more important things than winning ...

Available in paperback from all good bookshops and online stores. Visit www.choc-lit.com for details.

# A Second Christmas Wish

### Do you believe in Father Christmas?

For Melissa, Christmas has always been overrated. From her cold, distant parents to her manipulative ex-husband, Lawrence, she's never experienced the warmth and contentment of the festive season with a big, happy family sitting around the table.

And Melissa has learned to live with it, but it breaks her heart that her seven-year-old son, William, has had to live with it too. Whilst most little boys wait with excitement for the big day, William finds it difficult to believe that Father Christmas even exists.

But then Daniel McCormick comes into their lives. And with his help, Melissa and William might just be able to find their festive spirit, and finally have a Christmas where all of their wishes come true ...

Available in paperback from all good bookshops and online stores. Visit www.choc-lit.com for details.

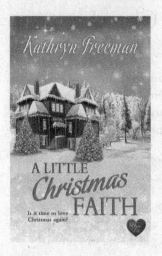

# A Little Christmas Faith

**Is it time to love Christmas again?**

Faith Watkins loves Christmas, which is why she's thrilled that her new hotel in the Lake District will be open in time for the festive season. And Faith has gone all out: huge Christmas tree, fairy lights, an entire family of decorative reindeer. Now all she needs are the guests …

But what she didn't bank on was her first paying customer being someone like Adam Hunter. Rugged, powerfully built and with a deep sadness in his eyes, Adam is a man that Faith is immediately drawn to – but unfortunately he also has an intense hatred of all things Christmassy.

As the countdown to the big day begins, Faith can't seem to keep away from her mysterious guest, but still finds herself with more questions than answers: just what happened to Adam Hunter? And why does he hate Christmas?

Available as an eBook on all platforms and will be released in paperback in October 2018. Visit www.choc-lit.com for details.

# Introducing Choc Lit